ECLIPSO'S
HAPPY
QUEST

Eclipso's Happy Quest
Book One: Goosed by an Iguanodon?
A Novel by David Taylor
ISBN: 978-1-63868-076-5(softcover)
ISBN 978-1-63868-077-2 (hardcover)
ISBN: 978-1-63868-078-9 (ebook)
Library of Congress Number on file with publisher.

ECLIPSO'S HAPPY QUEST

a Post-Planets Prequel by David Taylor

Book One:
Goosed by an Iguanodon?

dedicated to the memory of
Jonathan V.

Truths that are hidden are still truths; and maybe we can be guided by them only if they are hidden, just as we are guided by the sun only if we do not look at it.

-Roger Scranton

Chapter 1

Augustine "Augie" Matias must have reviewed the too-brief video at least a hundred times, featured in the latest episode of *Cryptomonster Hunt*. So what did he think his hundred-and-first review was going to reveal that he didn't discern already?

But maybe the thrill would suffice for a thousand more reviews, regardless of whether he picked up anything new. Augie believed a living, breathing, non-avian dinosaur might very possibly have been what put coconut palms and towering, wispy-branched casuarina trees into such commotion on an island off the coast of Papua, New Guinea the year prior, 1981. Wasn't that reason enough to continue magnifying every square millimeter of every last film frame? Keep searching for the least telltale glimmer of scaly, gator-type skin not entirely concealed by foliage and nightshade on that sweltering evening in the tropics?

The Expedition Channel could not budget officially for such an elaborate study, of course. Shades of the constraints Augie lived with as a renegade paleontologist at the Smithsonian Natural History Museum in Washington, D.C. That is, before world adventurer Jake Rumblehouse tapped him for his latest show.

What earned Jake's attention was Augie's 1977 field work along the Amazon River. Back then, Augie wasn't searching for a living dinosaur of the non-avian, non-bird variety. But he was scouring specific rock outcroppings for dinosaur fossils considerably younger than sixty-five million years. He sought to establish that a cataclysmic asteroid impact did not kill off every last flightless dinosaur, after all. That is, no more than it killed off every last turtle, gator, and frog, not to mention a host of other reptiles and amphibians.

A lone fossil tooth from the duck-billed dinosaur named Hadrosaur was all Augie Matias had to show for his efforts. He chipped it out of a twenty-million-year-old Miocene deposit. But fellow paleontologists had him mostly convinced the ancient tooth was actually from eighty-million-year-old Cretaceous strata reworked into the Miocene layer.

Mostly convinced; the dinosaur fossil was surrounded by a giant ground sloth rib cage, a significant discovery in its own right. If Augie didn't know better, he would guess that tooth remained inside the Megatherium's belly after he spit out Hadrosaur bones that went on to complete decay. And anyway, giant ground sloths did not come onto the scene until long after the Cretaceous-Tertiary boundary layer.

"Reworked strata reworks in mysterious ways!" chortled Dr. Gould in response. "But if you ask a creationist about this, he will tell you that doesn't really matter because none of the rocks are more than six thousand years old! Ha!"

The way Gould peered at Augie over his glasses' thick rims made his real message abundantly clear: There were the Bible-thumping creationist religious fanatics, and there were the even-keeled, scholarly scientists. The gap between those two groups was a no-person's land, as much as the iridium-littered layer separating age-of-reptile Cretaceous rock layers from age-of-mammal Tertiary rock layers was a no-fossil's land. Either you embraced the notion all life originated from evolutionary breezes purposelessly cascading chemical reactions certain directions like falling dominoes. Or you believed the Earth was only six thousand years old. Black and white, nothing in between; whose side are you on? *The minds of sworn atheists also rework in mysterious ways*, Augie often mused to himself.

In any event, yes, Augie Matias did fail to convince his colleagues they should revisit the taken-for-granted expiration date for non-avian dinosaurs. But he did succeed in garnering the flamboyant Mr. Jake Rumblehouse's attention.

Out of the blue, Jake paid for Augie's flight to Hollywood, California to meet with Expedition Channel executives, and pitch a show focused on fantastic rumors about living fossils the world over. Not thirty minutes after Jake explained the premise to Augie, he was rushing him into an elevator headed for the top floor. With virtually no prior preparation, Augie found himself put on the spot to explain how it was not impossible that dinosaurs and other prehistoric creatures of popular note still thrived, or at least hung on, in the planet's less-explored nooks and crannies.

All eyes were on Augie after Expedition Channel President Kim said, "To green-light *Cryptomonster Hunt*, Jake, you must first convince this young man here to climb on board, give it the necessary gravitas. Otherwise..." He shrugged his shoulders, but then added, "Of course, we'll want Washington D.C. as home plate, just out front of the Smithsonian Natural History Museum."

"Even though we can't expect the museum powers-that-be to officially sanction our missions," cautioned Jake. "But you do understand, Dr. Matias, that's where your 'gravitas' comes in, standing on those museum steps to discuss each proposed adventure."

"The next best thing to such a prestigious endorsement," enthused Seong Un "Sunny" Kim, making a my-point-exactly gesture.

"So you're saying I won't need to actually relocate to Hollywood for my participation." Augie couldn't tamp down his growing excitement. *Vicky might actually be cool with this!*

"Yes, you do have a wife and daughter back east, don't you? This would work for them," Kim went on encouragingly, though more interested in closing the deal than actually empathetic. "Especially if your wife has her own career she is pursuing?"

"You understand, Augie? I can call you Augie?" Jake asked.

"Of course."

"Augie, you will have to tag along on our critter hunts, and I'm just guessing we'll wind up in some very dodgy situations. But sure, even though this will likely require periodic leave from your museum gig, you'll be home with your family more often than not."

...one of the bonus pleasures from additional reviews of the tantalizing video clip was how they nostalgically returned Augie to his magical mood in the minutes before some unseen force sent ancient trees swaying. Back then, he was finally on the mend from an unnerving intestinal bug that hit him the evening of his first day on New Britain Island off the north coast of Papua, New Guinea. His appetite returning, a granola bar chased down by fresh coconut milk might as well have been a shrimp cocktail. They left him feeling refreshed despite the still air and oppressive, pea-soup humidity.

Also helpful was the bracing strawberry scent shed by a nearby stand of three-foot-tall dendobium orchids. Distant lightning flashes highlighted their splashes of lavender and burgundy far too briefly on that moonless night, but no matter. Augie's attention was far more on the vine-carpeted rainforest floor. If he could have, he would have willed a special critter into scampering about there, the size of an Anatole lizard, but with the unmistakable morphology of a non-avian dinosaur. Its legs would stick out from directly underneath its tiny torso, unlike gators with their limbs extending from their sides. And maybe it would feature a long, snakelike neck. A petite Apatosaurus; why not?

Augie had been so caught up in this fanciful reverie, he was taken completely by surprise when a hornbill swooped down close overhead. He felt a sudden draft from its majestic wing-flapping. And until the next lightning flash revealed its signature curved-down beak, he even wondered whether he was just punked by a prehistoric relic Pterodactyl.

In the aftermath of this too-brief encounter, Dr. Augie Matias, paleontologist, couldn't help asking himself whether the hornbill was any less amazing for not being a holdover from the Age of Reptiles. Such a question pestered him on several previous expeditions for *Cryptomonster Hunt*. To wit, weren't there already more than enough fantastical plants and animals extant for endlessly fascinating study? Do we really need living non-avian dinosaurs thrown into the mix that when you get down to it, are probably no more than wishful thinking anyway?

Knock! Knock!

Before Augie could lift a finger, Jake Rumblehouse threw open the door to his cubicle so hard, it banged against the wall.

"On your thousand-and-second look for the claws you couldn't spot on the thousand-and-first? Augie, we need to talk."

The bottom dropped out of Augie's stomach. He might as well have been back inside the biplane when it hit an air pocket during descent for landing on New Britain

Island. He was used to Jake's abrupt manner, but this occasion felt disturbingly different...so much so that before Jake got to what "we" need to talk about, Augie couldn't help prattling, "We've always complained about how little time we had in any one locale to really explore thoroughly-"

"I know you always complained-"

"No, I understand completely," Augie interrupted Jake's interruption, hands waving in protest. "We had this at the Smithsonian all the time. Just so much grant money, and no more, for particular field work. What we couldn't dig out-"

"Listen, Augie..." Eschewing the available nearby chair as always, Jake squat down off to one side of where Augie sat, leaving Augie in the elevated position.

For his insecurity, though, Augie might as well have been playing in a sandbox, with Jake looming over him. Self-consciousness over his awkwardly lanky physique didn't help; as usual, it left him continually shifting his legs about in a never-ending quest for comfort. "You're right as usual," he said, holding up one hand for Jake not to go any further. "I can obsess over this video on my own time, all I want. You need me ASAP to resume vetting proposals for season three."

Of course, Jake Rumblehouse barging in on Augie had nothing to do with third-season planning. But Augie was filibustering desperately to postpone the inevitable as long as possible.

"Look, Dr. Matias, about that..."

Dr. Matias?! Ouch! When was the last time he addressed me so formally??

"You know this has always been a ratings game. Shows live and die on audience share."

"But I thought that for *Cryptomonster*'s time slot-"

"It's been up against shit in its time slot! Big f-ing deal if we're one point better than *Fondu Smackdown*!"

"I'm just trying to understand." Augie held up his hand again, this time for Jake to calm down. "Didn't the head honchos commit to giving the *Cryptomonster Hunt* audience enough chance to grow? That they even saw us becoming a flagship for the network?"

"They did," Jake conceded in a most reluctant tone. "And if we had made just one spectacular discovery...Have you ever watched Road Runner cartoons?"

"Uh, of course."

"You remember the one where Wild E. Coyote is left holding a bundle of dynamite in mid-air off a cliff ledge?"

"Our Lizzy was watching that the other day."

"So when he started falling, he grabbed at each branch growing from the cliff side, right? But he kept pulling them out, roots and all, right? And just kept falling?"

Augie nodded with chagrin. Didn't take Nostradamus to predict where this was going.

Jake spelled it out, regardless. "Every episode, Dr. Matias, we were left with nothing more than a tantalizing bump in the night here, a blurry video there. No definitive evidence to create any kind of sensation." Jake's voice went confidentially low to conclude, "Wild E. Coyote has run out of branches, and he's about to hit rock bottom with his arm-full of lit dynamite sticks. You know what I'm saying?"

"The show's been cancelled, or at least my participation in it," Augie fatalistically stated rather than asked.

"Yes."

Augie sat all the way back in his chair, his lanky legs feeling ever more awkward. He made an inhale and exhale of exasperation. No small part of that was how Jake seemed to be awaiting his next reaction, like he was his therapist or something. "Again, I know all about budget constraints," Augie finally said, leaning a bit forward. "But must be frustrating, no?"

"How so?"

Augie required every last ounce of self-restraint not to meet Jake's question with, *You've got to be freakin' kidding me!!* But he still responded animatedly, "This last expedition, for example. What if we'd had an extra week on New Britain to explore more thoroughly where those casuarinas and coconut palms shook so violently? What might we have discovered, just snooping around the nearby coastal mangroves?"

"Any idea how much more that would have cost in bribes since all that land is claimed by the locals?"

"I know, Jake, I know! But this is a what-if question!"

"Waste of time, and money!"

"Really?!"

"Augie, I know how much you're like a little kid about this, how much fun it would be to stumble across a Brachiosaurus looking down at us from over a treetop. But if we're honest with ourselves, that was never going to actually happen. For a few years we indulged a steadily shrinking audience's childhood fantasy."

Augie's mouth hung open several seconds before he responded at last, "So what do you think did rustle that foliage so much?"

"You mean out in Papua? So many possibilities, does it really matter which? One of their huge-ass crocodiles might have been rubbing against the trees to itch itself. There could have been a sudden downdraft."

"That we didn't experience."

"Okay, well, the locals knew what we were up to. Are you sure a couple of them didn't hide in amidst the coconut palms, pushing their trunks into sway mode?"

"But how could that agitate the upper portions so much, give the impression something enormous was making its way through?"

"Augie, you remember that meal they insisted we share with them? What the betelnut did to us? Are you sure the food proper wasn't spiked with other hallucinogens that made us imagine we were in the presence of a hidden beast? Long after the betelnut effects wore off? Or maybe it was still the betelnut effects, a flashback trip."

"Those blue flower petals sprinkled atop the mashed tubers, in fact I am fairly certain that was Ipomoea, which is highly hallucinogenic," Augie conceded. "But our video that captured the upper foliage commotion was not subject to hallucinogenic effects. And studying it here in D.C., far far away from Ipomoea petals and betelnut alike, still gives the impression of some hidden enormous creature lumbering by."

"And you're positive our hallucinogenic impressions don't continue to color your impressions, no matter how many umpteen reviews you make of that video? Look, Augie," Jake went on while Augie was too taken aback to answer immediately, "these expeditions provided neat little travelogues, local color, short escapes to places our audience would otherwise never experience. Wasn't that enough?"

"What one woman shared about the upturned claw on the creature's forepaw, like a thumb's up that happens to fit the morphology of an Iguanodon: just a meaningless coincidence?"

"You mean just one person, who might have perused a book about dinosaurs that featured an Iguanodon?"

Augie would have objected that Jake leaned on one-too-many might-haves. He felt constrained, though, recalling Papuan children wearing Nike T-shirts. Dinosaur depictions could easily have made it onto New Britain Island, alongside the many other artifacts from western society. So he simply said, "I guess this is it for you as well."

"Regarding this particular project, yes. Look, Augie, you sometimes gave the impression you didn't have your whole heart in this."

Say what?!? Oh, I get it. You're the one who never did think we were going to flush a dinosaur out into the open, but I'm the one not fully on board!

"Aren't your wife and daughter going to appreciate having you around more?"

Augie nodded, but not about what Jake asked.

Over the past year, especially, on several occasions Jake and his film crew pushed Augie to join them for what Jake termed, "soldiers' R and R."

In places like New Britain Island, the whole gang needed to stick together nonstop whether working on the show or taking a break, for safety's sake. There was no such thing as "off-duty" under those particular circumstances.

But other places felt more secure, including of course Washington D.C., provided they weren't on an active search. Active searches usually took place at night, under the assumption most of their quarry was nocturnal.

That being said, the New Britain Island sightings reportedly happened mid-morning, at least for the locals.

Three different women reported seeing an enormous creature with alligator skin, standing on its thick hind legs to pick at pine-cone-lookalike fruit from a casuarina. Again, one of those women claimed to have observed a thumb's-up claw, consistent with the claw of a presumed-extinct plant-eating ornithopod dinosaur named Iguanodon. All three women also reported that rather than a long, gator-type snout, the creature's head was pug-faced, like a bulldog.

Whatever those women saw, the local police took them seriously enough to send out six officers on a fruitless investigation that still drew attention from local and Australian news media.

Anyway, Augie begged off most of Jake's R and R invites. He eschewed them in favor of going home to the wife and daughter when filming or episode planning was in D.C. When out of town, he claimed he was too busy emailing home.

Emailing had become all the rage by the mid 1970's, merely two years after a cache of incredibly transistorized computers was found left in place of truckloads of armaments meant for the El Salvadorean government to continue their bloody civil war. Anti-government insurgents' own weapons supplies disappeared around the same time, with boxes full of solar panels left in their place.

Anyhow, the one occasion Augie did accept Jake's invite, he wished he hadn't. Garish strobe lighting and stale odors from people's decadent carousing grossed him out plenty enough. But when one woman tried to lap-dance him, and another assaulted him to stuff a dollar bill under his belt...Augie did chuckle while Jake and company doubled over laughing, but he determined: Never again.

"C'mon, man!" Jake angrily protested Augie's rejection of his next invite. "None of us have cameras! Vicky will never know!"

"I'll know, okay?!"

*

"Folks, you'll never believe what our sound engineer just rushed into the studios!"

"What's that you're holding here, David?"

"Adam, it's the title track from the new Beatles album coming out next Tuesday! That same day it will also be released as a single. We've got it here in our grubby hands at WPXG-FM! Let's see: This press release says it's a concept work."

"Oh-oh. I mean, I'm a big Beatles fan and all, but..."

"No buts, dude! This is the freakin' Beatles!! And it's their first album featuring Linda McCartney and Yoko Ono as full-fledged members!"

"Hey David, think you could stop talking long enough to take the single for a spin?"

Augie Matias pulled his bike over to the side of the road, under maple tree shade near Rock Creek Park on his ride home from the Natural History Museum on a warm, sunny mid-May afternoon. A brand-new Beatles tune?! He needed to give that his full, undivided attention.

"From the album of the same name, both coming out next Tuesday, here is, for the first time, 'Careful What You Wish For,' by the Beatles."

Following an especially grungy introduction on multi-tracked electric guitars, classic Beatles harmonizing belted out:

"You say you want to stop confiscations
Of all ot the weapons
That otherwise would kill.
"You want to see the bloodshed from battles
That now you can't witness
For that special thrill.
"But think of your children, your families, your neighborhood,

The death and destruction they might have not withstood.

"Be careful what you wish for;
You don't know what's in store.
"Be careful-"
Ring! Ring!

"Crappadoodle-do!" Augie muttered as he switched from radio station to phone-line on his ear buds for the incoming call. "Hey Vicky!" His mood brightened instantly, happily anticipating his sweetie-pie's voice. But he remained bummed out over the news he would have to share with her. More bummed out, even, than over an interruption to his first screening of brand new Beatles music.

"Hey you," said Victoria Copplestone, sultry as ever, "want to talk dirty to me 'bout how your interview went?"

"If you mean with lots of expletives, oh yeah! I'm ready to cuss like a sailor!"

"That bad, huh? They can't return you to full time?"

"Castleman said he was about to contact me if I didn't beat him to it. They can't keep me even part time much longer. This fall they're bringing on this hotshot paleontologist from China who's already singlehandedly unearthed twenty new dinosaur species. He'll be here for five years. Meantime, the best Castleman could offer was a tour guide post, but he wasn't even sure about that. My GS position would drop through the floor, and that might not fly despite the career track being completely different."

"Could you apply like you never worked for the government in the first place?"

"He said I could, but might as well not bother. The wait list for museum guide applicants with no other government experience is a mile long."

Vicky sighed. So much for the heavy breathing portion of their call, except maybe to hyperventilate with stress. "Guess we might both end up retraining for different work. I think nursing wouldn't be so bad."

"Wait, is this about your kid with the UFO project?"

"'UFOs were not on the list of approved topics. None of the books you provided have been vetted by Media Resources. Not only for this student, but for the rest of your class as well, you've blown off essential tools in the language arts curriculum for quantified goal measurement. Including but not limited to time management prescriptions, rubric checklists, and formative assessments.'" Vicky recited effortlessly this laundry list of accusations from heart, as it had kept echoing through her head ever since her school's curriculum adviser hurled it at her in the principal's presence. "There's more," she went on to Augie over the phone, "but you get the gist."

"So how did you respond?"

"Not one of my more diplomatic moments, I'm afraid."

"Oh?"

"Went something like: 'You've blown off the most reasonable possible interpretation of much education research. Namely, that micromanaging children's language arts learning, trying to document in fine detail every last step of their progress, does far more harm than good.'"

"You might as well repeatedly weigh a cow," Vicky said at the review for placing her on probation. "Not going to result in extra milk, and in fact might make the cow so nervous, she reduces her output!"

"Are they going to fire you?"

"Worse. On Monday, they're going to have someone named a remediation coach second guess my every move two days a week. They said it's some master teacher."

"Master what?"

"Yeah, I wish I could lock her up in a closet to do that instead. Ditto for Muehler, who will occasionally second guess the second guessing. Think the only reason they aren't firing me outright is because my budding young ufologist's parents barged into the building and said all kinds of nice things about me."

"Did they write that terrific letter about their son doing more reading than they'd ever seen him do before, after you found him that account about Air Force Project Bluebook?"

"Yep, that's Jonathan. Supernatural possibilities are his element, his waterway for swimming upstream. Whenever I suggest more conventional topics to him, he reacts like I might as well have been asking the proverbial fish to ride the proverbial bicycle. And Augie, I'm sorry Augie, but what has pushed me seriously to the edge of dumping this gig and pursuing a career track in nursing is an admonishment I received from Lizzy's teacher, literally as I was leaving that rotten meeting with the curriculum adviser."

"Do I know what this is about?"

"I think you do, Professor Matias. And I quote, 'Your daughter's imagination is wonderful! Really it is!'" Vicky exaggerated Ms. Micara's girlishly high-pitched voice. "'But children rely on their parents and other responsible adults in their world to keep them well-grounded. Really responsible adults remind kids about the reality they must inevitably return to after any fanciful flights of fantasy! Now I can tell your daughter just worships your husband.'"

"That explains the incense I smelled burning-"

"Wait, Augie! Listen to what she said next! This is word-for-word. 'Dr. Matias is all the more obligated to make certain Elizabeth understands that nobody really expects to find a living dinosaur. His show is just for entertainment purposes only, am I correct? Whatever brings the highest ratings?'"

Augie could only close his eyes and shake his head in disgust over some people's narrow-mindedness. And then he noticed a split-open, empty cicada shell clinging to the trunk of the maple tree where he'd parked his bike to seek shade. On the end of the cicada's seventeen-year-long gestation period, it had dug out of the ground, climbed the trunk, and finally emerged from its larval stage as a large, red-eyed bug.

Inspired by the cicada shell's haunting insinuation of life after death, Augie conjured a most peculiar thought. Suppose non-avian dinosaurs, the last remaining ones, were still roaming about an inadequately explored wilderness. Could they have somehow managed to hypnotize large portions of humanity into stubborn skepticism of their existence? That's how they protected themselves from being hunted down and slaughtered, or captured for cooping up in zoos?

"Hello? Augie? You still there? Want to hear what I said to Nancy Micara?"

"Yes, of course. Sorry. I was just...Stunning arrogance on her part."

"Exactly my point! I told her neither one of us, neither she nor I, knows enough about the planet's climate and geologic history to say for certain what is or is not possible out there. Unless one is completely confident all the nooks and crannies have been sufficiently explored."

"How did she take that?"

"Cow in the pasture looking up from chewing its cud. You know the routine."

Augie knew exactly the routine. He always felt bottomless compassion for fellow human beings who did not enjoy his personal advantages on their own roads to adulthood. Grandparents' inheritance had freed him to devote high school summers and his university years to his non-lucrative passions for paleontology and cryptozoology. He was unencumbered by the need to hold down part-time work whether at a fast-food restaurant, a convenience store, or elsewhere. Not that his parents didn't make the occasional push for him to make some of his own money, rather than continuing to lean on their allowance up until his assistantship at the Smithsonian his last summer before graduation. But they were of too gentle a disposition to push too hard, and so it went.

Anyhow, despite empathy inspired by his assumption that most other people with whom he interacted did not share his good fortune, Augie still couldn't help an irritation that wife Victoria shared. No matter the venue, whenever he raised a subject off the beaten trail, or made an observation rarely made, if not breaking new ground altogether, more often than not he was met with a dumbfounded look. What occurred to him finally was to liken that look to a cow looking up at him from contentedly chewing her cud. Victoria had had his same experience in the realm of elementary school education, so she had easily embraced her husband's admittedly insulting imagery.

Over time, Augie grew to suspect something of the people who gave him that special look when, for example, he argued non-avian dinosaurs might still be extant. He grew to suspect that by and large, they were not a particularly happy lot. He often recalled one of Vicky's colleagues wistfully remarking that on her retirement, she would fill her days lounging on a deck chair in Myrtle Beach, South Carolina, sipping on a strawberry margarita. Really? There was no more to life than that? Wouldn't that become too boring? Then what? Whenever Augie recalled this little tidbit, he also imagined the colleague's deck chair slowly sinking into the sand until some years later, the only thing left was a lone hand holding a still-half-filled margarita glass out of the sand. A toast to self-burial.

Augie couldn't help wondering whether the key to many a person's true happiness didn't reside in one of the items met by the cow-in-the-pasture look. In other words, many people were doomed to never truly enjoy life, because they preemptively dismissed, slammed the door shut on the answer to that quest. For whatever reasons that was the case, Augie well knew he needed to ramp up, keep refreshing his empathy.

"Again, I pity anyone whose world view disallows for fantastical possibilities," is how Augie responded to Vicky's, "You know the routine." "We'll figure out something to keep a roof over Lizzy's head. But Vicky, this crap has been baked into the cake ever since the county hired you. You're really going to allow them to chase you out of teaching to become a nurse or whatever? You're so good at what you do. Look at all the fan mail you receive from parents and former students."

"I know."

"Aren't you going to run the risk of becoming that fish asked to ride a bike?"

"A fish that can sleep at night, untroubled by concern she'll be trampling over children's joie de vivre and creativity with her bike."

"I'm sure if you ask any good nurse, he or she will tell you all the b.s. they have to put up with..."

Bzzz! Bzzz!

"I better take this, Vicky. Could be the museum."

"We'll chew our cud together this evening. Bye!"

Click!

"Is this Augustine Matias?"

"It is." Augie's heart was already sinking. He didn't recognize the woman's voice on the other end. But he figured she was calling from a so-called boiler room, trolling for suckers. He should have checked the number displayed on his cell phone before...

"I'm connecting you with my son."

"This is Dr. Augustine Matias?"

"It is." Augie couldn't bring himself to hang up just yet, disarmed by "my son." His curiosity got the best of him, only compounded by the extremely nasal voice that took the mother's place.

"Dr. Matias, you may not know me, but I know all about your participation in that shameful TV spectacle, *Cryptomonster Hunt*. I read your profound frustration between the lines, and have formulated a proposal for your consideration.

"Call me at this number at your earliest convenience to discuss further. As an act of good faith, I have already deposited one-hundred-thirty-thousand dollars in your joint bank account. After taxes, you and your wife should clear an even hundred thousand, yours to keep even if you say no. Intrigued?"

Just before the line went dead, Augie could have sworn he heard reggae music starting up in the background, on the other end of the phone.

Chapter 2

"Praise Jesus, my big bro's back from the big city just in time for harvest!" Donald McDonald set down his bucket half-full of plucked mushrooms under tarpaulin shade, and via handshake pulled Scott McDonald into a tight embrace.

"Um, yes, praise Jesus. I did, you know, um, well," Scott stumbled about verbally. He imagined them both, decades later, and still finding himself overwhelmed by the ever-wild, wide-eyed look in Donald's eyes, accompanied by that uninhibited grin. Years ago, he used to attribute his younger brother's unhinged-feeling visage to his drug habit. But ever since Donald went cold turkey..."I might have stayed an extra hour or two for snooping about the bookstore after, um, after my reading, uhh..." Scott couldn't help continuing to stumble, despite relief over his brother finally relaxing the hug and stepping back, giving him space. "But, but clearly, clearly those shiitakes were only days away from sporing, last time I checked."

"So how did it go, bro? Sorry I couldn't attend, but like you said...look at how many are still left after I've spent all morning..." Donald waved Scott's attention under the tarpaulin tent pitched in an open field surrounded by towering oak trees.

Crisscross oak-log piles, four feet deep, sat just far enough apart for walking in between. Dotted by numerous shiitake mushrooms latched firmly to their bark despite Donald plucking them off for hours, enough spore dust blanketed the logs for semblance to a heavy frost. Add to that all the 'shrooms hidden away amidst the crisscrossings, in not-easily-accessed locations...

"Well," Scott self-consciously rubbed his paunchy belly, "there was some interest." Some interest indeed. Was he ever grateful that Donald did not attend. What a ruckus his uncompromising evangelical shtick might have fueled, hearing how his "big" brother handled one particular expression of that interest!

At Sir Readalot Books down a less-travelled side street in Louisville, Kentucky, polite applause from a sparse audience met the conclusion of Scott McDonald's slide show. He featured photos from the center of his recently published book, *Mokele-Mbembe: Real-Life Behemoth?*

"I have a question," said an attractive young African American woman Scott couldn't keep his eyes off when she took a front row seat.

"Oh, good," he reacted. The presence of anyone, attractive or not, interested enough to not even wait for him to ask if anyone had a question...

"The whole notion of searching for living dinosaurs in 'darkest Africa,'" she used her fingers for quotation marks as she affected an especially husky voice, and kept her chin raised defiantly high, "isn't that a racist trope?"

"A racist- racist trope? No, I- I want to hear this," Scott added when one of the guys sitting in the back row booed, who just happened to be of Scottish descent...same as the black woman on her father's side of the family. And Scott McDonald himself, of course. "If you will, please explain what you mean by that. I am very, very interested, Ms., um..."

As the guy who booed stood up and left with a dismissive hand wave, the woman answered, "Ms. Irene McDowell, and I thank you for the opportunity. Perhaps, um..." Irene stammered, taken by surprise over Scott not pushing back hard, rather professing a willingness to hear her out. She was rattled enough already by her inability to help feeling strangely attracted to this frumpy-looking fellow. "Maybe it never occurred to you before," she proceeded finally, "what that meant, calling Africa 'the dark continent.' (more finger quotation marks) Lots of talk was included about pygmies and headhunters. And now you add that possibly, the only location left on Earth where prehistoric monsters might still dwell...Isn't the upshot that black people are primitives from a primitive part of Earth?"

"Um, didn't I read yesterday there's a movement to coalesce several African nations into a United States of Africa? Freed from apartheid and other forms of colonial enslavement?" Scott strained to continue making eye contact with other people still in attendance for his book promotion. Part of him felt like Irene was the only other person in the bookstore with whom interaction truly mattered. They might as well have been cuddled together in the corner of a darkly lit restaurant.

"I read the same thing," Irene nodded, but with a tone that insisted, *Enough distraction; address my concern!*

"To your point, Ms. McDowell,-"

"Irene is okay."

"Yes, Irene. Well, like I was saying, to your point, I have had my own concerns about the role racial prejudice plays in getting to the bottom of the mokele-mbembe mystery. With other animals in Africa, it has always seemed their existence is not considered official until confirmation from a white man."

"Hm," Irene nodded, her affect leaving Scott uncertain whether he surprised her with something new, or she was expressing approval of his response.

Whichever, he went on, "Take the okapi, for example, like a combination of a zebra with a giraffe, actually part of the giraffe family. Its existence was not officially recognized until the turn of this century, even though the locals first described it over a thousand years ago. Similarly, peoples of the Congo and Cameroon claim to have known of our creature of interest for a very long time. As mentioned in my book, a missionary reports that one was killed to stop it from invading a fishing hole. And at the subsequent victory feast, its meat proved poisonous. Well, to repeat myself, it was described as having an elephant's body, a long tail, and a snakelike neck, entirely consistent with the morphology of a sauropod dinosaur. But again, since no white man has ever seen one from any closer than hundreds of yards away, as a head on a long neck sticking out of a river, its existence is not simply doubted. No, the skeptics of our culture suggest the locals are mistaken. They're misidentifying a rhinoceros, or an elephant making a river crossing with its trunk held skyward to keep from drowning. Or it's a fanciful mythology played for real to lure in tourist dollars.

"No, wait," Scott quickly went on, sensing Irene about to leap back in. "When we explore mysterious backwaters of Africa, this is not to suggest there are not other parts of the world that might conceal surprising, hitherto undiscovered relic beasts from prehistory, including one location not too very far away from here."

"Oh?"

"I am referring to the Scape-Ore Swamp in South Carolina. Only last year, reports came in from around its perimeter of a human-sized reptile that stood erect on its hind legs. Casual hikers find the swamp itself largely unwelcoming, too many poisonous snakes plus the occasional black bear."

"Weren't those reports from teenagers trying to get off the hook for scratching up their parents' cars?"

"That can't- That can't be ruled out, yes. But you also have parts of Alaska the size of Iowa completely untouched by civilization of whatever ethnic origin. Scattered stories from their outskirts speak of strange unknown beasts, one sounding maybe like a sabre tooth cat.

"Look, um, Irene it is, yes?" Scott stepped closer, opening his hands in supplication, showing nothing hidden in his palms...or about to be hidden in what he had to say.

"Irene it is, yes," Irene confirmed, keeping her chin raised high.

"Yes, thank you. What it comes down to, for me, is this. As a little boy, I enjoyed King Kong movies and comic books, wherein dinosaurs were imagined still thriving on some remote island in the Pacific. I always thought, wouldn't that be the neatest thing? So years down the line, when I learned we could not completely close the door on that possibility, well, well you wouldn't be unfair to accuse the little boy inside me of having never grown up."

"So this whole thing is you clinging to your childhood?"

By this time, Scott's audience had actually grown to a very obvious extent. Several other people in the bookstore gave up pretending they were browsing shelves that just happened to be nearby the corner set aside for book signings. They came over and filled chairs in the back rows. "That's not fair," a voice from among them could be discerned muttering in reaction to Irene's question.

"No-no-no-no-no," protested Scott, waving one hand emphatically. "I'm not sure that question isn't perfectly fair."

"You made reference to some dinosaurs having evolved into birds," Irene went on, emboldened by Scott essentially coming to the defense of her inquisition. "But wasn't your expedition to the Cameroons bankrolled by the anti-evolution Genesis Museum, which contains exhibits that argue for the Earth being only six thousand years old?"

"It is true that the Genesis Museum displays a literal interpretation of several Biblical claims, and the Earth's young age is one of them."

"How do you know how old the Earth really is, young lady?" a man raspy with old age and pack-a-day smoking asked reprovingly who was sitting behind Irene. "Were you here six thousand years ago?"

While a few other people laughed nervously, Irene turned around to respond directly in the fellow's face, "I wasn't here even two hundred years ago. But reading history books has given me some idea what was going on back then."

"History books written by people who were actually around to see what happened, I hope," the raspy man grumbled undaunted. "The best we have from thousands of years ago are the books of the Old Testament saying the world was created in six days, praise God!"

"Praise the Lord!" someone else chimed in.

"Were whoever wrote the Old Testament actually there to see those first six days?" Irene asked challengingly, also undaunted. "How was that supposed to work, if supposedly the creation of people was left for day six, after the stage was set?"

"They didn't need to be there because God told them what happened. It says so in the Bible."

"Amen!"

"Okay." Irene couldn't help becoming flustered, so much for unflappability. "So what you're saying, then, is that what's written in the Bible is true because it says so in the Bible."

"And what's so wrong with that, young lady?" the woman who said "Amen!" worked up the courage to butt in, emboldened by her anger.

"Where do you stand on all of this, Mr. Scott McDonald?" Irene redirected herself, worried whether she could maintain civility if she continued arguing with defenders of Christian fundamentalism. Clearly, rather than respond to her points, they were going to keep taking tangents that avoided ever facing the requirements of logical reasoning.

"From what we have learned in geology and physics, I think the evidence is unquestionably strong, that the Earth is at least four billion years old. Isn't to say I am not a man of deep religious convictions. But part of my belief is that God gave us brains to work on understanding the full magnificence of the creation."

"But you're still okay taking money from a museum that profits from presenting as fact that the Earth is only six thousand years old."

"Again, they are- they are presenting a particular point of view, a literalist interpretation of the Bible. And listen, I happen to know some people connected with the museum, um, their lives were turned around from certain self-destructive behavior by their engagement with such a belief system."

Scott left out that "some people" was his own brother, Donald. Not four years earlier, Donald's painkiller addiction in the wake of an injury on a building rehab job lost him his wife and the job as well. But one of his hard-hat construction work buddies literally dragged him out of a gutter, fed and cleaned him, then got him to a church service in a recreation center basement. There, plans for building a Bible museum threw him a lifeline to make it through his addiction withdrawal, followed by a second chance at construction job employment. Building the museum helped rebuild his life.

"Praise Jesus!"

"Um, indeed," Scott presently lukewarmly reacted to someone else in his growing audience. "But at the same time, on an almost daily basis we're learning more about the wonders of the universe, including through expeditions into the unknown such as my recent one that admittedly fell well short of the goal. My hope is that the more we learn, the more we can move away from literal interpretations of humanity's first attempts at deeply understanding the world around them. Then, we can put certain museum exhibits in, um, their proper perspective." Scott dreaded these words ever getting back to his brother, not to mention the numerous fellow parishioners who helped bankroll his Cameroon expedition. He had little to no faith they wouldn't take them the wrong way. But he had to be honest, especially for Irene. Even though he hardly knew her, she already felt like the voice of his conscience.

"So what exactly are your areas of formal training and expertise?" proceeded Irene with her inquisition.

Certain audience members felt she went way beyond rude, but Scott regarded her as more than fair, given the controversy he had waded into with total abandon.

"Yes, that."

"Don't answer her on my account."

"Amen!"

"No, wait," pleaded Scott to growing grumbles while Irene kept her chin held high, continuing to stare him down. "Given that I am pushing a notion that flies in the face of certain settled dogma, I do need to be able to establish my credentials. And so, well, my undergraduate work was in geology at Ohio University, with a minor in vertebrate paleontology. Then I went on to receive my doctorate in cultural anthropology."

"Oh, cultural anthropology! Was that so you could relate to the headhunters in deepest, darkest Africa when you went asking them, 'Which way to the Lost World'?"

"I need- I need to...Maybe this will clarify for you where I am coming from." For the first time, Scott was becoming genuinely pissed at Irene. He well understood her suspicions, but also knew that deep down inside, he was a better person than she was making him out to be. "Our missionaries in the Cameroons, they provided much of the logistical support for my team to safely reach those less-explored areas. But I also- We didn't want to go in there without doing something special for the people of that region, well beyond whatever the missionaries already offered."

Irene would have snidely remarked, *You mean, well beyond the missionaries warning them they were on the fast track to hell and eternal damnation if they didn't accept 'Jeeeeeeesussssss' as their personal savior?* However, she was not insensible to the considerable animosity she had garnered her direction, however racist its likely origin. So she kept quiet, albeit remaining chin held high, as Scott continued, "So we arranged college scholarships for two outstanding Cameroonian high school students. It was their choice whether to attend one of several good universities in the capital, Yaoundé, or the University of Kentucky. One of them chose to attend Yaoundé University 2, studying flood management, while the other is having a successful first year working towards a degree in agriculture on our home soil. It's all still little enough, but it's something."

"As long as they converted to Christianity, that is. Otherwise they are going to hell according to your missionaries, true?"

"Wait. That isn't fair," protested Scott.

"I think you might be the one who needs to worry about where you're going, young lady!" muttered the woman who earlier praised Jesus.

"And that isn't fair, either! Please, if I- if I can respond. Um, I got to know the student who selected Yaoundé University 2. He was raised a Muslim, but now he has his doubts about religion in general, and terms himself atheist-leaning. For my too-short interaction with Mohammed, he- he proved himself to be of the more honest and generous sort. In fact, it took some persuading for him not to turn down the scholarship altogether, on the basis of his thinking there must be others more worthy and needy than he. And that is the God's truth!

"Now about this other you brought up, about people going to hell if they don't believe a certain way: It never made any sense to me that a god of love, of- of the love that Jesus preached when He said we should even love our enemies, all that, how would such a god condemn anyone to eternal damnation simply because they doubted Her or His existence?"

That was it for the woman who implied Irene might be headed for hell; she got up and left, grumbling loud enough to be heard, "I can't listen to any more of this." Beside the cash register, she dropped off the copy of Scott's book she'd intended for him to autograph.

"So how many copies did you sell, big bro?"

"What was that?"

"Doesn't take you long to slip into a daydream, does it? I was just asking for the second time, hint hint, how many copies did you sell?"

Scott was daydreaming, about Irene. She caught up to him after the bookshop manager brought his book-signing event to an abrupt close before anyone else could leave in a huff without purchasing a copy. In a nearby coffee shop, he was studying his cup of hot chocolate, marveling at how the muddy liquid reminded him of the Sangha River's muddy waters. If only a teensy Apatosaurus would rear its long neck out of this cup of hot chocolate, that would save so much trouble…

When Irene found Scott so intently contemplating his refreshment, head bowed, she couldn't help asking, "So, has that body of water ever been previously explored?"

"My sonar picked up a strange lump at the bottom of the cup."

"Well that's just chocolate sludge not stirred in with the rest, the best part far as I'm concerned, and not some prehistoric relic sleeping off seventy million years," counseled Irene, reading Scott's embrace of her kidding around as a full welcome for her to sit beside him. After which she explained that where surviving dinosaurs were concerned, she would far prefer a prehistoric relic found still wandering around in the wilderness over some Jurassic-Park style, DNA-fueled resurrection. And she left him her phone number before, as she put it, she "had to go."

The copy of Scott's book she had him sign, she waited to purchase until everyone else left the bookstore, including Scott.

"I did sell a few copies, actually."

"Well there you go, big bro! Praise Jesus!"

"I can never thank the Lord enough for the blessing of my very existence," Scott diplomatically phrased his authentic sentiment. "But a few sales here, a few sales there are going to fall far short of funding a new expedition anytime soon, as in during our lifetime."

"I know, big bro, I know." Donald set down his bucket of harvested mushrooms to hold one hand high as in, *Don't interrupt me!* "Even with all the evidence you gathered for the survival of living dinosaurs, and what that means for the discrediting of evolution,-"

Scott flinched, but Donald didn't notice as he went on, "-there are still going to be a lot of intellectuals in their ivory towers who continue behaving like Doubting Thomas. 'Where's the proof you were crucified, Jesus? Show me the nail marks in your hands!' But you want to know something?" Again Donald was with those wild eyes and unhinged grin. "Those people will never be convinced! Never! But you know something else?!"

Scott had heard his brother ask this same question so many times before, and give the same answer, he had to wonder...

"God will find a way! God – will – find – a – way! Let's pray!"

Ring! Ring!

Ring! Ring!

"Um, yes?" Scott already regretted answering his cell phone instead of letting it ring. Again. He kept telling himself he needed to stop picking up when he didn't recognize the number. Those calls almost always concluded with his having to hang up on sales people instructed not to let a phone conversation finish until either they made a sale...or were hung up on. And Scott well knew he was too polite for his own good, seeking the genteel exit that the person on the other end was trained to never accept.

"This is Scott McDonald?"

"Um, yes." Scott found himself overwhelmed by an intuition he was talking to someone's mother, and that that mattered.

"I'm connecting you with my son."

Sure enough. What elaborate new scam is this? Scott couldn't help wondering.

"Dr. Scott McDonald?"

"Yes." Scott also couldn't help freighting that one simple word with on-the-alert suspicion, especially since so few people had any idea he'd earned his PhD. That was something he didn't even advertise on the back cover or inside flap of his book.

"Dr. McDonald, you may not know me, but I know all about your expedition to Cameroon. Between the lines of your impressive treatise, I read your profound frustration over the limits on how far you could actually journey into your quest.

"Call me at this number at a time of greatest convenience. As an act of good faith, I have already deposited sixty-four-thousand dollars in your bank account. After taxes, you should clear an even fifty thousand. Yours to keep even if you say no. Intrigued?"

Scott was too stunned to answer before the line went dead. Didn't help that whoever was on the other end spoke in the most nasal voice ever. And what was that music in the background that made its abrupt entrance on a most syncopated downbeat? Sounded like something from the tropics.

"I heard the phone click, bro. Did they get things reversed, and think you were trying to sell them something? You look like you've just seen a ghost!"

Scott finally collected himself enough to say, still stunned, "Someone who apparently, apparently he liked my book so much, he deposited a large sum in my bank account, no strings attached!"

Donald's eyes opened even wider than usual, and his grin expressed more dubiousness than joy to ask, "You really believe that?"

Funny, Scott thought to himself, *coming from a guy who just lectured me on Doubting Thomas Syndrome, and is willing to believe Jesus walked on water.* But as usual, he could not bring himself to express aloud his exasperation, constrained by gratitude for fundamentalist Christianity having helped his brother kick a drug habit, even if blind faith might accrue its own special hazards. *If fellow parishioners, not just my brother, ever had a window on my thoughts...*

"We can find out easily," Scott responded holding up his cell phone, instead of getting into the Doubting Thomas stuff. "I'll check my account." With a series of finger taps, Scott confirmed the sixty-four-thousand-dollar bank deposit. "Well there it is." The way he held forward his phone in the palm of his hand for Donald to see the evidence, Scott fancied he might as well have been showing him nail wounds.

"Huh," Scott's brother reacted noncommittally. "Well, don't try spending it yet, in case it bounces. And certainly don't write him a check for any amount."

"Don't worry. I know all about that scam."

"And I wouldn't call him. Whatever you do, don't call him."

Scott suddenly felt Donald glaring at him, even more unsettling than his, "Huh." So all he said was, "Okay, we better get on, get on with his harvest." He feared how his brother might react if he contradicted him. Where Scott was concerned, Donald might as well have been high on painkiller again, demanding they "drive somewhere to have some fun! Don't you want to have some fun?!"

Chapter 3

Bernie Coleman set aside his book about the Loch Ness Monster to stand up behind the check-in counter, and welcome a couple with their young son and daughter. When he heard wood block chimes announce their entrance, he assumed they came for directions to somewhere else in downtown Portland, Maine. Maybe the fire engine exhibit or the observatory. Or the Victorian Mansion which, unlike what he expected for his own operation, was saved from demolition at the last minute. Or maybe they wanted help on one of the tourist-oriented scavenger hunts. Or his recommendation for the best lobster roll. Least of Bernie's expectations was that they would actually want to check out his cryptozoology exhibits.

Yes, back in the day, during the 1960's, his storefront Triceratops head bursting through the brick wall above the entrance used to generate a steady stream of curiosity seekers of all ages. Hi-profile hunts for Bigfoot, sea serpents, and the creature named mokele-mbembe that bore a striking resemblance, as the locals described it, to a sauropod dinosaur: these certainly used to fuel interest in his exhibits, and expand membership in his Cryptozoological Fellowship. But the years wore on with strange creature hunts yielding little else than blurry videos, recordings of unusual sounds and the like. So public interest steadily waned in the notion of extraordinary beasts hidden in remote corners of the globe, maybe even non-avian dinosaurs that had escaped extinction. Periodically hoaxed evidence didn't help, nor did the notion that unexplored nooks and crannies were becoming scarce.

No wonder, then, that Cryptozoo World curator and sole remaining proprietor Bernie Coleman did a double-take when he realized the son was pulling on his father's arm to drag him up to the check-in counter.

"What is this place exactly?" the father asked Bernie noncommittally, while mother and daughter shook their heads disdainfully as in, *Here we go!*

"Oh, it's a little of this and a little of that," Bernie shrugged his shoulders. He had long since given up trying to make an impression. A curtain elaborately stitched with images of tropical foliage suggested exotic secrets concealed within. Beyond that, however, Bernie was through with the hard sell.

"You have special stuff about dinosaurs? Are there dinosaur skeletons inside there?" The boy leaned over to one side, stood on one leg to sneak a peek past the curtain.

"There is one replica of a Ceratosaurus skull, but that's not the main point of the dinosaur part of our exhibit. As you might already know, one kind of dinosaur flits all about us." Bernie made an effort to include the daughter in his attentive gaze. For which she rewarded him by anxiously grabbing hold of her mother's hand. Nevertheless, she did maintain eye contact with the wizened old fellow, whose unkempt white hair lent him a crazed visage where she was concerned. "They're called birds," Bernie continued, undaunted. "The dinosaur exhibit concerns the possibility non-bird dinosaurs, dinosaurs as we are most familiar with them, might somehow have survived to the present day, in some inadequately explored region of the Earth."

The whites showed clear around the boy's eyes as he laughed, "No way!" And he looked up at his father in a manner that said, *Please Pops, I have GOT to see this!*

Mother and daughter rolled their eyes as "Pops" asked, "So what's the admission charge?"

"Ten dollars for adults,-"

"And children get in for free?"

"Sure." Bernie Coleman couldn't bring himself to say otherwise. The sign by the cash register clearly indicated that children six and up were five dollars each; you had to be younger than six to get in free. But why bother? The exhibits were in their final days; three weeks hence, Cryptozoo World would close for good. And another week after that, who knew what the buyer of the storefront property would do? Gut the insides for a brew pub? Demolish the place altogether to start from scratch, no more Triceratops bursting through the wall?

"Sorry, Dad," Bernie could still hear his son's empathetic voice echoing in his head. "You know how much I'd like to keep this going for you. But with two daughters in college and a third starting next year..."

"You shouldn't apologize," Bernie had cut off Aaron. "You've already done far more than it was ever reasonable for me to expect."

"And at least you have a year to keep in storage those exhibits you don't have room for, until you can find a good home for them. Nothing will be lost."

"So where can I see a dinosaur that's still alive?" the seven-year-old boy asked Bernie with a tug on his green plaid sweater, while mother and sister posed for photos of each other beside the Bigfoot statue.

"Well that is a very good question, young man. I call your attention to this plaster cast." Bernie waved the "young man" over to the exhibit he referenced, encased by glass.

"So what's that supposed to be?" the boy asked after pressing his nose against the glass to take a closer look. "Dinosaur poop?"

"Jack Adkins! Watch your language!" Jack's mother admonished while his sister giggled.

"Several years ago, on an expedition to the border of Venezuela with Brazil," Bernie pointed at a map located beside the glass case, "I found a large, three-toed mud track. I filled the track with wet plaster, and when it hardened, this was the result."

"Guess I kind-a see the three toes," Jack said hesitantly after another intent look.

Bernie's heart never failed to sink when he heard such a remark, despite how often people made it. And he also never failed to find himself sounding defensive as a result, saying, "The problem, of course, is that the mud was excessively squishy. Once I poured the plaster in, it spread into the mud before drying out and hardening. That blurred the distinct three-toed shape you see in this photo. Well, should have been able to see in this photo. It's not nearly as distinct as it looked actually being there."

"So is it a foot track from a living dinosaur?"

"Can't say for sure. But where I discovered this, people speak of a strange beast named the stoa." Again, Bernie waved Jack's attention over to the exhibit, this time to an illustrated narration entitled: What is the stoa? Myth or reality? "Are you familiar with a novel named *The Lost World*? By Sir Arthur Conan Doyle who wrote the Sherlock Holmes stories?"

"Pops, didn't we see an old movie on TV named *The Lost World*?"

"That was based on the book."

"Well the book," Bernie went on, not missing a beat, "was inspired by something Sir Arthur Conan Doyle learned during travel to South America. There are stretches of land along the border of Brazil with Venezuela that are hundreds of millions of years old. But rivers have carved them into what are termed tabletop plateaus, as you see here in this photo. Conan Doyle learned that around some of them, legends abound of strange beasts that sound a lot like they could be actual living dinosaurs."

Jack gave his father another of his youthful, wide-eyed looks of wondrous amazement which he couldn't help meeting with a skeptical head shake.

"At the base of one of those plateaus in particular, that's where the stoa is said to have made a rare appearance. It has, supposedly, very big and wide muscular legs, small forearms, and two small horns on its head."

"Like this drawing," Jack's father observed in dubious mode.

"Exactly. And here is the especially interesting thing about that drawing: As the caption reads, it is an artist's rendering of the theropod dinosaur, Carnotaurus, as it might have appeared in real life, based on a fossil skeleton excavated from late Cretaceous rock in Argentina. Which of course is on the same continent, South America, as Venezuela and Brazil." Bernie hastened to add that last factoid, as he sensed puzzlement over the big deal regarding Argentina. "The great zoologist, Dr. Karl Shuker, has written extensively on this subject," he couldn't help prattling on while the father studied the caption.

"Near which plateau, exactly, was this creature allegedly seen?"

"The natives call it Kurupira."

"Kurupira," the father repeated as he whipped out his cell phone to fact-check. "How is that spelled?"

"As it is pronounced: K–u–r–u–p–i–r–a."

"Except for a reference to it by that Dr. Shukar you mentioned, I'm finding no other information."

"Ah, yes, well, things do get a bit complicated, don't you know. The Brazilian government renamed it something in Portuguese I don't presently remember. And they've gone to great lengths to keep people from approaching anywhere near. They don't even have it on a map."

"So how did you locate it?" Jack asked.

"An excellent question, young man. You see this star on the map? It covers hundreds of square miles on the Brazil/Venezuela border. Locals named the Yanomani, living on the Venezuela side, brought me there in exchange for a certain mushroom they had never seen before. But they insisted my team and I make our journey wearing no more than a pair of boxer underpants. And we were forbidden from carrying along anything beyond food supplies, snake venom serum, a camera, and that plaster I used to make the footprint cast. Indeed, they frisked us for compasses so we very quickly became completely disoriented, lost before we were anywhere near the Kurupira tabletop mountain, also known as a tepui."

Unnoticed by Bernie were the anxious looks Jack's mother and father were exchanging, especially after he mentioned the boxer shorts and the mushrooms. So the father took him by surprise when he made a show of looking at his watch, then said, "Gee, Lisa, weren't we supposed to meet our friends at the harbor for lunch?"

"What time is it?"

"Almost eleven," said the father, checking his watch again.

"Can I give you directions? Where at the harbor?" Bernie asked to be helpful despite a creepy feeling he was being fed a fabrication.

"That's okay, we know the way. Say thank you to the nice man, Jack," said Jack's father even as he dragged his son nearly off balance towards the exit, the same as his mother with his sister.

"I hope you find the stoa, mister. But he looks awful dangerous, so be careful."

"You have an excellent lunch, young man."

From inside the exhibit room, Bernie Coleman could hear Jack's older sister past the entrance curtain, coincident with the wood block chimes on the family's hasty exit. She was asking, "Why only one foot track? Shouldn't there have been several? And how do you hide a-"

The door closed shut the sister's final word, but Bernie knew it was "dinosaur."

Part of Bernie wanted to run after the family to answer their daughter's questions. Where foot tracks were concerned, there was only that one bare, muddy spot. Fallen leaves, fronds and twigs blanketed the rest. And they did appear matted down in a manner consistent with a large creature of massive weight have lumbered through. And as for hiding a dinosaur, the mists of trans evaporation after daily rainforest soakings would do very nicely, thank you, for concealing an entire herd of them. There was also the matter of informed speculation and local legend suggesting the stoa's actual habitat was atop Kurupira, alongside other mysterious creatures mentioned by the locals. What happened, perhaps, was that on rare occasion, a stoa would accidentally make its way through a crevasse down off the three-thousand-foot-high plateau. Maybe that's what the Brazilian government was trying to protect people from when they obstructed exploration. Or might that be yet another region where solar panels and cell phones were mysteriously showing up while various armaments were just as mysteriously disappearing? Another chapter in the reigning enigma of the past century? An enigma responsible, according to best estimates, for humanity's technological progress exceeding what would have been otherwise expected, on the order of at least three decades?

There was one basic thing Bernie would have had to concede, had he pursued the discussion with his unexpected customers. If, indeed, non-bird dinosaurs still roamed the Earth, the evidence for their existence sure seemed paltry. But then again, why wasn't it zero? Why had he come across that three-toed track, far larger than even the largest known ostrich could make? Rather than no track at all? The Yanomanis went to the trouble of hoaxing it just for him? Really?

Far more significantly, he wouldn't ever forget the first morning he woke up in camp near the base of Kurupira. He could have sworn he saw a lizard's head emerge from behind a palm tree when he poked his nose out from his tent to contemplate the mist-enshrouded landscape. That head appeared the size of a basketball, maybe even bigger, and had a short horn above each eye. And it was gone from sight as fast as a shooting star. Too much undergrowth around the palm for foot tracks, of course. Maybe he hallucinated, fueled by wishful thinking combined with a stray whiff the night before of whatever the Yanomanis were smoking...

Ring! Ring!

"Coleman here."

"Bernie Coleman?" asked the woman.

"Yes," Bernie confirmed regretfully, feeling foolish for having picked up the receiver instead of making whoever leave a message...probably a junk-call sales person. He also, quite strangely, found sorrow over his wife's recent passing hitting him again, hard. Suppose she did still live beyond the grave, like a relic dinosaur beyond the sixty-five-million-year-old Cretaceous chalk layer boundary. Why so little evidence, comparable to the so little evidence for surviving dinosaurs? Why wasn't there either no evidence at all, or abundant, incontrovertible evidence? Why those peculiar experiences, for example of someone rolling over on the bed beside him when he couldn't see anyone there? As elusive and frustrating as that lone foot track that proved impossible to distinctly plaster cast?

"Mr. Coleman," said a male unusually nasal, "it might seem no one really cares about your mission. But I care. At your earliest convenience, please call this number for further details. Meanwhile, as an act of good faith, I have deposited sixty-three-thousand dollars in your personal account, yours to keep whatever you should decide. You will also find an additional hundred thousand in your business account for upkeep while you are gone. Of course, if you choose not to be gone, not to participate, simply consider that a no-strings-attached donation."

Bernie Coleman could not have been more shocked had a Carnotaurus poked its head out from behind the exhibit-cloaking curtain.

Chapter 4

"Finally!" exhaled Skip Newton as Irene McDowell stepped from a taxi along South Market Street in Frederick, Maryland. "If you'd taken much longer, girl, I was going to film the interview without you!"

"Oh yeah? And just how was that going to work?" Irene got in Skip's face with her chin once again raised defiantly high. "You were going to listen for what the book had to say for itself?" She gestured towards the paperback copy of *At The Crossroads of Folklore and Reality: a Cryptozoological Inquiry*. Skip left it lying on an unfolded metal chair in the small front yard of Irene's parents' row-house.

Skip wondered whether he could get away with giving Irene a passionate lip smooch in response. But she'd already sat down for the interview. If he didn't know better, she labored to avoid just such a thing from happening. So his head shake had as much to do with her evasiveness, a creepy sense she was continuing to forestall any intimacy, as it did with her brazen wit. "I heard you correctly on the phone that you've returned from a side trip to Kentucky? Kentucky?!?!" Skip repeated with his exclamation going high-pitched screech on the "tuc." "What were you doing in Kentucky?! Recruiting for the local KKK?!?"

"I told you on the phone, Skipper." Irene was getting really pissed; out the corner of her eye she espied her mom and dad approaching while their front screen door slammed shut. She knew "Skipper" went on like he did to alert her parents where she'd been. He damn well wasn't at all uncertain what he'd heard her say over the phone! "There was a book reading about a dinosaur hunt in the

Cameroons," she explained, addressing her parents more than her budding film-maker friend. "Gotta keep current."

"Everybody's writing a book," Amber McDowell, Irene's mom, shook her head in disdaining wonder.

"That's right, Mom. Where's yours?"

"People are paying me good money to keep my mouth shut and my pen dry," Irene's mom responded with a husky laugh.

"A dinosaur hunt," father Ian McDowell said in his fathomlessly deep voice. "And you're not talking about bones, are you?"

"You know I'm not, Daddy."

"So where in Kentucky were you, exactly, for your crypto-whatever-you-call-it?"

"Downtown Louisville, Daddy, safe as safe can be." Irene pretended too much preoccupation locating a particular passage in her heavily researched tract for her usual defiantly-held-high chin.

"Mmm-hmm," Ian nodded dubiously. "Seeing whereas you're unwilling to look me in the eye, I'm guessing it would have been much less worrying had you been deep-sea diving Loch Ness instead."

"That's right," said Skip, again with his high-pitched screech. "You're from Scotland originally aren't you, Mr. McDowell? Scotland! How'd that happen?"

"How'd a black man end up born in Scotland? The way most good things happen," Ian McDowell answered in his deeply booming voice, not missing a beat. "Love."

"Hey, if we're going to do this interview outdoors, we better boogie," warned Irene. "It's almost sunset."

"I hear you, girl."

"And knock it off with that 'girl' stuff!"

"Damn! Okay," agreed Skip as he finished focusing his tripod camcorder on Irene. "We're on in three, two, one-"

Slam!

Irene shrugged her shoulders, resigned to the likelihood her father made a point of slamming the screen door shut at the exact right time to mess up the start of the filmed interview. Pessimistic disgust over the prospects for any news channel, even cable, featuring Skip's interview probably fueled his anger. Not to mention mounting frustration over his daughter's waste of so much time chasing fantasies she ought to have spent pursuing a career worthy of her genius.

"Okay, we're here speaking with Ms. Irene McDowell, author of the newly published book, *At The Crossroads of Folklore and Reality: a Cryptozoological Inquiry*. That's quite a mouthful, Ms. McDowell. What does it mean exactly?"

"Well I want to thank you for this opportunity to explain what it means, Mr. Newton." Irene coincidentally on purpose held up her book for the camera. "Across multiple cultures, rich traditions celebrate the wonderful diversity of life on our planet. You have Native American totems in the northwest United States and Canada, engraved with everything from bald eagles to an ape-like creature variously named Sasquatch or Bigfoot. And that's the whole point, maybe. In those traditions, creatures we all accept do actually exist are accompanied by creatures that must either be fanciful imaginings, or are real but not officially confirmed. In the case of some previously unidentified whale or dolphin depicted in ancient drawings and engravings, no big deal. For example, a new species of orca whale was discovered off the coast of Peru that the locals have known about for centuries. But what gets really interesting is when such traditions speak to something that looks like a sauropod dinosaur, or a prehistoric sea reptile."

"But Ms. McDowell, c'mon." Skip ladled on a skeptical tone easily, no matter how attractive he found Irene. "Aren't there other explanations we can lean on before we're carried away by dreams of living dinosaurs? The legend of the gryphon, thought I read that probably originated with the discovery of Protoceratops skulls in the Gobi Desert."

"Protoceratops skulls! Well you have been doing your homework! Maybe we should explain for your audience..." Irene ground to a halt because the harsh rumble from an eight-cylinder engine unmitigated by a muffler had finally grown deafening. She easily imagined it the roar from a Tyrannosaurus Rex directly in her ear.

The reconditioned, bright red 1969 Camaro emblazoned with a Confederate flag and outfitted with oversized tires slowed alongside where Skip was filming. Then someone in the back seat tossed an object out the window, and someone in the front passenger seat fired at that object with a blowtorch, setting it ablaze.

The burning wooden cross landed mere inches from Irene's sandaled feet as a young man harshly shouted, "Go back where you came from!" Pursuant to which, the Camaro's rumble intensified for acceleration deeper into downtown Frederick.

By the time Irene's dad ran back outside, Skip had already lost sight of the car thanks to other traffic filling in behind it.

Where Irene was concerned, might as well have been one of those legendary prehistoric relics rearing its extraordinary dragon's head out of primordial wilderness all too briefly before disappearing again.

Splash! Irene's mom drenched the burning cross as well as the smoldering, tinder-dry grass underneath with a bucket of tap water. By then, Irene's father had come up behind Irene at the street curb, staring defiantly downtown. "Those mysterious angels of mercy might still be confiscating weapons by the truckload from random battle zones around the world," Ian muttered. "But they still haven't found a way to confiscate the hate, Irene honey! And until they do, that's why your old man fears for your life when you wander certain regions in search of stories about monsters that should have gone extinct millions of years ago. God protect you from these other monsters that also should have gone extinct!"

"That's what I've been telling her!" complained Skip.

Irene didn't fully key in on what her dad and would-be boyfriend were saying, for puzzlement over whether the phone she heard ringing faintly was from her parents' row-house, or elsewhere.

"Baby girl," Amber addressed her daughter Irene as she hurried back out onto the front steps, "a woman wants you to speak with her son! Now what's that all about?"

"Doesn't sound like any scam I've ever heard of," Irene's dad remarked. "But in case it has something to do with our drive-by cross burners, think you better just hang up."

"Wait!" Irene rushed indoors past her mom. Who knew that someone didn't talk with someone else after reading her book, and wanted to hook her up with a solid lead on serious cryptozoological evidence? ...or that that cute if insecure guy from Kentucky had already done a gut check after pondering the phone number she wrote down for him only a few hours ago? Although, she did find herself half hoping it wasn't him. She didn't like the idea of his mother making phone calls on his behalf, rather than him taking that initiative on his own.

Chapter 5

"Hi, Mom!" joyfully exclaimed Heidi Letterman.

"Hi, Mrs. Rosenberg!" added Harry Letterman, behind Heidi with hands on her shoulders. "Your daughter is my wife, and we are so happy you arrived here at exactly three pm!"

"Harry is my husband, Mom," said Heidi, reaching back to give one of his hands a loving squeeze.

"Yes," emoted Sally Rosenberg in her girlish voice, "and you have been married for almost two years already! Mazel tov!" Sally understood the importance of routine restatements of the obvious for both her daughter and son-in-law with Down Syndrome. But her enthusiasm came naturally, as she envied the couple's evident bliss.

"How long have you had your own place?" asked Stu Rosenberg, also sensitive from long experience to the importance of routine in his daughter and son-in-law's lives. "Has it been a year already?"

"One year, one month, three days, sixteen hours, twenty minutes..."

"Days are good enough, remember," Harry took advantage of Heidi's pause to say, with another gentle loving squeeze of her shoulders while she looked at her watch.

"Days are good enough," Heidi nodded. "He's my check," she told her parents as if for the very first time.

"And she's my balance," Harry added. "We are so happy you arrived here at exactly three pm."

"This is very exciting," Sally emoted again in her girlish voice. But intent on moving along the conversation before it got stuck in a repetitive groove, she hastily proceeded, "You will finally let us see what you have been doing with your spare room?"

Sally and Stu did have to wonder why Heidi and Harry kept their extra room project so top secret. But they always came back to figuring it had something to do with their need for routine. And so, neither Sally nor Stu's imaginations ran at all wild over what was soon to be revealed. A library? A hi-tech entertainment center? An indoor garden since the room's large window afforded plenty of natural lighting? Or maybe even - Well Stu especially thought this particular speculation did run a little off the rails – a baby nursery? Couples with Down Syndrome could expect to have trouble giving birth, but it was far from unheard of.

"My parents are going to think we are crazy. No they are not," Heidi shook her head as she argued with herself.

"They are nice people, sweetie pie," Harry counseled as though her parents were not present.

"He's my check," Heidi turned to her parents to repeat.

"And she's my balance."

"So what is your agenda, Heidi and Harry?" asked Stu, intent like his wife to move things along before his daughter and son-in-law bogged down in another feedback loop where they repeated the same stuff over and over. "Maybe you make the big reveal, and then we talk about it over lunch?" Years raising Heidi had impressed on him the supreme importance of schedules and routines for her.

"The big reveal, yes! I like that," laughed Harry. "It is going to be a big reveal, yes, sweetie pie?"

"And then we talk about it over lunch, just like my father said, my handsome man." Heidi encircled Harry with her arm to drag him from behind her to beside her. "He's my check," she explained.

"And she's my balance."

"That's the room right there, isn't it?" Sally pointed at a closed door down the hallway from the living room. Over the years, she had learned patience and even a certain respect for the sort of interactions required to, again, keep matters moving along for her daughter and now son-in-law.

"That is the room, and after we show you inside and explain what it's about, we will talk about it over lunch."

"Which we will eat in the sun room," Heidi noted.

"You hear how she completes me?" asked Harry as he opened the door and ushered his in-laws inside.

What greeted Sally and Stu's eager examination was unlike anything they ever imagined or expected.

Maps of each continent and its accompanying islands covered the four walls. Color-coded thumbtacks scattered about them tied into special charts that specified times, places, and guesses as to reliability and truthfulness. And they also featured artist renderings of various dinosaurs, plus a few photos of such extant creatures as the monitor lizard and the rhinoceros. Bulletin boards featured laminated photocopies of newspaper clippings.

Sally and Stu knew that their daughter worked on book returns and cataloguing at the local public library, while Harry did maintenance at a nearby office complex. So their first reaction was dread. Maybe Heidi cut up parts of books, and stole maps for the elaborate display they anxiously beheld? And Harry assisted all the way, stealing thumbtacks and such from the office where he worked? The Rosenbergs knew they would need to tiptoe slowly towards any dealing with such unfortunate possibilities, if they weren't going to set off a load of upset.

Stu waited for Sally to make the first move.

"Um, gee," Sally started hesitantly.

"You don't like it?" Harry asked worriedly, strongly feeling his in-law's unsettled state.

"Oh, no," Sally emphatically, if disingenuously, shook her head. "I'm just wondering, did you do all of this? It looks like you document where various dinosaur fossils have been dug up?" Sally suspected that wasn't at all what the stuff covering the walls was about. But she couldn't bring herself to peer too closely at any of it, especially the laminated news clippings, for fear what she would learn.

"Actually, Mommy," Heidi answered without hesitation, "my handsome man and I have been documenting every occasion we can find, when somebody thinks they have seen or heard a living dinosaur."

"From anywhere around the world," added Harry proudly.

"That is...wow. Dinosaurs, honey."

"Where did you kids get the maps from?" Stu ignored his wife's shocked reaction to say, unable to help an accusatory tone.

"We didn't steal them from anywhere," Harry responded defensively. The same as so often before, he amazed his father-in-law with his eerie ability to read Stu's mind. "We bought them from a travel store named Triple A.

"Heidi's mom and dad don't like me," he went on to sob. "That is not true," he shook his head, arguing with himself. "They are just afraid of the unknown."

"Mommy!" whined Heidi tearfully.

"That's not true at all," protested Sally rushing over to Harry's other side, from the side Heidi leaned into him for support against so much upset. Nevertheless, a chill traveled down her spine over the son-in-law's clairvoyant assessment of exactly what set off both Stu and herself, which was indeed fear of the unknown. "We just were not anticipating you two would have so much interest in, um, actually looking for living dinosaurs, is it?"

"Living dinosaurs!" Heidi exclaimed. Her eyes lit up, just thinking about it.

"Our compilation of all known evidence has become an important resource for international cryptozoologists," Harry boasted proudly. "They consult us all the time."

"Three times already this month," said Heidi, bending back her pinkie finger with her thumb to hold up the other three fingers.

"Oh, that's my cellphone," said Stu.

"Your cellphone? I don't hear any cellphone," reacted Harry matter-of-factly.

"I put it on vibration, Harry," explained Stu, affecting a nonchalance he wasn't really feeling. "I'm very sorry to have to interrupt the plans, but something at the office...if this is what I think it is..."

"We have to make new plans," Heidi groaned in alarm.

"Remember what Dr. Murphy told us," said Harry, referring to their family therapist. "Interruptions sometimes happen. You face the interruptions..."

"...and calmly make new plans. He's my check."

"And she's my balance. And she completes me."

"You better take your call before they hang up." Harry pointed at Stu Rosenberg's cellphone.

"Okay," Stu said on his hurry out of the chart-strewn room, thinking of nothing better to say.

"You know, Heidi, I was waiting to go to the bathroom until just before we sit down to lunch," said Sally, also affecting a nonchalance definitely not felt. "But if I go now, maybe that will be one less interruption later on?"

"I can show you where the bathroom is?"

"I think your mother already knows, sweetie-pie."

"Thank you, Harry," Sally emoted with genuine relief; she wasn't sure how she would have navigated telling her daughter "no" without making the situation even more awkward. "Now you two just wait here and...maybe you can tell us about your favorite dinosaur at lunch." As Sally rushed off, she thought, *Here Harry gave me an easy out, and I couldn't have made matters more awkward if I tried!*

Sally and Stu met inside the bathroom, shutting the door quietly, and held hands for moral support.

"I thought they were doing so well," said Sally, trading a knowing look with her husband that said, *This stuff about living dinosaurs is too crazy to even require verbalization.*

"Well, I think it's more than we can deal with on our own. We need to bring in Murphy. I'm wondering whether they already told him how they use their spare time. And if so, why he didn't give us a heads-up."

"What they said about some 'ologist' consulting with them, you don't think they've been taken in by a cult?"

"I'm also worried about how they secured those maps and all that other stuff."

Looking in each other's eyes lasted for long sorrowful moments before Sally tearfully said, "After Henley disowned us, at least things seemed to be going so successfully for Heidi and Harry..."

Stu flushed the toilet to mask his wife's sobbing, just in case such sounds could carry through the townhouse walls.

Son Henley Rosenberg had fallen in with a white nationalist group intent on uncovering who was mysteriously defanging random military operations around the world. On the verge of particular conflicts turning really violent, of all-out war breaking out, who was making guns, tanks and the like suddenly disappear in a matter of hours? Then leaving behind curious items such as solar panels and super-transistorized computational devices? That physics engineers guesstimated accelerated technological advances decades ahead of where they otherwise would have reached?

The United States government, among others, kept pushing an insinuation that wise counsel and breakthrough research, both kept well hidden from the public domain, were acting as guardian angels repeatedly protecting humanity from its baser instincts. Significant numbers of people, however, agreed this was a cover story to prevent general panic. That in reality, some truly extraordinary other-worldly force had taken to regular disruption of Earth civilization's recent history. Consisted of either an extraterrestrial intelligence, time travelers from Earth's own future, or, what many evangelical Christians preferred to believe, the hand of God.

But across the globe there were also small groups of paranoid conspiracy theorists who read something far more sinister into the violence-preventing enigma. Henley was lured into one of them that wanted to prove a group of Jews were working in tandem with a group of Africans and African Americans, to achieve enslavement of the so-called white race.

Sally and Stu missed or didn't take seriously enough signs their son was being step-by-step brainwashed, recruited into Swords Before Plowshares.

"I tried to make time with him on weekends; I actually thought we were doing a pretty good job of not neglecting him while we met Heidi's needs. But," Stu laughed in the middle of a rehash he and Sally had done on multiple other occasions, word for word, "how could I compete with fishing trips offered by other guys his age?"

"Remember, Stu, those were summer weekday trips when you had to be at work." Again, a word-for-word repeat of what Sally had reminded her husband of on so many prior occasions, before also repeating, "I know you didn't think it was that big a deal. But the fact we couldn't afford as big a bar mitzvah as many of his schoolmates..."

"I'm not sure that mattered," Stu shook his head, going on further with the word-for-word rehash. "What I keep coming back to, what still haunts me to this day, is that time I found him in the backyard when he was only six years old, plucking legs off a praying mantis one by one. He was giggling about it!"

"We're having the same awful conversation again, aren't we?"

Stu drew Sally into his arms. "I heard someone else say something that certainly applies: You're my check."

Smiling wanly, Sally was about to respond, And you're my balance. But then there was a knock at the door. Took a moment to sort out that it wasn't the one to the bathroom where Stu and Sally were cramped inside. Rather, it issued from outside the townhouse.

"Don't worry about the door! You are our special guests! I'll answer it!" Harry Letterman shouted as he hurriedly stomped down the hall in a manner that reminded Stu of a lumbering beast. Chinaware in a display cabinet rattled tinkle-tinkle at the same time Harry's voice groaned deeply.

Stu snuck out of the bathroom first, unnoticed by either Harry or daughter Heidi. He was just in time to watch Harry open the front door to a most genial-looking fellow sporting a cream-colored cardigan sweater and a winning grin. Stu motioned Sally to join him outside the bathroom as Harry asked the stranger, "How can I help you? You are interrupting our schedule."

"Sorry about that. I am sure your schedule is very important," the fellow at the door reacted with earnest empathy, if still standing his ground. "I am here to represent someone who holds the work of you and your wife in the highest esteem. You are Mr. Harry Letterman, and that's Mrs. Heidi Letterman just behind you?" he asked in an uncertain tone, noticing Heidi's parents even further down the entrance hall than Heidi.

"That is correct. I am Harry Letterman. That is my wife, Heidi Letterman..."

"He's my check."

"And she's my balance. And," Harry surprised himself with being able to move right on along and complete his introduction, not find himself sidetracked by his wife's interruption into another feedback loop, "here are Heidi's mom and dad, Mr. and Mrs. Rosenberg."

"You must be very proud of your daughter and son-in-law," enthused the stranger at the door, reaching in to shake Stu and Sally's hands.

"So you know them from..." Stu trailed off.

"They have compiled the definitive chronological summation of experiences worldwide that might, and I do emphasize the word, might, suggest the survival of non-avian dinosaurs into the modern era, maybe even into the present day."

Heidi and Harry nodded proudly.

"I don't know how much they have told you, Mr. and Mrs. Rosenberg, but their data collection has become an important gold standard resource for cryptozoologists around the world."

"They were just starting to tell us about, uh, cryptozoologists was it?" said Stu. "And who are you?"

"The name is Samuel Longbottom, and cryptozoology is the study of animals whose existence is in question, but can't yet be discounted entirely, if at all. Harry, Heidi, as a good faith gesture, the person I represent has deposited one-hundred-twenty-five-thousand dollars in your joint bank account, no strings attached. After taxes, you should clear an even hundred-thousand."

Harry and Heidi hi-fived one another while Stu said dubiously, "No strings attached, but that person you represent must be expecting something in return."

"All he is expecting is a phone call to this number, to discuss an opportunity to do more with your data, Mr. and Mrs. Letterman, than you might have ever dreamed possible. Your parents are certainly welcome to listen in, Mrs. Letterman. But you can wait until after you complete that schedule I am so sorry to have interrupted."

"And if they say no to everything, even the phone call?"

"The money is still theirs to keep as a small token of gratitude for what they have already accomplished. And we will never bother them, ever again."

"It's no bother," protested Heidi. "Please stay for lunch."

"We move with the flow," agreed Harry, beaming.

"Let's move with the flow, dear," said Sally, encircling Stu's arm with an urgency not much different from what she would have felt were she pulling him back from the edge of a cliff.

Chapter 6

That Sherman Peabody found the courage to remove his protective helmet before he entered the baby pool meant nothing to nearby parents. They every last one of them couldn't evacuate their infant sons and daughters fast enough. A grown man exhibiting so much trepidation on his descent into one foot of water, and encumbered not only by an inner tube, but by a life jacket as well: This was not a man to be trusted around children until more measures of his behavior had been taken.

Oblivious to all that, Sherman reminded himself what the odds were of a meteorite surviving its fiery descent through the atmosphere long enough to reach the ground, and then happening to strike someone. "You're far more likely to be hit by a stray bullet," he could hear the sweet voice of his girlfriend Esther echoing in his head from a few days ago. "Or struck by lightning. Or run over by a car. Or, or bitten by a poisonous snake. So why stop at the helmet? Why not also always wear a bulletproof vest? And ride around in a tank fitted with a portable lightning rod, while carrying an assortment of venom antidotes? Where does your security from every conceivable threat, no matter how remote, end?"

Baby steps, Sherman thought smugly, figuratively patting himself on the back. And was most pleasantly surprised to discover that even seated in the pool, the water proved too shallow for flotation devices to much matter...unless he lay back, became so relaxed that he drifted off to sleep. Danger still lurked.

But feeling secure enough, despite his head left vulnerably unprotected from the astrophysical elements, Sherman returned to his latest thought experiment. The idea was to live forever in a very particular way. He figured he better start practicing sooner rather than later, when old age encroached.

The principle was very simple, really. Take a ten-minute time frame, and focus on the first five minutes. Then focus on the remaining two-and-a-half minutes. Then the remaining minute and a quarter, so on and so forth until he found the remaining half-life too short to give a thought. With enough practice, shouldn't he be able to make ten minutes feel like ten years? After all, if you stood ten feet away from a wall, and walked half way towards it, then half of the remaining way forward, and kept moving accordingly, you never did reach the wall, did you? Because you only walked half of whatever distance was left?

When Sherman Peabody thought too much about this, he had to wonder how anything ever reached anywhere, whether through time or space. Maybe that was how someone was able to see their whole life pass before their eyes just before they died. Although there was the issue of how anybody could actually discover that was what happened, and live to tell about it.

Rats! So distracted from my exercise, ten minutes seem to have flown by, if anything. Have to start all over again!

Ring! Ring!

Sherman's phone took him by such surprise, he started flapping his arms wildly, so wildly he found himself floundering even in such a shallow pool, and got water up his nose.

The life guard shook her head in disbelief; was she really going to have to rescue a youngish adult male from drowning in the kiddie area?

Parents once more evacuated their infant sons and daughters, after having allowed them back in the pool one by one as their confidence grew that Sherman didn't pose a threat to anyone other than his own self.

Meanwhile, Sherman coughed up enough water to return his attention to his still-ringing phone. He hastily extracted a zip-lock baggie from his swimming trunks, opened it, opened the smaller baggie inside of that and then the smaller one inside of that. He feared his cell phone would go quiet before he ever reached it, but miraculously it did not. And even more miraculously, all his discombobulation did not prove for naught, didn't end up being over a junk phone call.

"I have a very particular need for the very unusual perspectives you bring to each situation you deign to address," the nasal-voiced person on the other end spoke admiringly, after that person's purported mother ascertained the renown Sherman Peabody was on the line.

What Sherman learned was that a week from then, he would be transported from a nearby bus station to an undisclosed location, for full disclosure of exactly what Mr. Nasal Voice had in mind. In the meantime, no other strings attached, some sixty-seven thousand dollars had already been deposited in his bank account, calculated to leave him with an even fifty thousand after taxes.

Half a week amounting to three-and-a-half days, half of three-and-a-half days amounting to one-and-three-quarter days, so on and so forth...Sherman had to wonder whether he would end up experiencing eternity far sooner than imagined, such was his excited anticipation.

Chapter 7

"Human beings have a propensity for seeing what they want to see, and not seeing what they don't want to see. Yes?" Stephen Feldman noticed a raised hand, even with the lights low.

"Can we assume you include yourself among that subset?" the wise guy managed to ask keeping a straight face, to the scattered snickers he hoped to garner.

"You mean the subset of human beings? Well yes, there have been questions raised in that regard. You are not the first to wonder," Stephen kept his own straight face to respond deadpan in his characteristically deep voice. "I don't see any fangs dripping blood from you, so I assume we can also include you among our number." Stephen triumphantly cleared his throat amidst far more numerous snickers than the college sophomore student precipitated. So did he continue as guest lecturer in Professor Mitchell's class on contemporary culture at Ohio University, central to a small town named Athens in the rural southeast corner of the state. "I am going to show you a short video that makes the point far more elegantly than anything I could say. That is, about humans seeing what they want to see, not about my being one of them," he resumed addressing his more general audience. "But first, I need to give you a simple direction. You are going to see a group of young men and women, much like yourselves. Please count how many times they pass around a basketball."

Indeed, the people on the video made a circle in some gymnasium, and were variously bouncing or tossing a basketball back and forth.

"So," said Stephen after he turned off the video, "any of you notice anything unusual?"

"The ball was passed around fourteen times?" one woman asked without bothering to raise her hand.

"You are correct, but I'm not really interested in that. I just told you to concentrate on that as a distraction. I repeat: Notice anything unusual?"

"A bunch of people with nothing better to do than pass around a basketball?" said Mr. Wise Guy, though more interested in learning the real answer than showing off his self-fancied wit.

"What if I told you someone in a gorilla costume was prancing around the men and women?"

"Huh?"

"No way!"

Gasps and mumbles broke out as students found the rerun video absolutely mind-blowing.

The guy in the gorilla costume made a real spectacle of himself, running back and forth in amidst the circle of bouncers.

How could we have missed that?

When the rerun ended and Professor Mitchell turned up the lights, no more wise guy remarks, Stephen Feldman said, "You're probably wondering, 'How could I possibly have not seen Apeman's hijinks? That doesn't seem possible!'"

"Yeah!"

"You sure you didn't show us a different video the second time?"

"Good for you, asking that question!" Stephen made a triumphant forefinger stab towards the woman who raised the possibility of trickery. As chief editor of *Doubting Thomas: the Official Journal of the Society for Clearer Thinking*, he couldn't be prouder that his presentation prompted such a display of healthy skepticism. "I assure you I reran the exact same video. But I also assure you that you ought not to take my word for it," he responded further. Then stepping aside from his laptop that had projected the video onto a big screen, he went on, "Feel free to come up here and check out my equipment. Make certain there are no other files on the DVR disc than the one I shared."

"She might get nauseous checking out your equipment, dude," wisecracked the same student from before while the young lady demurred from accepting Feldman's offer.

Speaking loudly enough to be heard above the raucous laughter, Professor Mitchell said to Mr. Wise Guy, "Danny, maybe to spare Carla from throwing up, you are volunteering to check out Mr. Feldman's equipment yourself."

For once, Danny found himself the target of laughter as he grumbled, "Okay," and stood up.

"Actually," Carla overcame her shyness again to further involve herself, "he could have switched out the DVR in the darkness without our noticing, and hidden it where you really will have to..." she trailed off with a shoulder shrug as applause and laughter erupted.

Stephen Feldman spread his arms. "Right," he said. "So give me a full pat-down."

To his classmates' further amusement, a chagrin-faced Danny proceeded to quickly pat down Stephen from top to bottom, seeking a hidden-away DVR disc. But standing back up from stooping down low for the cuffs of Stephen Feldman's pant legs, he smugly sighed, "There's no point to this. He just as easily could have switched from the disc to a file on his hard drive, or vice versa."

"And we don't have enough time to wade through the hard drive and rule out that possibility," said Professor

Mitchell. "I think the point has been fairly, amply made, about the rigorous standards that have to be applied to evaluating any amazing claim. Amazing claims require amazingly indisputable evidence with no other explanations possible. But for the purpose of concluding this lecture some time before midnight, I think we can agree Mr. Feldman wouldn't risk his reputation to pull off an elaborate con in a freshman college class. So if you will proceed..."

"Thank you, professor. You have made a most persuasive point, even if I do say so myself.

"Back to the video: The first time you viewed it, you were so focused on the task I assigned, none of you noticed the guy wearing the ape suit. You saw only what you were instructed to look for.

"Now, we could have had someone tiptoeing through like a ballerina, or juggling five oranges on a unicycle. But the fellow in a gorilla suit is especially apropos, because there are people who claim to have seen an unusually large primate often referred to as Bigfoot. Consequently, it has become commonplace for expeditions to comb forests in fruitless search for him, yes?"

From early on in his lecture, Stephen noticed a genial-looking fellow seated near the back in a cream-colored cardigan sweater, and sporting a most pleasant smile. So Stephen hastened to call on him when he ventured to raise his hand.

"Are you suggesting our failure to notice this man in a monkey suit, the first time we watched your video, demonstrates how people could be mistaken about seeing Bigfoot?" the genial-looking fellow asked.

"Yes, that is a fair conclusion."

"But doesn't our failure actually make a whole different point?"

Stephen's mouth literally dropped open, dumbfounded, and he said, "I don't understand."

Unfailing in his pleasant demeanor, cream-colored cardigan sweater guy went on, "Haven't you just proven that if, for example, let's say someone goes camping who has no interest in Bigfoot. They are so caught up in camping details, such as pitching a tent and starting a campfire, they don't notice some hairy guy nine feet tall who keeps peeking at them from behind a nearby tree. Haven't you shown us how that is a very real possibility?"

Stephen shook his head like he was shaking off some irritating insect buzzing his face. "No, I don't think you understand. Let's say your campers are very interested in Bigfoot. And so a bear comes along that they don't see is a bear, rather they mistake it for your hairy guy who's nine feet tall."

"But in your video, what are they seeing that they are mistaking for something else? Wouldn't you have to show them mistaking the basketball for a soccer ball, if that is the point you're trying to make?"

"Okay, then please allow me to make that point since the video doesn't seem to have worked for you." Stephen strained to maintain a dispassionate tone with who he initially misperceived, so he thought, being well in the corner of rational thinkers. "It might surprise you to learn that in my youth, I was a true believer UFOs were spaceships from other planets."

"And here I thought you had just been dropped off by one."

"Enough, Danny," warned Professor Mitchell.

"You're not the first to suggest that." Stephen mentally patted himself on the back for so quickly and affably making such a self-deprecating remark as he proceeded, "I really wanted to see a UFO, other than the one that dropped me off. Preferably, it would land in my parents' backyard, and little bug-eyed beings come out to wave hello. Well, one evening from the balcony of my grandparents' high-rise apartment, I imagined genuinely getting my chance. A classic flying saucer appeared to come closer and closer, complete with an impressive array of multi-colored lights circling its rim. Closer and closer, closer and closer...until I realized it was only a small plane with landing lights. I would guess it flew a good couple thousand feet above the roof of the high-rise."

"So you want to argue with me some more?" Stephen asked Cardigan Sweater Guy when he made a beeline for him directly following the conclusion of his lecture.

"I was actually very impressed by your entire presentation, and how you fielded my objection. I am here on behalf of someone who requires your fierce skepticism for his project."

"And what project would that be? Look," Stephen added before his question could be addressed, suddenly rethinking the wisdom of giving in to his curiosity, "I am so busy, really don't have time for anything additional, let alone some 'project.'"

"Fully understood." Cardigan Guy raised his hands in surrendering concession. "But my client hopes to move his project to the top of your priority list by making a good-faith gesture."

"And what good-faith gesture would that be?"

"If you check your bank account, you will find a seventy-three-thousand-dollar deposit that should clear you an even fifty thousand after taxes. Yours to keep even if you tell me to buzz off. Absolutely no strings attached."

Stephen Feldman had long since bowed his head to busy himself packing away the materials he brought for his lecture. He was intent on communicating to this increasing nuisance of an irritatingly genial fellow that he would soon be leaving him behind in the dust of his departure. But he couldn't help pausing to look up at him, upon mention of the no-strings-attached deposit.

Chapter 8

"Ms. Gómez!" Charley Puffington exclaimed when she was the one entering his office after he wearily said, "Come in," to her gentle rap at his door. "This must be big," he went on while reaching for his security blanket Cuban cigar. "I thought our arrangement was I come to you about assignments and updates, and you don't come to me about anything unless there is a death in the family." Charley pushed away from his desk, and leaned back in his swivel chair, turning his year-old Havana Humidor side to side without ever actually smoking it. Rather, savoring the connection to his late father who always used to reek of the stuff. "So who died?"

Laura Gómez curled up like a cat, Charley mused, on the armchair that faced his desk, tucking her tennis-shoed feet to one side. And only then did she finally respond, or purr as Charley would have likened it, "Yes, that would seem to be our arrangement. And yes, I am coming to you with something big that might be my most 'out there' assignment yet."

Laura's regular column for the bi-weekly journal, The Puffington Post (managing editor, Charley Puffington), was entitled "Out There." She covered the weird news beat, from UFOs to the Loch Ness Monster, and every crazy thing in between.

"Okay, doesn't really matter whether I come to you or you come to me; you always call the tune on what you're going to tackle, regardless. My only say has been when it goes to print, and word count." Charley addressed his unlit, never-to-be-lit cigar. "So what do you have this time that's so special, you couldn't wait for me to drop by to assign you what you were hell-bent on covering in any event?"

"I should make you wait for your cigar to respond. Then we would have the ultimate 'out there' story, assuming I was willing to vouch for your claim of a talking cigar."

"Ah, hahaha," Charley laughed as he might have, had Laura just checkmated him in chess. "Whisper it in my ear, ciggy," he said, holding his cigar to his ear like a phone. "What's she got going on?"

"I received a phone call from someone who claims to represent Eclipso Sunray Smith."

Charley looked into Laura's beaming eyes, enough with the cigar foolishness. "Eclipso Sunray Smith; now there's a name I thought we'd never hear again until his corpse washed ashore. Okay, now you really have stoked my curiosity, well beyond your previous woo-woo hijinks."

Eclipso Sunray Smith made his fortune reverse engineering some of the more complex technological wonders left behind when weapons caches mysteriously vanished. Which vanishings always happened on the verge of major conflicts scattered about the globe dating back to the early nineteen hundreds. As a result of Eclipso's efforts, people were using cell phones, laptop computers and sundry other devices decades earlier than might otherwise have been the case. But Eclipso was always a strangely reclusive fellow. And not more than a decade ago, in the early 1970's, he vanished altogether after rumors of some strange illness. Did that have anything to do with grieving over his wife's tragic death in the Amazon, on her last in a series of mysterious expeditions? Did Eclipso himself perish, and leave instructions in his will for his family to keep his fate impenetrably secret? Or rather than from rumored illness, did his disappearance result from coming too close to unraveling the century-old mystery of super-advanced technology left in the wake of confiscated weaponry?

"A Mr. Samuel Longbottom said my 'attendance is desired,' that's how he put it, at a meeting about a 'very special project.'" Laura made finger quotation marks for each word-for-word phrase she repeated from Mr. Longbottom.

"And presumably you would make direct contact with Eclipso at that meeting."

"I did ask if he would be there."

"And?"

"That's when I was offered the tidy sum after taxes of fifty thousand dollars, in exchange for at least consideration of attending the meeting in question. With the promise of larger fortunes to come, should I go all-in on their project."

"Their project."

"Just before arriving here, I checked my bank account. They did make the deposit."

"So you accepted their terms," concluded Charley, "and blabbed about it to me."

"Because I trust you to be discreet." Laura reached across Charley's desk to pat his arm. "I also thought you deserved an explanation, should I go deep cover with this thing for any length of time."

"Did you ask how long their 'project' might last?"

"'That's uncertain.'" More quotation mark fingers.

Charley's subsequent furrowed-brow squinting conveyed to Laura what made words unnecessary.

She needed to offer him something more.

"Look on the bright side," Laura said finally. "In addition to perhaps landing some incredible scoop, albeit on an eventual basis, obviously I'll easily be able to afford unpaid leave."

"Unpaid leave? So what happens to Out There during 'the project'? Do we just shut it down for the time being?"

"Tom Funiciello..."

"But Tom is stock market beat."

"That doesn't stop him from regularly dropping by my office to offer a chocolate croissant in exchange for what I've got in the pipeline."

"I didn't know Tom was into the 'woo-woo.'"

"I'm not sure whether it's genuine interest, or he has a thing for me."

"So it might be more the 'hey-hey!' than the 'woo-woo.'"

Laura couldn't help blushing as she said, "Either way, I suspect he would jump at the chance to temporarily hold down the 'woo-woo' fort until I return...or you have to find a permanent replacement."

Charley set down his security blanket cigar, to bring forefinger to chin for a long, hard, contemplative stare-down of Laura, orange-streaked hair and all. "I always considered you one of our top investigative journalists, probably one of the tops anywhere," he said finally. "That's made it especially frustrating that I couldn't ever get you anywhere near as excited over more conventional science or politics, even. You could have become one of the regular talking heads representing us on a cable news show, take your pick."

"'Conventional science,'" Laura bristled. "What does that even mean? Oh, I know: Reporting on the latest findings about the sleeping habits of Emperor Penguins, etc. etc. Learning they take short naps standing up isn't going to challenge anyone's world view, now is it? I'm not saying that's not all really interesting stuff," Laura added quickly, anxious to take the contemptuous edge off her voice.

"With my ability to drift off on my feet, waiting in the wings for someone to finish introducing me," said Charley, also wanting to turn down the heat, "have to wonder whether I might not have been an Emperor Penguin in my previous life. Oh-oh! Now you'll go on about reincarnation."

"That report I did last month on the suppressed psi study?" Laura returned to bristling. "That ought to have become major, mainstream media news because it highlighted everything wrong with labeling scientific inquiry as being either conventional or unconventional."

"I know," said Charley meekly. How could he argue, given what Laura discovered? A study of whether people could tell when they were being stared at from behind their backs had passed numerous strict research protocols to be published in a prestigious, refereed psychology journal. But two months after publication, the editor abruptly retracted the article, a rare extraordinary move. Even worse, that editor violated the norms for such an occasion. He should have explained why the retraction, and allowed the study's authors to offer a rebuttal. Well, there was no explanation, and no rebuttal allowed. And when Laura interviewed the editor, he said he couldn't reinstate the article until its authors conceded that paranormal events were impossible. "It's like arguing that trees can sprout wings and fly," said the editor. "We're not going to allow that."

"The editor of a world-renown prestigious psychology journal was treating science like a religion; you have your blasphemers and heretics," Laura presently piled on further. "How is that not major news?!?"

"I know," Charley repeated ever more meekly. "I'm just thinking how you might have redirected that clear-headed investigative genius to illuminating the reigning enigma of our time, with advanced technology left in place of mysteriously absconded weapons. There's some high-visibility woo-woo for you."

"Hey, give me a lead and a budget, and I already would have been all over it! And I'm still not sure my story last week about the medium isn't a lead of sorts."

"That woman with the alternate universe stuff?!" Charley sat up and leaned forward over his desk. "Bullshit! Bullshit!" he cursed, so much for meekness. "She could make up anything, and no one could ever prove or disprove any of it! Okay, in an alternate universe, I grew an elephant trunk and played it like a trombone for the New York Philharmonic! There! Prove that didn't happen!"

"As I'm sure you remember from the article, she's much more circumspect about what she can accomplish during a séance than your usual trickster. And there's the stuff about John Lennon..."

"Shameless! Shameless! That's your usual trickster's number one gimmick to draw attention, saying something about a famous personality!"

The medium in question told Laura that ever since 1980, she had been picking up a strange, discomforting vibe from near her residence in New York City. Always happened early December, and seemed to have something to do with John Lennon of the ridiculously popular and still-prolific art-rock group, The Beatles. Well last December, 1982, the medium claimed to have experienced an astounding revelation: in an alternate universe John Lennon moved to New York City and was fatally shot near the condo complex where she lived.

Subsequent to medium Charlene Busybody sharing this bizarre purported psychic revelation, Laura obtained a short phone interview with Lennon, who lived with wife Yoko Ono on a small sheep farm in southern Wales when they weren't recording. Concealing what Busybody told her, she asked the Beatle if he had been having any strange dreams on a regular basis since 1980. "Bees knees, Ms. Gómez, how did you know?" he reacted. "Three Decembers in a row, I have been having the worst nightmare about someone emerging from the darkness to take a shot at me. And it's in some big city not London, maybe New York. You're the first person I've shared this with. Not even my dearie Yoko knows, for fear she'd want to howl like a banshee about it on our next album. Bloody hell!"

"You still don't think Lennon's dreams are a bit too much of a coincidence? And the time of year he's having them? And that the alternate universe aspect might tie in somehow with those mysterious weapons confiscations?"

"Busybody went on a fishing expedition, and managed to land a whopper. I know Mr. Peace and Love claims he never shared his recurrent nightmare with anyone. But you don't know that for sure, and that Busybody didn't somehow catch wind of it. Or that on the other hand, Johnny Boy didn't catch wind of her crap, and is hatching a plot to discredit her. Look," Charley Puffington finally calmed himself down enough to say more even-temperedly, "if you do meet Eclipso, maybe all your investigative work into the woo-woo will pay off with one of the biggest scoops by anyone, ever, woo-woo or no woo-woo. And you're intent on going all-in on this no matter what, even if I threaten to fire you on the spot. Okay," Charley added after Laura kept quiet in response. On this occasion the same as too many others, he felt her silence acting like a vacuum sucking the assent out of him after she spoke her full peace. And so, likewise the same as before, he reached for his unlit cigar and gestured at her with it to say, "Vaya con Dios or however that goes."

"Gracias, Señor."

"Yeah, yeah," he answered resignedly, leaving Laura a look at his balding forehead, only, on her departure from his office.

The bottom line for Charley was that he could tell how absolutely thrilled his best reporter became on the trail of weird mysteries, the weirder the better. So who was he to ruin her fun? At least she knew what she really enjoyed doing. Which was more than he could say for himself...apart from the whisky on ice he was about to bring out from under his desk. He would have offered to share it with Laura, but she always turned down drinks in the past though adding, "Don't let me stop you." And he didn't think he could have endured her sorrowful regard again, how she pitied his inability to get joyfully worked up over, say, a UFO sighting with potential supporting evidence.

Chapter 9

"So much to tell, Vicky-Shmicky; where to begin? And I'm still not sure what I was brought here for specifically." Augie sat on the edge of a regal four-post bed, talking on speaker phone. He wondered how he could ever do justice describing all the antique wonders that filled the room he'd been assigned. The cuckoo that popped out of the gold-plated ceiling molding every fifteen minutes, for example... What the hell?

"Well, Augie-doggie, why don't you begin with where they put you up for, um, what is it? An overnighter?"

"Actually, the bus driver promised he'd have us back to the rendezvous point by no later than eight. Tonight, that is." I'll meet you here right after your orientation, Augustine Matias remembered him saying.

"The rendezvous point being the train station by BWI Airport?"

"Exactly," Augie nodded. "Meanwhile, until I'm called down for what the bus driver termed 'orientation,' I have the run of this luxury suite inside some humongous mansion the middle of nowhere."

"The middle of nowhere?"

"I'm guessing west central Pennsylvania."

"Guessing? You didn't pay attention to the highway signs? Or they blindfolded you?"

"They blindfolded us."

"Oh!" gasped Vicky.

"But not for the entire trip. The guy seated beside me plus a few others started complaining about motion sickness."

"So then you did get to see where you were going!"

"Not exactly. The windows are fitted with these special slats that only allow you to see bits of road shoulder, and the base of occasional concrete barriers."

"But what about the front windshield?" Vicky asked insistently. "The driver had to be able to see where he was going, certainly. So couldn't you sneak a peek out there as well?"

"Funny thing about that," Augie shook his head in wonder all over again. "Some opaque material completely covered the front windshield. And the driver just sat there watching the steering wheel turn on its own."

"Good God, Augie!"

"Yeah, calling him the driver almost seemed a misnomer. But there was something he kept checking down below the steering wheel. Probably a TV monitor; in a pinch, I assume he could have overridden the computer program.

"So anyway, as we approached our destination, the window slats and opaque material were retracted, allowing an unobstructed view of the final stretch. That's also when the driver resumed control by flipping a few switches and grabbing the steering wheel."

"Okay, Augie, so he took the bus off automatic pilot like he was flying a plane?"

"Exactly."

"And you said you were seated beside someone? Anybody you knew, or knew about?"

"Actually, he was one of the only folks I didn't know, aside from the bus driver, of course."

"Oh?"

"Wait; before that, might not have much time before they call us wherever, but wish you could have seen how the actual arrival went down."

"Oh, wow."

"Wow is right. Remember those special pictures that look like kaleidoscopic art? And if you stare at them long enough, these three-dimensional images of animals, you name it, seem to magically lift into the foreground?"

"Like on that calendar one of my students gave me?"

"Exactly! That's what happened when we were allowed the full view outside on our final approach. There was a stand of yellow birches in the middle of a big wheat field, most unusual."

"I know," said Vicky emphatically. "Don't yellow birches prefer hanging out in nightclubs where they can do the limbo? Limb-o, tree limb, get it?"

"What I've said before, Vicksen: You missed your calling as a standup comedian."

"Then I'd have to be funny all the time. Too much pressure. No thanks! So about those birches..."

"Yeah, the closer we got to them, the clearer something else emerged. But it wasn't a trick of the eye like on your calendar. It was an actual palatial mansion."

"Palatial, no less?"

"With a turret on every corner. Three stories tall, like something transplanted from Bath, England complete with yellow oolitic Jurassic limestone."

"Zzzzzz," Vicky snored loudly, then with a snort like she just woke up said, "Oh, sorry, what was that again?"

"What I was about to say was that what distinguishes this place from anything we saw in Bath is its bizarre design. Could have been a disciple of Gaudi turned loose."

"Gaudi?"

"You know, the guy with that cathedral in Barcelona that looks like a coral reef."

"So this mansion looks like a coral reef?"

"Actually, looks more like a particular dinosaur."

"A dinosaur? Oh boy."

"A stumpy claw is carved into the base of each corner tower with the turret on top. And the French door front entrance makes absolutely clear a dinosaur has been invoked, not anything else."

"What, does it say, 'Je suis le Oo-la-la-odon'?"

"Hey, I thought it was too much work being funny all the time! Anyway, those French doors are crafted in the shape of an Ankylosaurus skull, complete with horns."

"And let me guess: There are only two front windows, located as eyes?"

"Yes, and from what little I could see of the roof, I suspect it sits like a turtle shell embedded with rows of spiky nobs. And that there is a narrow hallway extension out the rear that ends in a circular room, perhaps a greenhouse. That would represent the Ankylosaurus's club-shaped tail."

"Are you on the phone with Daddy?" Augie could suddenly hear his daughter Elizabeth in the background.

"Want to say hello?"

"Hi, Daddy!"

"Hi, there, Lizzysaurus Lex. Or is it Lizzyliptodon?"

Augie loved hearing "Lizzyliptodon" giggle. Someone could have been tickling her.

"Are you on another dinosaur hunt, Daddy?"

"You mean, when there's a dinosaur at home that I could easily stick in a cage for the zoo, named Lizzyliptodon?"

"Nooo, Daddy," Elizabeth giggled some more, though this time with an edge that warned Augie she wasn't going to be sidetracked from her intended question, which was, "When can I join you to look for a dinosaur that isn't a bird?"

"Very good! You know the difference! I'm impressed! Lizzyliptodon is the smartest dinosaur ever!"

"Nooo," complained Elizabeth, this time far more whine than giggle.

"You're not the smartest dinosaur ever?"

"Nooo," complained Elizabeth again, all whine.

"Lizzy, they're going to call Daddy off soon to a mystery meeting, and I need to finish talking to him first. But he'll be back early enough this evening for you to pester him some more."

"Ooookay," Lizzy sighed in resignation.

"Lizzy honey, a part of me thinks I should give up the dinosaur searches altogether, just sort through old bones at a museum. Then I can come home to you and Mommy every single evening, and all weekend as well. We can watch television specials about other people finding living dinosaurs, when I'm not busy tickling you!"

"Hey!" shouted Elizabeth in giggling protest.

"You know, 'Daddy,'" said Vicky, "there's a name for people who sit back and watch while everyone else goes exploring."

"Oh?"

"Yes. They're called ghosts."

"Lizzyliptodon, I have to send lots of kisses over the phone to Mommy."

"Yuck! I'm out of here!" Elizabeth's voice was already fading from whence it emerged, well before she finished her declaration.

That's when Augie stopped his kissy noises.

"Okay," Vicky went on, "so who was the guy you didn't know, and all the ones you did?"

"The guy who sat next to me, he is such a character I could spend the next twenty minutes describing him. Let's just leave it at this: His thought process wanders so far outside the box, I'm not sure he's even aware the box exists."

"Interesting observation from the man of conventional disposition who searches for a living, non-avian dinosaur."

Augie didn't have to wait long for Sherman Peabody to make clear he was not one of the usual suspects. Soon as Sherman sat beside him on the bus, even before he formally introduced himself he announced, "Please don't fret over my not using the seat belt. I am wearing an airbag outfit."

"An airbag outfit..."

"Correct," nodded Sherman. "Suppose, heaven forbid, we experience a collision. My airbag outfit will inflate automatically, engulfing the entirety of my corporeal existence. You will suddenly find yourself seated beside what looks like a small blimp standing on one end. However, were I to buckle myself in, there's a chance you would see the seatbelt decapitate me at the waist."

"We wouldn't want that."

Thereafter, Augie met every bump in the road with not a little trepidation over the possibility Sherman's airbag would inflate.

Sherman offered up more odd comments along the way, including the statistical odds of a passenger experiencing bodily harm from a meteorite hitting the bus. But the one Augie found most striking concerned the Ankylosaurus mansion, after they arrived there safe from any celestial object inflicting harm.

A most friendly fellow sporting a cream-colored cardigan sweater was leading Augie and company to rooms for freshening up in advance of the meeting where presumably all would be revealed. Augie paused on a winding marble staircase to ponder a curious, elegantly framed painting that depicted two native Americans dressed in traditional native American garb. Their bows and arrows were drawn at a charging Triceratops. It was an odd painting indeed where normally, Augie would have expected to see someone's portrait from a century or more ago. Perhaps a captain of industry, or a woman of impelled leisure showing off the most elegant jewelry as well as offering a subtly prurient glimpse at her cleavage. Even weirder, Augie could have sworn he'd seen the Triceratops painting before, but just couldn't place it.

"I suspect," said Sherman, pausing beside him, "this edifice was shipped over here from England, brick by brick, for reassembly. After all that work, though, either its owner died, or quickly realized that the relocation project itself provided him with much more joy than the end result. Either way, he became a hermit crab moving on from the shell he'd outgrown. And that's when the new owner, quite likely the present owner, moved in with all his unique, dinosaur-related adaptations that clash so glaringly with the rather staid aesthetics of the original owner. But say," he turned to face Augie who continued pondering the man-versus-Triceratops oil painting, "do you share my curiosity over whether this edifice is as effectively camouflaged from aerial view as it is from surface view?"

"I do, and rather suspect it is."

"Okay, Augie my dinosaur-hunting hero," went on Victoria Copplestone-Matias presently, "so what about the fellow travelers you do know?"

"Many of them are a who's-who of reputable cryptozoologists."

"As opposed to the 'who-dat' of disreputable clowns?"

"Exactly. So there are Heidi and Harry Letterman."

"Aren't they known as the Compilers?"

"They are, but I never knew they had Down Syndrome."

"Really?"

"Really."

"Well that's just awesome! I'll have to share that with a certain colleague."

"You mean the one who told you not to expect much from your Down Syndrome student, just prepare him for becoming a cashier or some such?"

"An amazingly resourceful insult to both Down Syndrome people and cashiers, yeah that's the one."

"Well, to rub her face deep into that mud pie of her own prejudiced making, don't forget to mention that criminal forensics experts have expressed special admiration for the Letterman family's database, even if they don't buy into the entire cryptozoological endeavor."

"You can scratch that off your worry list. So who else?"

"At the sound of the Cuckoosaurus, please make your way to the conference room following the green arrows," came a feminine voice over a hidden intercom in Augie's room. Sounded like the mother who connected him on the phone with her unnamed son to start the mysterious ball rolling the previous week.

"The Cuckoosaurus, Augie? Good grief!"

"Good grief, indeed. But there's no reason I can't keep going with you until we're actually called down, or roared down depending on the sound a Cuckoosaurus makes.

"Remember my mentioning a certain Scott McDonald?"

"The creationist buff who believes that finding a living dinosaur would disprove evolution?"

"Yeah, I asked him about that while we were waiting at the train station. He had a very interesting response that also peaked the attention of this collector of cryptozoological-related folklore named Irene McDowell. If I didn't know better, in fact, I'd say there is some electricity arcing between them."

"Well then to hell with his response! I want to hear more about the electricity!"

"Um, yes, well," Scott's hesitating voice still echoed in Augie's head, "I do hear what you're saying." It was at this point that Scott realized Irene hung on his every word, which made for a couple more "um"s sprinkled with "and so"s before he continued, "There's a whole salad mix of issues I'd rather not dwell on. Am more focused on a scientifically rigorous search for the identities of certain creatures reputed to roam parts of Africa. The mokele-mbembe, for example. Where religious matters go, I do consider myself a person of faith. Faith has saved my brother from self-destructive behavior. But-But also, regarding the Bible museum, I consider it more as- more as a documentation of certain religious dogma, rather than beliefs I can entirely endorse, myself."

"Let me finish telling you the rest of who's here before the Cuckoosaurus erupts," went on Augie presently over the phone to Vicky. "Maybe to avoid more sparks flying between her and Scott McDonald, Irene McDowell has been hanging out a lot with Dr. Roberta Quiñones from the University of Maryland."

"The one who discovered that weird, missing-link whale with the hind leg stumps near the mouth of the Amazon River?"

"And also founder of the International Society of Cryptozoologists, don't forget."

"Do I need to be jealous?"

"Only if I need to be jealous of that bachelor P.E. teacher at your school, what was his name? Adkins?"

"Rob Adkins, but we like to call him Mr. Hunky-Hunk behind his back. Not to worry; I could never get it on with a guy who rocks out to Kiss."

"But if he were a big Lila Sosa fan...?"

"I would have to find another excuse to keep my distance. And speaking of Lila Sosa, glad you reminded me. Just read that for the first time ever, she's leaving the shelter of a recording studio to actually go on tour."

"Really?! I would almost be willing to travel somewhere far, like overseas even, to see that!"

"You make me very happy indeed, Augie-doggie, putting a Lila Sosa concert right up there alongside catching a relic Brachiosaurus on Candid Camera!"

"I intend to make you forget all about Mr. Hunky-Hunk."

"Should I let you go preen yourself? Won't that Cuckoosaurus thingie be calling you away any second now?"

"I prefer remaining un-preened for anyone but you, sweet stuff. And a few more peeps to tell you about, anyway."

"A few more? Wow! Whoever this is must already be out a lot of money, if they paid those others what they paid you just to listen to- I assume this isn't a pitch for the craziest time-share resort, ever."

"Let's hope not. That presentation we were suckered into, that was so torturous, not sure I could endure a second one, even for a hundred thousand. Anyway, Bernie Coleman is also here, a super friendly guy a bit up in his years. Bless his heart, he has kept open a cryptozoology museum in Portland, Maine, despite great personal expense."

"The windfall from our mysterious benefactor should help."

"I hope so!"

"And there's one more?"

"Two more. There's a reporter from the *Puffington Post* named Laura Gómez. Her byline is on a column called Out There that occasionally dips into my neck of the woo-

woo woods. And lastly there's our arch-nemesis, Stephen Feldman."

"The professional skeptic who wrote that nasty article about your show?"

"The same."

"Oh, well, then I know exactly what this is all about!" exclaimed Vicky. "Your mysterious benefactor is going to throw each of you onto the floor of a coliseum to face Feldman, one by one! Then the reporter will document each mauling."

Cuckoo, cuck-

ROAR!

Eek!

CHOMP!

"That must be Mr. Feldman now."

"What was that, Augie?"

"Would probably take too long to describe before I should be going downstairs. Tell you tonight after I return. Kisses."

"Okay. Be careful!"

At fifteen minute intervals, a cuckoo popped out of a section of ceiling molding. But this time, the supposed Cuckoosaurus stopped it mid-cuckoo, the second time through. A much larger section of molding around the cuckoo swung open to reveal a sizeable, wooden, reptilian-looking head stretching its mouth wide for a loud roar. Then the cuckoo could only let out an "Eek!" before the Cuckoosaurus engulfed it, chomping down, and withdrew into the molding, no trace left of what happened.

Chapter 10

Augustine "Augie" Matias descended a spiral marble staircase, joined his distinguished associates following green arrows to the conference room. En route, he wondered whether he'd already spent too much time in Sherman Peabody's company, for the odd thought that intruded on his fevered-enough-as-it-was imagination. Sherman likened the mansion to a hermit crab shell its builder shed, to be inhabited by someone else. But Augie found himself conjuring a no-less-peculiar alternative narrative. Namely, that there was something quite epochal about the palatially large edifice, well beyond having been constructed of very old rocks. Each room represented a geological era, and where the big meeting was to be held, that was the surface, the present era piled atop all the rest.

In any event, immediately upon entering the conference room, Augie found his attention drawn to a long, wide, rectangular table. Monstrous spiders could have covered the arched cathedral ceiling, and desiccated corpses been mounted on all four walls. They weren't, but the point is that even if they were, there was no getting past what occupied most of the tabletop.

Initially, Augie defaulted to the most conventional explanation possible: he beheld an ornately elaborate, miniaturized mock-up of a swamp affixed to the tabletop. Other such tabletops sported complex model railroad layouts. Track ran in and out of paper mâché hills, and wound through small villages populated by plastic figures. And artificial trees made from a variety of materials dotted the landscape.

However, the closer Augie looked, the closer he came to realizing the palms, cypresses, draping Spanish moss and more were actual living plants encircled by actual muddy water, no HO-scale train tracks anywhere to be seen.

This must be one of the most ambitious bonsai plant projects ever, Augie marveled. He even noticed the sort of mugginess he associated with venturing into a swamp.

As Augie took a seat near one end, Sherman on his immediate left, he noticed mists swirling about the real-life, pint-sized diorama. They originated from tiny nozzles hidden amidst the foliage, producing faint hisses every time they sprayed. The only thing missing was fake thunder like accompanied misting of carrots and green peppers at Augie's local grocery store.

What drew Augie's attention next he found no less unexpected, to the point he was braced for anything.

Turned out Augie along with Harry seated directly across the table from him had stationed themselves closest to the person at the head. That bulky, middle-aged fellow wore a dark plaid shirt and oversized spectacles. His mother, presumably, stood just behind him, spreading hummus on pretzels. Munch-munch, munch-munch, he appeared to eat the pretzels as fast as the woman could prepare them. Augie sensed that so many men and women sitting either side of the swamp-embedded table made the fellow nervous in a way that could only be tempered by devouring hummus-smeared pretzels.

Wait. I've seen that face somewhere before. No, he can't be...Well he would certainly have the money for this extravagance.

Journalist Laura Gómez's eyes practically popped from their sockets, pursuant to which she fell to furious note-taking. Augie wanted to ask whether her reaction had to do with the pretzel muncher's identity. But before he could open his mouth, the fellow left off from his apparent pretzel binging to say in a voice equal parts nasal and crusty, "Some of you might recognize me from photos taken by paparazzi some years ago. For those of you who do not, my name is Eclipso Sunray Smith. Yes, I'm that Eclipso, the one who reverse-engineered many of the hi-tech items mysteriously left behind when weapons were just as mysteriously confiscated from circumstances on the precipice of war. Yes, I'm that Eclipso you can blame for cellphones, laptop computers, and many other items we otherwise might not have developed on our own until decades from now. I'm that Eclipso, as opposed to all the many other Eclipsos you might know."

"But I don't know any other Eclipsos!" protested Harry Letterman.

"I think he was joking, dearie," said Harriet, gently patting Harry on the back of one hand.

"She's my balance," he said.

"And he's my check," she said.

Eclipso's pained frown flashed by so fast, Augie barely caught a glimpse before the man's determined-looking, thin-lipped expression returned. It seemed Eclipso tucked away his sorrow for another time.

"This magnificent building," Eclipso gestured with both hands, "was originally constructed outside Bath, England by a mining tycoon. He might as well have constructed the world's largest spider web, because he used it to entrap attractive women until alcohol and old age withered him away. Afterwards, the economics of maintaining such an edifice with all the necessary personnel threatened to bankrupt his family. They were more than happy to unload it on me at a bargain price. I had every last brick transported to the states, but made certain changes. As a result, there's great difficulty distinguishing it from the encircling stand of yellow birch until you are almost at the front door.

"Which is all my longwinded way of saying welcome, and thank you for indulging my request."

"Does it have a name?" asked professional skeptic Stephen Feldman.

Eclipso Sunray Smith gave Stephen a long, hard stare that he met without a flinch.

What was going through Eclipso's mind? Augie wondered. Was he asking himself whether Stephen's impertinence was worth enduring? Was he formulating a devastatingly witty response? Or, as Stephen proceeded to interpret his stare, was Eclipso simply awaiting elaboration on exactly what Stephen expected for a response?

"Usually," Stephen Feldman went on, striving to make clear that Eclipso's stare-down didn't faze him in the least, "a residence of such grandiosity is given a specific title that goes well beyond mere street address."

"Mr. Feldman, I am not in the habit of naming inanimate objects. Though that isn't to say this 'residence of such grandiosity,' as you put it, isn't in many ways intimately connected to things that are or were quite animate indeed, at least when viewed from a fifth dimensional perspective. The oolitic limestone bricks from the Bath region, for example, consist of the compacted detritus from creatures who filled the sea millions of years ago. Very well, then, let our inspiration from that fact lead us to a name for my Ankylosaurus-shaped mansion. Let us name it God's Toenail. Welcome to God's Toenail!"

"I feel very close to having already earned my hundred thousand," Irene McDonald whispered to journalist Laura Gómez seated beside her. She wanted to sneak in her snark under the minor hubbub over Eclipso's odd concluding remark. But somehow, just as she opened her mouth, her fellow travelers went dead quiet.

Eclipso made clear he heard every word, nodding, "Yes, there is that question of just how much that people are willing to put up with for a certain sum of money. Take these, for example."

Eclipso reached into a small bowel set before him, and with his thick fingers he extracted half-a-dozen small, spherical dark objects. Then he held them out for all to see in the palm of his hand. "They bear a striking resemblance to defecated rabbit pellets, do they not? Mother, please eat them for a quick ten thousand smackeroos."

Augie had to wonder at how hastily Eclipso's mother gobbled the pellets and in fact appeared to bliss out on them, closing her eyes as she chewed.

Eyes darted every which way, nonverbally communicating, *What the hell?*

"As a matter of fact," said Eclipso in his most nasal, crustiest voice yet, "you are all grossing out over nothing. For ten thousand dollars, I just had my mother feast on nuggets of rich dark chocolate. The best of both worlds, wouldn't you agree? Being paid to do something you would happily do anyway for its intrinsic value? For the joy it brings you?" Before Eclipso's assembled company could recover from this little stunt, he lifted a thin little magazine and said, "This is a comic book entitled *Turok Son of Stone*. Yes, it's another inanimate object with a name, but stories always are given a title, are they not?"

"Along with most everything else we know exists, yes," Stephen deadpanned in his deepest voice.

Eclipso gave Stephen another of his stare-downs, though not nearly as long as before. Wasn't worth arguing, he decided, over the difference between categories of objects and unique titles for each object. Instead he quickly went on, "A certain Gaylord Dubois created Turok and his sidekick, Andar, as two Native Americans of the Mandan affiliation. In the first issue thirty years ago, Turok and Andar became lost in a strange valley hidden somewhere in the southwest United States, a valley full of dinosaurs and our cave-dwelling ancestors. Issue after issue, they fought off deadly dinosaurs, plus our ancestors' deadly stupidity, at the same time they kept searching for a way out of the valley, back home."

Paid a small fortune to be there, Eclipso's audience were too stunned by the turn his remarks took to verbalize any immediate reaction while he paused to hold the comic book facing their way.

Nevertheless, Augie noticed a small ripple across the surface of the table-embedded miniature swamp's placid waters, waters that wound in and around cypresses and mangroves the size of broccoli florets. Whether due to someone's exhalation or something moving through the swamp water, he couldn't say. But when he keyed in on the comic book cover, he recognized both the characters and the sort of artwork from the painting many times larger, elegantly framed beside the marble staircase. The *Turok Son of Stone* comic book cover featured GOLD KEY, the publisher's logo, in the upper left-hand corner, and the price, 12 cents, in the upper right-hand corner. And the painting itself depicted bare-chested Turok and Andar in their leather pants and moccasins, a dinosaur stampede chasing them away from an erupting volcano.

"In this issue, number 44, an enormous meteorite collapses part of the rock-wall that closed off Lost Valley from the rest of the world. At long last, Turok and Andar can escape, no more dinosaurs or hostile cavemen. A big problem, however: A meat-eating theropod dinosaur and a herd of ceratopsian dinosaurs named Styracosaurus also escape Lost Valley, threatening Turok and Andar's homeland. The two men set a prairie fire to herd the dinosaurs back into the valley, inadvertently herding themselves back in as well. And before they can escape again, an aftershock quake from the meteoric impact causes tremendous rockslides that reseal the rock wall, once more entrapping our heroes."

Augie sensed Eclipso choking up.

No matter, where Stephen was concerned. "You do realize, Mr. Smith, sir, that that is not documentary evidence for the survival of dinosaurs into the modern day," he bluntly observed. "It is only, as you yourself admitted, a comic book."

"But it does provide a mirror image of the world we find ourselves trapped in, every bit as much as Turok and Andar feel trapped. Our world seemingly harbors no such wondrous things as surviving non-avian dinosaurs. So that most ironically when we read a *Turok* comic book, perhaps we are intent on escaping into the very world they labor to exit. Part of us wishes they never do escape so there will always be another issue, containing ever more dinosaurs."

Irene crossed her arms as she thought, *And by "we," he means himself*, not repeating the mistake of a sidebar whisper that risked Eclipso overhearing.

"I must strenuously object to your characterization of our world as lacking in wondrous subjects," sternly and loudly objected Stephen Feldman, intent on Eclipso not missing a single word he said. "Just the other day, a woman gardening in Thailand encountered an orchid praying mantis. Are you familiar with the orchid praying mantis?"

"The male is small, nondescript, and rather reclusive when not searching for a mate. But the female is large, and has evolved to most colorfully blend in with orchid blooms, the better to entrap other insects," answered Eclipso with emphatic nonchalance. "But your point is certainly well taken, Stephen. I misspoke when I implied the orchid mantis is any less wondrous than the largest sauropod dinosaur to roam the Earth. However, is our craving for the wondrous ever really satisfied? Consider your lifespan. Imagine you could live life gloriously, surrounded by loved ones, for a thousand years. If you are honest with yourself, would that really satiate you to the point that all curiosity about and desire for an afterlife, or simply an additional thousand years, would fade away?"

"A thousand-year lifespan would more than suffice," said Stephen. "In fact, no surprise if I became too deadly bored a few centuries in."

Eclipso Sunray Smith glared at Stephen Feldman anew, but this time he upturned the corners of his lips just enough to finally unnerve him. "So you're suggesting," said Eclipso, "that our world is not so full of wonders, you might not exhaust their supply well before your thousand years were up?"

"Ah ha ha," Stephen laughed in his deep voice, the same you-got-me reaction he had whenever he realized an opponent was about to checkmate him in chess.

"Either you have not yet come to understand what brings real joy to your life," proceeded Eclipso, piling it on, "or by your nine-hundred-ninety-ninth year, you would find your remark much more difficult to so flippantly make than you are finding it to make, halfway through your first century. In either case, I would concede that a surviving non-avian dinosaur is not necessary for our world to be considered the proverbial garden of Earthly Delights. But I would also strenuously argue that a world where there is a chance non-avian dinosaurs have survived into the present era is far preferable to a world where there is zero chance.

"So consider this, everyone." Eclipso left off from focus on Stephen seated the furthest away from him to his right, favoring a more inclusive regard of his paid audience. "In the Lost Valley, Turok occasionally stumbles across an artifact that could only have originated from his home world. A feathered headdress here, a buffalo cave wall painting there. In our world, we find the occasional comparable hint at the persistence into recent history of non-avian dinosaurs. A centuries old wood carving of a sauropod dinosaur from long before our arbiters of reality recognized they ever existed, a three-toed foot-track in fresh mud, larger than the largest ostrich could ever produce..."

"There's another name for those 'hints,'" said Stephen with more edge to his voice. "They're called hoaxes." No matter, whether or not the wonders of the world could keep him engaged for anything close to a thousand years. He was already grown weary of Eclipso's wondrously eccentric outlook, maybe not worth sitting through even for a hundred thousand bucks.

"Extraordinary possibilities often do act as a magnet for hoaxers," admitted Bernie Coleman interceding on Eclipso's behalf, leaning forward to look past Scott McDonald at Stephen. "But what do you say when a missionary in the Cameroons tells you his parishioners claim their great grandparents killed a beast that fit the description of an Apatosaurus, to stop it from eating all their fish?"

"I say show me the bones," answered Stephen. "I also say that such a story is excellent for tourism."

"I just wrote about what is likely the same event, in my book about mokele-mbembe," piped up Scott McDonald caught between Stephen and Bernie. "Not only did I speak with the missionary. Through a translator, I spoke with residents of a region over two hundred miles away who I established had no previous contact with the missionary parishioners. They reported hearing of the same event, occurring in the same time frame. And incidentally, bones left out in the open, especially in such a hot and humid climate, rot away pretty fast."

"That's one of the pieces of evidence we have compiled," Harriet seated beside Bernie Coleman nodded.

"From all over the world!" added Harry triumphantly, seated beside her.

"He completes me," Harriet announced proudly, then gave Harry a peck on the cheek.

"That report included a claim that some of the fishermen died from eating the meat," Harry beamed, albeit with red-faced embarrassment.

I'm guessing that look on his face has more to do with Harriet completing him than with a gruesome poisoning from Apatosaurus steak, Irene wanted to whisper for Dr. Quiñones. But she feared being overheard by the Lettermans.

Meanwhile, Augie noticed Sherman Peabody seated beside him nod his head knowingly. And could have sworn he heard Sherman accompany that nod with an "mm-hm." All of this, while Irene did say to Harry and Harriet, "Maybe you two should get a room." Pursuant to which, when she realized Scott was looking on in shock at her having made such a comment, she flashed him a pucker face. To which he reacted with bowed head and crossing himself.

"We already own a two-bedroom apartment," said Harriet. "I don't think we need another."

"If I could get back to this matter of evidence for the present-day survival of non-avian dinosaurs as you phrase it, Eclipso," said Stephen, irritated, "there's a whole other problem nobody here has even mentioned yet. Let's grant you a mysterious three-toed foot-track here and rumors of a slaughtered sauropod there. For such a creature to have survived for so many million years, there can't be just one or two of them. You need a large enough breeding population for the gene pool not to weaken to nonviable status."

"He has a point," said Laura Gómez from the *Puffington Post*, to many agreeing nods.

"Maybe," said Eclipso. "But consider this. Lights please, Samuel?"

The genial fellow in a tan cardigan sweater, who inconspicuously took a seat at the end of the swamp-embedded table opposite from Eclipso, headed for the light switches.

"That's my assistant, Samuel Longbottom, who drove you here and was first to reach out to some of you."

As lights dimmed, a framed, enlarged *Turok* comic book cover over the fireplace split wide open, revealing a spacious film screen.

"First," said Eclipso, "you'll see a painting from the National History Museum in New York that depicts a supposed typical landscape during the Jurassic Era, some hundred-twenty-million years ago."

The iconic painting depicted a long-necked Apatosaurus, formerly known as Brontosaurus, dominating the foreground, mouth overflowing with swamp reeds. Numerous other dinosaurs crowded the background, including an Allosaurus chasing after a duck-billed dinosaur named Trachodon. And flying reptile Pterosaurs filled the sky.

"As you can plainly see, so many dinosaurs are practically bumping into each other. Standing room only! Now keep that image in mind for the next photo."

The next photo could have been a close-up of the swamp embedded into the table around which Eclipso's company sat. That is, if not for telltale bits of blue sky amidst the tops of palm trees and cypresses.

"Now you're looking at a Louisiana bayou. The best estimate is that it contains dozens of poisonous snakes, a half-dozen gators and crocodiles, tens of turtles, and literally hundreds of small lizards. I challenge you to spot even one of them. The best I can do is wonder whether one branch is really a branch, or whether a tiny lump sticking out of the water might be alligator nostrils.

"Mr. Feldman, I am surprised you haven't already remarked it's a lot easier for a ten-foot gator to hide than a forty-foot sauropod dinosaur. But let's say you have. Consider this."

The next photo showed a shoreline variously sandy and crowded by tall reeds.

"This was taken along a stretch of the Nile River in Egypt. Present there at the time, I happen to know for a fact, were exactly nine Nile crocodiles. They ranged in length from fourteen to nineteen feet, lying in wait for some hapless prey to linger for a drink."

"Be that as it may," Stephen pounced, every bit as much lying in wait for Eclipso to stumble, "I have seen several more photos of Nile crocodiles quite visibly sunning themselves on river banks." Stephen restrained himself from adding *So there!* or *Ha!*

"You still have to admit," spoke up Professor Roberta Quiñones for the first time, and in an authoritative voice, "that when a large motorboat approaches gators or crocodiles, they usually run or dive into hiding."

"As a group," Eclipso hastened to add, "reptiles are among the most instinctively reclusive creatures on Earth. So ponder this additional photo, if you will."

The additional photo revealed a small sandbar in the foreground framed by dense jungle crowding the background.

"We see here part of a tributary off Lake Tele in the Central Republic of Africa. This is a region I understand has been of great interest to you, Mr. Scott McDonald, for the locals' reports of creatures with an elephant's body, a snake's long neck, and an alligator's tail. Imagine them hiding in this very photo. After all, dinosaurs enjoyed one-hundred-fifty-million years of evolutionary adaptation. Might not some sauropod dinosaurs have evolved unimaginably sophisticated ways of concealing themselves from predators over those endless-seeming eons?

"The asteroid that struck the Earth sixty-six million years ago, in tandem with an unfortunate confluence of super volcanos, was not enough to wipe out all the turtles, snakes, alligators, etcetera etcetera. And yet, Mr. Stephen Feldman, you are willing to so casually assume those events were enough to completely eradicate the planet's rulers of, again, one-hundred-fifty-million years?"

"Don't forget birds," said Stephen. "I've always conceded birds are latter-day, miniaturized theropod dinosaurs. Look," he hastened to add as the lights came up, and Turok aiming a drawn arrow at a Tyrannosaurus Rex resumed dominance over the fireplace mantel, "it is absurd to argue that since gators, snakes and what-all are hiding in the one photo, dinosaurs might be hiding in the other."

All the talk of concealed critters sent a chill down Augie's neck. How close might he have come to an Iguanodon or some other surviving ornithopod dinosaur, making palms and casuarinas sway from side to side off the coast of Papua, New Guinea?

"For that matter," went on Stephen, "you might as well argue we don't know for sure a flying green giraffe isn't hidden in that African jungle."

"But there is an important distinction," countered Eclipso. Or was Augie reading those words into his sigh? he couldn't help most curiously wondering. "We do have that paltry evidence already mentioned, concerning the possible survival of non-avian dinosaurs into the present day. Eyewitnesses, foot-tracks and such... But there is not a shred of evidence I am aware of for the existence of flying green giraffes. Okay, let us stipulate the living dinosaur evidence is indeed most paltry. We also must admit that while it is too little to take too seriously, it is also too considerable to outright dismiss. ISN'T THAT RIGHT, BONSAI GATOR?!?!"

Swamp water closest to where Eclipso sat started churning like it had been brought to a boil, Augie imagined. The next thing anyone knew, an alligator six inches long, at best, leapt from the swamp and landed on the table top not a foot away from Eclipso. Dripping wet, he did several pushups before settling down on his belly and swinging his head wildly from side to side.

"Bonsai Gator wants his Beatles reggae, does he?" asked Eclipso indulgently. "Play 'You Won't See Me' by Yellow Dubmarine!" he seemed to command thin air.

Within seconds, a reggae downbeat filled the conference room from wall-embedded speakers. What ensued was the reggae group Yellow Dubmarine's peculiarly infectious version of a Beatles song entitled, "You Won't See Me."

Even more amazing than Bonsai Gator showing up in the first place, where Augie and company were concerned, was how he stood on his two hind legs, tail providing balance, of course, and danced to the reggae music.

Augie reckoned he couldn't have found himself that much more surprised if instead, a green giraffe had suddenly flitted about the room.

"This 'Bonsai Gator' of yours," said Stephen, straining to maintain a calm yet assertive demeanor. It didn't help that as soon as he said "Bonsai Gator," Bonsai Gator froze in mid-reggae-boogie and swung his inch-long snout Stephen's direction. "No," Stephen shook his head at the teensy reptile, "I'm not talking to you, though maybe I should be. I'm addressing your keeper. Mr. Eclipso Smith, sir," continued Stephen Feldman while Bonsai Gator resumed his boogie to reggae-fied Beatles music, "I take it you produced that creature by breeding successively smaller generations of gators?"

Eclipso seemingly munched on a bit-off piece of hummus-dipped pretzel. His mother's mouth moved curiously in tandem like she was munching on something as well, Augie thought. All that, before finally he answered, "A reasonable supposition, especially since the swamp vegetation is bonsai, as are the midget dragonflies you might have noticed flitting about."

Coincidental to these revelations, Bonsai Gator worked the snapping-up of one dragonfly into his dance routine.

"But Bonsai Gator has a different origin," went on Eclipso. "True, he will never grow any larger than he already has. However, the name I've given him is a misnomer. He is more accurately described as a pygmy alligator, quite possibly the very last of his kind. My late wife, Agnes, discovered him on a lone island in the South Pacific hardly a square mile across."

Augie noticed Bernie Coleman's grin grown so wide, he could imagine it stretched clear round the back of his head, were that possible.

Most everyone else appeared in bug-eyed shock.

"On my account," continued Eclipso, clearly unfazed by any reactions from his well-paid audience, "Agnes was hoping actually that she would come across pygmy dinosaurs."

"Wait." Stephen closed his eyes and held up his hands before them. Eclipso might as well have kicked sand in his face. "You said your wife was searching for dinosaurs?"

"Pygmy dinosaurs."

"Okay, pygmy dinosaurs. She was searching for pygmy dinosaurs on a ridiculously tiny island in the South Pacific."

"Not far from the Fiji Islands, yes."

"Well there you go," Stephen spread his hands apart, confident. "Aren't those volcanic atolls only thousands of years old like the Hawaiian Islands? How were dinosaurs of any size going to swim all the way out there from New Zealand or wherever, millions of years after their extinction?"

"Actually, the complex geology of the Fijis goes back well over a hundred million years, when dinosaurs were reigning supreme worldwide. The particular island Agnes investigated remained enshrouded by heavy mists from its lone geyser until she boated close enough to shore. Bonsai Gator came running to her not five minutes after she hit the beach. But her thorough search of every nook and cranny turned up no other pygmy gators or dinosaurs. There were only a few Anatole lizards, plus giant hermit crabs carrying empty coconut shells on their backs. We're not even sure Bonsai Gator didn't swim there from elsewhere, some other still-undiscovered island perhaps. But at least for now, we have to assume he is all alone. Anyway, he thought it would be a great idea if there was a fresh search for living non-avian dinosaurs, no expense spared."

"You said your late wife, correct?" reporter Laura Gómez found herself nearly shouting above the continuing reggae version of "You Won't See Me," about not being able to endure if the singer's true love won't see him.

"Correct," Eclipso confirmed.

"Did you accompany her to the South Pacific, or…?"

In Laura's estimation, Eclipso filled his chair like he could have been a sack of potatoes unceremoniously dumped there, spread out extra wide at the base. She empathetically guessed his grief over Agnes's death had left him immobilized, pigging out on his pretzels and hummus.

"I never accompanied Agnes anywhere," declared Eclipso. "We were a classic case of opposites attracting. I hate stepping outside God's Toenail, while she couldn't stand being home more than two days before she was off on another adventure. And her pygmy dinosaur search was only a small part; her main 'jam' was helping less fortunate people around the world as a do-it-yourself one-person Peace Corps.

"So no, I did not join Agnes on her Fiji sojourn. Nor, again, did I accompany her on any of her other travels."

"Would it be too indelicate to inquire as to the circumstances of her demise?" Bernie Coleman asked in such a gentle voice, he completely undermined any suggestion of indelicacy.

"No, not at all," Eclipso shook his head vigorously, "far less indelicate than the circumstances themselves. According to witnesses, she was engulfed by a sinkhole near the Amazon. This happened some years ago." Eclipso's voice cracked falsetto, and with one trembling hand he reached for another hummus-buttered pretzel.

Bonsai Gator settled down on a small patch of sand beside the swamp water after the Beatles' song concluded. But sensing Eclipso's distress, he lifted his head, followed by his entire cigar-thin body on his four tiny legs. And he trotted over beside Eclipso's empty hand. There, he sank his pale yellow belly down onto the smoothly varnished mahogany, and consolingly rubbed his long, tooth-bristling snout up against Eclipso's pinkie finger.

Eclipso shut his eyes in blissful contemplation of Bonsai Gator's kindness. Then he said, "Suppose any or all of you take up what Bonsai Gator considers a good idea, and your consequent travels bring you near where Agnes vanished. I will ask that you devote at least a small part of your time there to seeking further information as to her fate. There's reason to believe such information will prove not entirely irrelevant to our mission."

If Augie Matias had grown Bugs Bunny rabbit ears, they would have shot straight up. As matters stood, he felt a new chill down his spine, recollecting his search along the banks of the Amazon River for dinosaur fossils from well past the infamous Cretaceous-Tertiary boundary layer.

"So this, um, good idea, um, you want to finance us conducting a thorough search for living non-avian dinosaurs? Does that sum up what this is about?" Scott McDonald found the courage to ask despite feeling all eyes on him, especially Irene's, and even Bonsai Gator's from where he had settled back down into the miniature swamp up to his snout.

"There are multiple possibilities, of course," said Eclipso, his excitement making his already very nasal voice sound like he'd inhaled a large quantity of helium. "We can hope non-avian dinosaurs are still roaming about, despite the paltry amount of evidence. But we can't yet rule out the possibility that people have been experiencing quite literally ghosts, hauntings from millions of years ago. Human ghosts are often associated with violent deaths. Assuming dinosaurs are endowed with spirits the same as our selves..."

"Assuming," deadpanned Stephen, dubious of even the human spirit notion, let alone dinosaur spirits.

Bonsai Gator's eyes just above the swamp water line looked towards Stephen; if Augie didn't know better, they squinted to express no uncertain irritation.

"Yes, assuming that," went on Eclipso, undaunted, "why wouldn't a dinosaur's violent death in the jaws of a Tyrannosaurus Rex, or buried in lava from a super volcano eruption, also leave behind a troubled non-corporeal entity? But of course," Eclipso added, noting how Stephen Feldman rolled his eyes and shook his head, "if we are honest with ourselves, we can't yet rule out a far grimmer possibility. That at the end of the figurative day, we will have to conclude, even if with the greatest reluctance, that neither dinosaurs nor their tormented spirits are alive or haunt us today. That what has been taken for possible evidence is merely an unfortunate convergence of wishful-thinking-fueled misidentification with hoaxes. And it won't matter whether those hoaxes are of the self-deluding variety or intentionally, mockingly misleading."

"Ding-ding-ding-ding-ding!" said Stephen, like someone in a TV game show just gave the correct answer.

"Mm-mm-mmm," Sherman Peabody cleared his throat.

Bonsai Gator plus everyone else turned their attention to Sherman seated between Laura and Augie along the left side of the swamp-embedded table from Eclipso.

Sherman's chin tucked firmly into his neck so he was looking around at his audience over his spectacles, he proceeded, "Processing the situation, I'm not sure we can yet dismiss other possibilities, however remote, that might explain why so little evidence, but evidence nonetheless."

Stephen's forehead wedged down between thumb and forefinger suggested he was suffering a headache that wouldn't quit. The miniature dragonfly buzzing him certainly didn't help.

"Ghost dinosaurs would not be able to leave fresh foot-tracks anywhere. But dinosaurs that made short jaunts through portals from an alternate universe…"

"Oh, we might find ourselves quite surprised, indeed, at the impact a ghost can have on the corporeal world," advised Eclipso, his mother nodding thoughtfully behind him. "But it's your careful consideration of even the most extreme-seeming possibilities that makes you such a valuable member of our team, Mr. Peabody, should you honor us by signing on."

"I hope you haven't ruled out the possibility that what distinguish flying pink giraffes are their three-toed foot-tracks," said Stephen edgily, while still resting his forehead against forefinger and thumb.

"Yes, Mr. Feldman," nodded Eclipso. "And while your relentless skepticism can become quite tedious, it can also be the perfect antidote to gullible naiveté. Which is what makes you so valuable to the cause. In fact, I will say right now that any conclusions failing to convince you will automatically fail to convince me."

"Oh?" That got Stephen's forehead up off his cradling hand.

"While I am at it, let me continue around the room. Scott McDonald…"

Scott couldn't help jumping in his chair.

"...Can't say I have any patience for creationist fantasies of the Earth being only six thousand years old, nor of human evolution being completely unconnected to the rest of the animal kingdom, etcetera etcetera. But there is no denying that in your quest for mokele-mbembe, the 'one who stops the flow of rivers,' you have very carefully gone where the evidence leads. I sense that despite your most evident timidity, you will prove fearless in pursuit of the truth.

"Bernie Coleman seated beside you, an honest broker in the field of cryptozoology for nearly half a century: Your accumulated wisdom should help us as much as our professional skeptic, Mr. Feldman, to ferret out fraud and misdirection from authentic leads.

"And Heidi with Harry Letterman: The evidence for the survival of non-avian dinosaurs might be paltry. But what evidence there is, whether fraudulent or real, you have compiled and organized in ways that might help us discern significant patterns."

Heidi and Harry gave each other high fives, grinning proudly.

"How you fit new evidence we might gather into your structural framework could ultimately crack the code.

"Which brings me to Dr. Roberta Quiñones seated all the way the other side of Bonsai Swamp. Dr. Quiñones, you carry the unique distinction of having actually confirmed the living existence of a previously unidentified creature of no small proportions. I'm talking about the Cetiñones, an evolutionary missing link between whales and their land-dwelling ancestors."

Roberta Quiñones flashed a shy smile, then resumed her head modestly bowed for intense taking-in of Eclipso's meeting.

"And having also founded the International Society of Cryptozoologists, clearly is no wonder why I wanted you here.

"Why I invited Irene McDowell, seated beside you, might seem a bit less obvious, as her specialty is more folkloric traditions than science. However, folkloric traditions are where we would expect to find tales of dinosaur-like creatures if such creatures have survived into recent times. And that is exactly part of what she described finding in her fascinating read, *At The Crossroads of Folklore and Reality: A Cryptozoological Inquiry*."

Scott wasn't sure whether Irene's bemused-looking smile was over the flattery she received from Eclipso. Or was it from the puppy dog looks he kept trying to sneak her direction without anyone else noticing?

The sneaking part wasn't going well for Scott, because even Heidi and Harry caught on, as much as they were still happily absorbed in each other.

"Yes," pounced Stephen, emboldened by the role Eclipso envisioned for him. "There's the gryphon, like a sort of dragon, clearly inspired by fossil Protoceratops skulls brought back to England from Mongolia."

"My book covers that," said Irene. "But there's also the experience by Africans named the Wambutti and the Monbuttu. Both speak of an odd-looking creature called the atti. Their reports were dismissed as folk myth until white people 'discovered' and renamed it the okapi, because nothing officially exists until there's confirmation by the white man."

"Point well taken," Stephen conceded.

"As you just heard," Eclipso said, gesturing towards Stephen, "Mr. Feldman might fancy himself a professional skeptic. But he is not impervious to full and sufficient evidence. Which, again, is why I want him manning the gates through which proof of living non-avian dinosaurs must pass before I accept it. I also intend strong backup for him. That's where Laura Gómez seated beside Irene comes in. As reporter-in-charge of so-called 'woo-woo' at the *Puffington Post*, she brings a depth of experience separating the authentically 'woo-woo' wheat from the chafe, whether a matter of fraud or misidentification.

"Then there's my hoped-for brainstormer-in-chief, Dr. Sherman Peabody. He is one of the leading lights in Artificial Intelligence robotics, who might end up providing that key piece of outside-the-box thinking that allows us to definitively establish non-avian dinosaur survival...or prove a negative."

Sherman might have been keeping his chin tucked into his neck, but with attention drawn to him, Augie sensed he would have buried it from sight there altogether, if he could have.

"Last but certainly not least, seated closest to my left we have Dr. Augustine Matias, or Augie as I understand he likes to be called."

Augie's ears turned beet red, a physiological reaction he wished he could control, and hoped would never work to his actual detriment, for example by giving away his presence when at long last finally privileged to sneak a peek at a living dinosaur.

"Augie," went on Eclipso, "brings to our swamp-embedded conference table not only his expertise as a vertebrate paleontologist at the Smithsonian Natural History Museum in Washington, D.C. For two seasons, he also acted as professional adviser to the notorious Jake Rumblehouse on the latter's scattershot worldwide investigation of cryptozoological phenomena, including the occasional possible living dinosaur. Dr. Matias, my sources inform me one of your chief complaints with

Rumblehouse's work was that it didn't matter how interesting a particular expedition turned. They were always brought to an abrupt close."

"That's correct," acknowledged Augie, his ears paling back to normal. "On one of the last episodes, we had to depart Papua, New Guinea literally twenty-four hours after we saw palm trees sway at night, seemingly agitated by something enormous. Happened close to where a group of women reported a monstrous reptile stood on its hind legs to feed off a casuarina. Although in defense of Mr. Rumblehouse, he was working under budgetary constraints with which I am well familiar. On more than a few fossil digs, we had to leave promising rock outcroppings untouched because the money ran out."

"An important observation, yes, Dr. Matias," said Eclipso while Laura found herself stunned by how Bonsai Gator's eyes poking just above swamp water level bounced back and forth between Augie and Eclipso as they spoke. "I am very, very delighted to report that all of you who sign on to my dinosaur search will have virtually unlimited time and resources at your disposal. The next occasion of your finding trees mysteriously set in motion, or you otherwise develop a promising lead, you can take an extra week, an extra month, as much time as you need to dig deep."

Bonsai Gator lifted his head from the swamp water to nod it with seeming enthusiasm before settling back down up to his eyeballs again.

"So that's as big as he'll ever get," Irene remarked, overcoming her general amazement to make any noise at all.

Bonsai's eyes travelled from Irene over towards Eclipso when he said, "We could even keep him in a swamp one thousand times larger. Unlike certain creatures whose proportions enlarge to fill their habitat, he wouldn't grow even another millimeter in length. Most curious, given the general predisposition of gators to grow bigger and bigger, the longer they live."

"How will you afford to do that, I mean what you said about granting us unlimited resources?" asked Laura Gómez, trying to ignore Bonsai Gator's attention turned her direction. "I realize that adapting the hi-tech devices left in place of weapons has proven highly profitable. But don't you risk exhausting your fortune by making such a pledge? Does finding a living non-avian dinosaur really mean that much to you?"

Eclipso's head tilt from side to side during Laura's question oddly struck Augie as similar to a small Anatole lizard's when alertly contemplating its surroundings.

"Definitively establishing non-avian dinosaur survival to the present: Perhaps that means far more than we could ever imagine. Doesn't it, Bonsai Gator?"

Bonsai Gator lifted his head from the swamp water again.

Augie reminded himself that reptiles' permanently set jaw line made them always appear grinning. Nevertheless, he couldn't help reading genuine joy into the expression on Bonsai's long snout.

"There's a design engineer whose success has been nearly equal to my own," went on Eclipso. "He's also exploited the hi-tech artifacts left behind by whoever's withdrawing weaponry from our midst. But unlike myself, he's managed to stay out of the spotlight. And happily, he's pledged to split the costs. Has a somewhat different agenda from mine, yet is very much dependent on my success. I draw your attention to the fellow on my left, Mr. Alistair Frump. Alistair, if you would care to explain the horse you have in this race, or maybe I should call it a horse-o-saurus?"

Alistair rose to his feet from where he had been sitting beside Eclipso, unnoticed until then by Augie what with so many wondrous distractions. He'd long since removed his Navy blue jacket and yellow silk tie, but still sweated heavily in his white short-sleeve shirt and navy blue pants, thanks to the swamp-enhancing humidity. Rather than look up at his audience, he kept his head bowed forward. Where Augie was concerned, he might as well have been a bull about to charge through. "Ladies, gents, I keep company with other wealthy people; Eclipso's not the only tiger in that jungle. But unlike Eclipso, they really have no idea what to do with all their riches."

"If everything else fails, they could try helping the poor," Irene McDowell observed drily.

"I'm getting to that," Alistair looked up at Irene just long enough to say. Then lowering his figurative bull horns to continue charging, he went on, "'They' need a gimmick, a special something that leads them to surrender big chunks of their wealth, some of which will indeed be redirected to those less fortunate."

"So other chunks will comprise your take, to compensate for your investment," Irene once more drily observed.

"Very true," Alistair Frump conceded. "But for just a minute, I want everyone here to take off your wariness hats and I mean especially you, Ms. McDowell, and you too, Mr. Professional Skeptic Stephen Feldman. And I want you to try on a pair of rose-tinted lens."

The way Mr. Frump kept his head bowed, Augie was reminded of certain meetings at the Smithsonian when the speaker read from notes. Said speaker seemed so lost in those notes, he or she forgot about eye contact with their audience. That is, unless he or she was using their notes as a convenient crutch to avoid eye contact.

However, Alistair didn't have anything in front of him at all. This left Augie wondering how ashamed the man felt, versus how adamant he was on plowing through whatever he had to say.

"Okay," Alistair went on, "now how many of you have ever played mini-golf? I see a few hands raised." He lifted his eyes the minimum necessary to make this observation, forehead furrowing considerably. "Well, if you have ever had the pleasure of playing that exquisitely silly little game along the main thoroughfare of Ocean City, Maryland, you cannot have missed the wide variety of mini-golf themes."

Augie and company exchanged looks of *What the hell is he talking about?*

"You have everything from a pirate ship to a space ship, a down-under motif featuring kangaroos to a simulated volcano spouting red-dyed water," Alistair plowed forward, undaunted by his audience's reaction if he was even aware of it. "But my favorites, and I suspect many children's favorites as well, have to be the layouts featuring dinosaurs, some of them animatronic."

"You think some real ones might be hiding in their midst?" Irene snarked.

"Wouldn't that be something?" Alistair looked up to laugh, totally disarmed. "But no," he bowed his head to resume plowing forward. "Imagine, if you will, a full-sized golf course bordering where it has been confirmed, where *you* have confirmed, the persistence of living dinosaurs. The golfers' caddies are not only armed with yardage booklets to help them navigate the course. They are also armed with powerful tranquillizer dart rifles, in case one of our prehistoric cash-cow-o-saurs finds a way to break through the electrified fences that will surround the resort."

Augie imagined Bernie Coleman's grin making a second circuit round his head while Alistair added, "Ideally, an occasional patron of the Mesozoic Links Resort will see a Brachiosaurus head loom on its long neck above a palm tree, or catch a glimpse of a scaly, twenty-foot-long tail sticking out from behind a mangrove, I don't know!" exclaimed Alistair, hunching his shoulders and holding out his hands in supplication. "I'm just guessing! But a golf trip to Mesozoic Links, just think about it! A ball sliced or hooked out of bounds might come to rest beside a Triceratops, an Iguanodon or some other such fantastical beastie. The mere prospect is certain to separate some obscenely wealthy guys from a share of their vast fortunes, in search of whatever new thrill to keep from becoming bored silly! In fact, I could easily see especially addictive personalities return multiple times in hopes of joining those lucky elite few who do sneak a peek into the primordial past! Think what that would mean for the locals who doubtless would be paid well for operating the resort, working as rifle-toting caddies, so on and so forth!"

"And you think these filthy rich resort patrons will spread around enough of their wealth to make it worth your while ponying up for Eclipso's dinosaur hunt," Laura Gómez said more as a statement than a question.

"Dinosaur search," Eclipso corrected. "'Hunt' connotes killing animals. But if we do succeed, we can safely assume we will be dealing with singularly rare, endangered species.

"We have been skirting the edges of my full conception for far too long, now. It is a wonder Bonsai Gator hasn't yet petitioned for another reggae-fied Beatles tune. So here we go." Eclipso Smith clutched at the conference table, it struck Augie, like he was bracing himself for a roller coaster ride.

Everyone else, Augie included, found they couldn't help following suit.

"Alistair and I will pay you one million dollars each – that's after taxes – to work together, or separately, in aid of securing definitive proof that non-avian dinosaurs have survived to the present day."

"So we don't have to actually bring you a caged Suck-on-this-o-don," said Irene, leaving Scott to wonder whether she was constitutionally capable of ever not sounding snarky, despite his infatuation with her. "Or is that what you will require for definitive proof?"

"Video combined with something we can examine for DNA evidence should suffice. But please let me paint the full picture for you. After a year of earnest endeavor, if none of you have succeeded, you are welcome to throw in the towel, as it were. But you will also be welcome to carry on, aided as before by the virtually unlimited resources we are placing at your disposal.

"Moreover, at any point one of you succeeds, whether next month or next decade, you will each receive an additional two-million-dollar bonus, again after taxes."

"We may work together or separately," said Laura, referring to her already-extensive notes. "But success for one means a two-million-dollar bonus for all."

"Correct on both counts. Munch!" Eclipso Sunray Smith nonchalantly bit into a new hummus-battered pretzel, apparently.

"Okay," Laura went on, "let's imagine only one of us actually sets to work. The others merely pay lip service while basically doing so little, they might as well join your Bonsai Gator, squatting down up to their eyeballs in swamp water. And then our one hard worker, bingo! She brings you a Protoceratops on a leash."

"You're asking whether all but one of you could deceive me into paying you a fortune for sitting on your hands? I suppose anything is possible."

"Such as happening across a living dinosaur. Okay," Stephen held forward a hand to pre-empt the correction he knew Eclipso was about to make, "a living, non-avian dinosaur."

"Actually, I believe that happening-across bit is far more likely than even one of you, let alone all but one of you, undergoing such an abrupt character transformation into lazy bums from the intrinsically motivated, principled creatures my extensive research documents."

"You might have reached a mistaken conclusion in my case," said Stephen in his usual I-hate-to-break-it-to-you-but-actually-am-delighted-to-rub-your-nose-in-it   mode. "I'm only here for the money; if I decide to climb aboard your crazy train, it will only be for the million bucks. I mean for the million bucks only. There is no honest way anyone here will be able to satisfy what you require for the additional two million. In fact, why not have us search for something slightly more plausible, like Bigfoot? The possibility one of the hominid candidates for its identity managed to survive an additional couple hundred thousand years or so past its last known date of existence isn't great. But it's definitely larger than the possibility a non-avian dinosaur managed to survive an additional seventy million years, dodging all manner of apocalyptic natural disasters along the way, and keeping itself out of the fossil record since the Cretaceous."

"The prospect of a relic Gigantopithecus might prove fascinating for some, but really doesn't interest us does it, Bonsai Gator?"

Bonsai Gator lifted his long snout out of the swamp water and vigorously shook it from side to side. Whether in response to Eclipso's question or, as Stephen was intent on believing, by mere coincidence, who could say?

"In that case, I can save you and Mr. Frump both a whole lot of time and money."

"What you're saying, Mr. Feldman, is that you already can provide proof of non-avian dinosaur survival to the present day?" Eclipso asked in such an unusually stern and less-nasal voice, for him, that even his mother took a step back from where she stood most attentively by his side. "If so, you save us little money at all because to celebrate, I will promptly make whatever bank deposits are necessary for each of you to clear three million dollars after taxes."

"Wow!" Stephen couldn't help exclaiming, stunned. "No," he shook his head, quickly collecting himself. "To prove a negative lies well beyond my modest talents, even for such an absurd proposition as extant dinosaurs. But I have no doubt that you could send a thousand people on your quest, and still end up with the same result: nothing, nada. They won't find anything more than, exactly as you put it earlier, mistaken identities fueled by wishful thinking, and hoaxes. Now, I really would like to take your million dollars. However, whatever small element of decency remains to my constitution recoils at that prospect. In fact, I don't sit comfortably with that hundred thousand you've already awarded me, now that I fully grasp your objective."

"That is precisely how I know you will earn every penny I give you or have already given you," declared Eclipso. "But now, a little confession of my own. Yes, Bonsai Gator and I look forward to savoring definitive proof of non-avian dinosaur survival. But I would be less than honest if I did not admit that such proof will be all the sweeter for the shocked-speechless expression it is likely to leave across your face, Mr. Feldman." With that, a big bite disappeared out of Eclipso's freshly hummus-battered pretzel. And staring down Stephen Feldman, Eclipso made slow munching motions that seemed to Augie Matias to be daring the professional skeptic to contradict him.

"No doubt," said Stephen. At the same time, he wished Bonsai would stop directing its long snout towards each person who spoke as though it could actually follow the conversation. He did try to assure himself the miniature-sized reptile was merely attending to each noise, rather than going on to grasp its meaning. And he held out the possibility Bonsai Gator's snout swings had zero to do with people's voices. Rather, it was following one of the mini dragonflies in a manner that accidentally coincided with the ebb and flow of the conversation.

"I have to admit that of the many cryptozoological subjects, non-avian dinosaur survival fascinates me the most," said Professor Roberta Quiñones. "Unfortunately, they also seem the least likely of all possible living fossils. Although I am not as certain on that score as you are, Mr. Feldman.

"Other commitments already consume much of my time, including of course my duties with the Cryptozoological Society. No doubt, fellow society members will happily cover for me. And if I kick in some of that million you are promising us, there should be enough biology department funds to have graduate students teach my more basic classes such as the introduction to paleontology. But there are specialized lectures, new excavations from Utah, hmmm. Suppose I might be able to swing an unpaid sabbatical."

Eclipso nodded understandingly. And to Stephen's growing consternation, Bonsai Gator nodded as well. *Has to be simply another coincidence.*

"Full time dedication to the search would be ideal, of course," Eclipso said, more nasal than ever. "But we value most profoundly the input each and every one of you could provide. I am not going to turn down your help, or dock you any of the pay I have pledged, if your participation needs to be squeezed in round the edges of other commitments. I simply ask that you sustain whichever level of input, limited or full time, hope hope, for at least one full year. Maybe less if you prove Mr. Feldman, there, wrong sooner rather than later."

"And we can choose whether we all work together in one big group, or in two or more smaller groups," said Scott McDonald while trying not to be too obvious about snatching glimpses at Irene...again; never expected to find hair weaves so attractive. His head was spinning in any event, wondering whether his joining Eclipso's quest to the neglect of the Bible museum wouldn't earn him all kinds of estrangement. His brother was ticked off plenty enough with his having accepted the invitation onto a bus headed for parts unknown. And the rest of his family already feared there was too much science in his life, and not enough faith, like science and faith were mutually exclusive.

"As I said before, you can even split yourselves up into ten groups of one each," confirmed Eclipso. "You're likely to stick together at the outset. The longer you go without success, though, the greater the odds you will break apart, developing conflicting theories of the case."

"What if we need, uh, what if some of us, one or more of us need time to think about this?" Scott asked with his usual hesitancy.

"What is there to think about, Mr. McDonald?" asked Irene before Eclipso could open his mouth again. "This offer might expire when Bonsai Gator sinks out of sight into Bonsai Swamp."

Scott guessed he looked like the proverbial deer caught in the headlights.

Finally, Irene busted out laughing. "Just baiting you, Mr. McDonald! But how about it, Eclipso?" she abruptly turned away from Scott McDonald to ask. "Are we going to have any time to give your proposal a good ponder?"

"Here is what I find fascinating," said Sherman Peabody, chin still lodged firmly into his neck. "In a sense, the shoe has been jammed on the wrong foot. Should be ourselves, Eclipso, piled high with flipcharts and the like, trying to persuade you to part with so many millions of dollars. Instead, you're practically begging us to do something I gather that many here would pay for the opportunity to indulge, let alone have a fortune land in their laps because of. Most fascinating, indeed!"

"What we discussed, dear," Eclipso's mother whispered, but not softly enough to escape Augie's notice.

"Yes I know, Mom," Eclipso whispered back, unable to hide his irritation, nor to speak quietly enough to not also be heard by Augie. "No matter whoever is doing the selling here," he proceeded loudly. "Given the huge investment of your time and personal resources I am asking for, quite unreasonable to expect any final decision right this minute. So true, regardless how enthused you might feel over the prospect of a definitive search for a living, non-avian dinosaur. Therefore, I grant two full weeks to make up your minds, explore how you will deal with conflicting demands on your time, etcetera etcetera."

Harriet and Harry turned each other's way, and Harry asked ecstatically, "Two weeks?"

"Two weeks!" just as ecstatically responded Harriet.

The couple nodded at one another, both thinking the same thing: Over two weeks, they could gently ease their families into accepting their going off heaven-knows-where, searching for dinosaurs of the non-fossil, up-and-moving-around variety.

"Two weeks, okay," Stephen Feldman said in a voice Augie found intentionally putting a damper on Harriet and Harry's enthusiasm. "Then what?"

"Then we form a circle and dance the hokey-pokey," Irene answered with her unrelenting snark, effectively cloaking her own thrill. "I'm sure Bonsai Gator would be totally up for that."

Bonsai Gator vigorously nodded its long snout, thrashing the swamp water enough to send it spraying in people's faces despite its compact size. What Stephen desperately wanted to dismiss as behavior having absolutely nothing to do with Irene McDowell's remark.

"If I might, Maestro," said Alistair Frump, hesitating to speak further until "Maestro" Eclipso nodded his assent. "My idea actually might have worked well enough for this initial encounter. As they say, though, better late than never. How many of you already have the video conference call ap on your smart phone?"

"I'm afraid I don't have a smart phone," said Bernie Coleman in a woeful tone.

"That's okay..."

"My phone says I've already reached my data limit," Stephen interrupted Alistair to once more sound like the voice of doom, where Augie was concerned. Seeming to only further that purpose, he added, "Most of my aps stall when I try using them."

"What's an ap?"

Augie didn't catch who asked this question. But Stephen was shaking his head "No," eyes closed, after noticing Bonsai Gator slowly sink beneath the swamp water until only its nostrils remained visible.

"I appreciate where you were going with your question, Alistair," said Eclipso, seeing his human partner lost in puzzlement. "But I think it will be easier to simply reconvene here in two weeks. That is, except for any of those who to our great disappointment choose to bow out. What's that, Bonsai? Time for more reggae Beatles?

"Samuel Longbottom, if you will lead our future heroes back out to the bus..."

Wow, where did that come from? Augie asked himself as Mr. Longbottom, the perpetually pleasantly smiling chap in the cream-colored cardigan sweater, started ushering him and others out of the conference room dominated by the swamp-embedded table. Not only had Bonsai Gator re-emerged fully from the swamp onto the smallest sand bank Augie had ever seen. He was wearing a tiny woolen hat tied in a neat bow underneath his short scaly neck, a tiny woolen hat shaded red, green, and black, the colors of the Jamaican flag.

Just outside the room, past the French double doors, Augie could hear a reggae downbeat followed by the members of Yellow Dubmarine harmonizing, "He's a real nowhere man..."

Meanwhile, Sherman Peabody didn't look where he was going, so lost in thought. *I have never previously lent any attention to the notion of certain regions still sufficiently unexplored, prehistoric beasts are able to roam largely undetected beyond that occasional rare encounter. Hmm. Perhaps my assistance in discovering certain subatomic particles together with my work on artificial intelligence..."*

THUD!

The more lost Sherman became in thought, the faster he walked as his pulse quickened with excitement. And the less he attended to exactly where he was walking. No surprise, then, that he crashed with considerable forward momentum into one of the cement fangs of the Ankylosaur façade, just outside the front doors. He crashed with enough force to set off his airbags so the next thing anyone knew, he seemed engulfed by one big gray oblong balloon, bouncing down the driveway towards the bus.

"...just sees what he wants to see..." Augie heard leaking from the conference room, in Yellow Dubmarine's reggae version of the Beatles song, "Nowhere Man."

Meanwhile, others ran past Augie out of the mansion, to catch Sherman before he could bounce colliding into the bus. That's when Augie realized nobody thought to address the matter of confidentiality. Not even journalist Laura Gómez, to his amazement.

Eclipso Sunray Smith obviously had gone to a lot of trouble hiding from public view. So wasn't he concerned one or more of his recruits for his dinosaur search might make a beeline for the nearest media outlet to tell all? Especially Laura Gómez of Puffington Post fame?

On the other hand, say someone, Laura even, did rat out Eclipso? She'd have to say he was living in a mansion designed to look like an Ankylosaurus, camouflaged to blend in with a stand of yellow birch in a field in western Pennsylvania. And furthermore, that he was bankrolling a massive search for a living, non-avian dinosaur so Alistair Frump could open a golf resort only the wealthiest people with nothing better to do could afford. Moreover, he claims a full-grown alligator the size of a pencil "thought it was a good idea." Who would believe any of it? Aside from, most worrisomely, certain hoaxers who might want to gum up the operation?

Chapter 11

As promised, Eclipso Sunray Smith reconvened the chosen ones for his extraordinary quest exactly two weeks later. Same as before, a bus labeled "Turok Tours" waited for Augie Matias and company at a train station parking garage near Baltimore-Washington International Airport. For the casual observer, the bus could have been taking passengers to Gettysburg Pennsylvania, the Skyline Drive along the Blue Ridge Mountains, or any number of other sightseeing destinations. But the ever-pleasantly-smiling Samuel Longbottom, this time wearing a burgundy-colored cardigan sweater, drove back to the Ankylosaurus mansion somewhere out in the wilderness of western Pennsylvania, best as Augie could tell. Again, special window shades only allowed passengers to see slivers of roads, road shoulders, and bits of greenery just off the roadside where the shoulders narrowed. No road signs or other helpful clues, but there was just enough of a view to minimize motion sickness.

Of the ten people originally invited to form the living non-avian dinosaur search party, all ten returned. As Eclipso quickly learned, their question was not so much, "Should I do this?" as it was, "How am I going to explain this to people I care about who might regard the entire matter as a bit crazy, million dollars or not?"

Inside the large conference room peculiarly dominated by the swamp-embedded conference table, Eclipso zestfully popped a small hummus-lathered pretzel ring out of sight, so pleased was he to behold every last invite back for more. "This is marvelous. Marvelous!" he enthused in tandem with munching noises. "So let's get right to it," he went on after he swallowed. But then in the harshest whisper, "I'm asking, Mother. I'm asking, okay?" Of course, he was addressing the thin wraith of a woman still standing attentively behind him.

Certainly can't be the case, Augie tried to assure himself, fighting a creepy feeling, *that this guy's mother has been standing there at his side, essentially unmoved, for the entire two weeks since we first arrived here.*

"So, then," went on Eclipso, slapping at remnant pretzel crumbs on his stubby-fingered hands.

Augie found himself reminded of the many times he unsuccessfully tried to slap away clay particles that pickaxes sprayed all over him during a fossil dig. Only Eclipso's crumbs showed not the slightest inclination to remain stuck to his skin or clothes.

"What I want to hear first is exactly how the important people in your life reacted when they learned you would be devoting so much time to searching for a living dinosaur."

"In other words, if I might interrupt," said Sherman, his chin pressed so firmly into his neck, Augie mused he could have been addressing one of the buttons on his green-and-purple plaid shirt, "you want to know whether we were as successful brushing off their concerns as you have been, brushing pretzel crumbs off your fingers."

"The important people in your life, whether relatives, friends, or both are most certainly important in every sense of the word imaginable," responded Eclipso without, to Stephen's way of thinking, responding to Sherman Peabody's remark. "In many great works of music and literature, you start at home, go on a marvelous adventure, then return home. In issue 115 of *Turok Son of Stone,* Turok and Andar are distracted from their search for a way out of Lost Valley by a young theropod dinosaur. Andar believes the dinosaur has befriended him, or that he has befriended the dinosaur. But he soon learns that Turok is right; his pet Allosaurus was just biding time until the time felt ripe for eating him. After Turok saves Andar from his lesson learned the hard way, that you can't trust a dinosaur, especially a meat-eating one, they return to their perpetual quest for a way back home, that much wiser."

"So home base in your typical *Turok* comic book tale," said Sherman, "is not really home base. It's the search for home base."

"A search some might argue we embark on from the time we are born," nodded Eclipso, "but a destination we never actually reach until our supposed deaths return us to whatever mysterious state we were in prior to our births."

"Nothing, in other words," deadpanned Stephen.

"How absolutely absurd!" protested Eclipso while Scott McDonald thought to himself, *My brother would have a field day with Stephen Feldman!* "But enough of this dilly-dally; let's hear from each one of you about your home base. Starting to my left with you, Augustine Matias, but you go by Augie, yes?"

"Augie, yes. And happily, when I brought up the matter with my better half, the first words out of her mouth were, 'You have to do this!'"

"Maybe she's trying to get rid of you," deadpanned Stephen again.

"You wouldn't try to get rid of me would you, Harriet?" Harry turned to ask Harriet in sudden alarm.

"Of course I wouldn't, sweetie," answered Harriet. "You're too big to pile into a trash can."

"And you're too big to pile into a trash can, also. I'm stuck with her," Harry announced to the group.

"And I'm stuck with him!"

"Actually," Augie laughed, "I did tell Vicky she sounded a little too excited about my possibly being gone for far longer than the one-to-two-week stints *Cryptomonster Hunt* usually entailed. But that's when she admitted her total infatuation with the financial windfall you have so generously offered for our mere good-faith effort, Eclipso. You see, one of her teacher supervisors has been cramping her pedagogical approach. She likes knowing that if the probation they've put her on doesn't work out, won't be the end of the world."

As much as he revealed, Augie couldn't bring himself to repeat what Vicky said, even though he remembered her exact words: "What I'm excited about, Augie-doggie, is saying, 'Bite me!' if they threaten to end my career altogether!"

Augie also decided it wouldn't be prudent to mention daughter Lizzy's reaction. That she was counting on him to set up a video eavesdropping system so she could follow vicariously his dinosaur-searching exploits…similar to how Vicky hoped he could make those exploits available for her students to enjoy an ultimate learning experience.

"And you, Sherman Peabody," Eclipso looked past Augie towards Sherman seated beside him, "how are your family or whoever handling your news? Certainly they can't be fretting over your safety, given all the many several precautions you take for your well-being."

"Actually, my girlfriend's reaction had me wondering something similar to Dr. Matias here."

Soon as Irene heard the word, girlfriend, she leaned way forward, looking past Laura to confirm she didn't confuse who uttered it. *Now that's someone I'm going to have to meet*, she told herself while Sherman continued, "Esther clapped her hands so delightedly, I couldn't help bursting out, 'Do you have any idea what dangers I'll be facing?! Between exposure to deadly viruses and bacteria, extremely poisonous snakes, frogs, bugs and who knows what else?! If I didn't know better, I would guess you want me killed!!'"

"I want you living!" Esther protested. "But say something else that dumb, and I might stage a major extinction event right here in this living room!"

"What about your loved ones, Ms. Laura Gómez?" Eclipso asked, looking past Sherman. "Did important people in your life clap their hands delightedly, by any chance?"

"My Aunt Gladys waved her hands dismissively as in, 'Tell me when you're not chasing after something crazy.' But my Aunt Filomena sounded more worried than usual. She wondered why I don't take up a safer hobby, like having my body parts pierced. Oh, and there's the editor-in-chief at *Puffington Post*. He's cool with my unpaid sabbatical for a year so I can fully devote myself to aiding your search. He hopes for award-winning pot-of-gold reporting at the end of this rainbow if you actually succeed."

"Nothing wrong with that, certainly. And what about your family, Ms. Irene McDowell?" Eclipso looked past Laura to ask. "Would they prefer you do body-piercing instead?"

Irene raised her chin haughtily high at the outset of Eclipso turning his attention to her. But on his question about body piercing, for once she bowed her head, though not nearly as far down as Sherman Peabody usually kept his. And with what Scott found the most endearing smile, she responded, "Think my Dad is still talking my Mom down off the panic cliff. For all I know, she might well have rather seen me show off a belly button ring, but they're okay." Uncharacteristically where

Scott was concerned, she seemed a bit choked up. He couldn't have known the two recent experiences weighing on her. One entailed breaking the news to her parents, that she was basically dropping everything to join the search for a living dinosaur. "You're going to love this," she said.

"Meaning we won't," her father remarked so quickly, could have been part of her same sentence.

Once Irene finished laying out her plan, wishing along the way she could stop sounding so defiantly defensive, her father gave her a long, hard stare. Then maintaining that stare, he said, "Wish I could join you."

"Oh, Daddy!" gushed Irene rushing to wrap her arms around him, and nuzzling her head against his chest. Although she just as quickly stepped back to ask, "So why don't you join us? I'm sure-"

"Your mother would kill me."

"You've got that right, honey," Amber McDowell held her own chin high to confirm with as much of her own defiance as she could muster, despite her eyes watering.

Irene's other experience entailed Skip, who she had already resolved to definitely not invite along even were he to express an intense desire. Talk about searching for elusive strange beasts, there was the matter of whether that peculiar creature called love was hiding away somewhere inside her, in regards to Skip. She figured a lengthy time spent away from him would flush it out into the open, if it existed.

Skip pressed the same search, reacting to Irene's announced intent with an off-the-cuff marriage proposal. "I haven't touched a whisky bottle or a cigarette in months, all because of you," he started.

Well at least we know what you're *getting out of our relationship,* Irene couldn't help thinking, though she well knew that would be too cruel for even her to voice aloud. What she did go on to say, once Skip awkwardly concluded "So how about we get married?" was, "Let me think about it. Wait, to clarify: I'll think about it." *I don't need your permission.*

When it came to University of Maryland zoology professor Dr. Roberta Quiñones, like Irene she kept the bulk of her own soap opera details to herself. Hurrying past a breezy assertion her family respected her work, she expounded at length on rearranging her schedule, passing off most of her duties to others so she could go all-in on Eclipso's search. "No worries."

In reality, there were big worries with Roberta's significant other, Daniela. "You know who Scott McDonald is, don't you?" Daniela asked in a cold voice that Roberta knew from past experience foretold another of her ranting bipolar meltdowns.

"I know that cryptozoology attracts some real characters. No doubt, Scott is one of them," Roberta answered with as much nonchalance as she could muster, trying her best to pre-emptively defuse the situation.

But Daniela would have none of that. "Scott's a real character, alright!" she suddenly shrieked. And in one violent wriggle, she shook off Roberta's affectionate effort to entwine her arms round her neck. "He's a real character who believes if he finds a living dinosaur, he'll prove evolution wrong!! He'll acquire the best exhibit yet for his f-ing Bible museum with its holy order of willful ignoramuses!!"

"Of course a living dinosaur would prove no such thing. It would join the ranks of other living fossils that evolution didn't necessarily require go extinct when left by the wayside. What some evangelicals push along that line is, like you say, a case of willful ignorance," Roberta conceded, albeit fighting down trembles as she strove not to give up on defusing her lover of five years. How many more of Daniela's irrational rages could she endure before needing to pull the plug on their relationship? "But, but…"

"No buts!" Daniela literally snarled.

"Please hear me out, Daniela. The discovery of a surviving non-avian dinosaur-"

"I don't give a f—k about your surviving non-avian dinosaur!!"

Smash!

Daniela picked up the nearest loose object, a framed photo from their trip to New Orleans three years back, and threw it at the wall with all her might. She missed their flat-screen TV by mere inches.

"They're as plentiful as flying pigs!" Daniela vented further. "So all you'll do is burn up lots of free time you could have spent with me, that we could have enjoyed together!"

Yeah, I'm having a laugh riot with you at the moment, Roberta stewed inside while she gave Daniela a you've-got-to-be-kidding-me look.

But the irony was not lost on Daniela. One minute she's raging at Roberta and in the process angrily smashing to bits a photo of them together. The next she's complaining over their spending too much time apart. So with forlorn meekness she added, "I just wish, sometimes, you took more interest in banning cruelty to animals we know for sure exist, than in creatures that might be more figments of the imagination. If you weren't gone so often, we might have been able to take in extra dogs from the animal shelter."

"Ruff-ruff-ruff!"

"Awoooo!!"

"Who's your mommy? Who's your mommy?" Daniela asked their two dachshunds Queenie and Prince Charles. They competed for her attention, having just pushed past a black rubber flap to re-enter the kitchen from a small back yard.

"Well think of it as kindness to endangered dinos," Roberta finally responded while stewing inside even further, *If you didn't insist on so many pets, we could have traveled together more.*

Daniela might have appreciated Stephen Feldman, had she been present at the Ankylosaur mansion to hear him answer how family and friends reacted to his planning to accompany Eclipso's dinosaur search.

"I was hesitant at first to break the word to myself," he deadpanned. "But once I got good and soused on Jack Daniels..."

"And how did you take it when you finally admitted to yourself what you would be about?" Eclipso was of enough wit to ask. "I should hope you didn't throw yourself out of your residence, or otherwise disown yourself."

"It took a lot of effort, actually, to keep from pummeling myself senseless for proposing to waste so much time on a fruitless mission. What saved the day, just before I would have passed out from my hand choking my neck, was my pledge that when your search is ultimately abandoned, I'll prepare an extensive report on the folly of it for the skepticism journal. Hopefully, I'll convince readers that the plight of real life animals is far more worthy of their time and resources than are fanciful chimeras. Help end the barbarity of bull fights and cockfights, and leave hopeless chases after nonexistent prehistoric survivors sequestered inside your *Turok* comic books."

"Fine by me if that line of reasoning secures your participation!" Eclipso reacted with special gusto. "But what about your families, Harriet and Harry Letterman? Do they regard my quest as being after 'fanciful chimeras'? And is that a family member you brought here?"

"Mr. Smith, I've been to time-share introductions, investment opportunity seminars, you name it," blustered Harriet's father Stu Rosenberg who up until then had been standing patiently quiet behind his daughter and son-in-law. "But I'm still trying to figure out what kind of scam you're running that makes you enough payoff to afford a hundred-thousand-dollar lure!"

"When we told my Daddy you were paying us gobs of money to look for a living dinosaur, he freaked out," said Harriet tearfully. "He yelled and screamed he would need to accompany us here."

"Which he wouldn't have done if he didn't love you so much," said Harry giving his wife a comforting pat on the shoulder.

"He completes me," sniffled Harriet like she was revealing this notion for the very first time, rather than having repeated it on numerous other occasions.

"And she completes me."

"What I'm trying to wrap my head around," said Harriet's father, Stu, "is how this works. Maybe you're about to introduce some lame reason your targets here have to make withdrawals on their accounts? And turn over that money to you before those hundred-thousand-dollar checks bounce?"

With a small splash Bonsai Gator leapt from the mini-swamp. He landed on his two hind legs, and gave Stu Rosenberg a staring look by turns puzzled and severe.

"Has it not occurred to you yet, Mr. Father of Harriet Letterman, that those checks were deposited in their accounts weeks ago? They would have bounced long before now were I not of sufficient resources to cover them."

Harriet's father found himself shifting his attention with increasing anxiety between Eclipso Sunray Smith and Bonsai Gator. What was the smallest alligator he'd ever seen doing there, standing on its hind legs like he'd never seen an alligator able to do, and continuing to stare him down like that? And for that matter, what was up with this swamp-embedded conference table?

Most likely, sweat would have been trickling down Stu Rosenberg's neck, even were humid greenhouse warmth not permeating the conference room.

"I don't think you need worry about Mr. Eclipso Smith taking financial advantage of your daughter and son-in-law," said Stephen Feldman. "He might be throwing away money by the bucket-load on a fool's errand. He might be totally delusional and have several other issues as well," Stephen nodded towards Eclipso's mother standing ever-present behind him. "But I don't think he's a crook."

"Please. So much flattery," Eclipso waved his hands in protest. "You're making me blush."

"These are nice people, Daddy," said Harriet. She craned her head around to look up at Daddy Stu standing behind her, and gave him a comforting pat on his hand protectively clinging to her shoulder. "They're not going to allow anything bad to happen to us."

Stu's attention was still drawn to Bonsai Gator's unsettling glare at him, while Irene McDowall sitting across the swamp-embedded table from Harriet added, "Nice is probably not the first word that comes to mind when people think about me, but your daughter is right. Can't guarantee how it will turn out if we are ever chased by a surviving Velociraptor. But as for any con operations, whoever is responsible will have to deal with me first before they get anywhere near Harriet and Harry."

Addressed by Irene, Stu couldn't help turning his attention her way. On completion of her assurance, though, he also couldn't help returning his attention to Bonsai Gator. He found the small reptile nodding at him as in, what Irene and his daughter said ought to more than suffice.

Stephen Feldman closed his eyes and shook his head. *Most unfortunate,* he told himself, *when Bonsai Gator happened to move his snout up and down. Harriet's father is going to leave here believing the impossible.*

"Um, if I could go home now, I'll call a taxi," said Stu. "But you and Harry please be very careful."

"Any Velociraptor will have to eat me first before he takes a bite out of my Harriet, Mr. Rosenberg," said Harry.

That should leave it too full to have room for Harriet, Irene thought better of reacting out loud.

"I won't hear of it," protested Eclipso. "Samuel Longbottom will be happy to take you home personally, free of charge. And he won't hear of you giving him a tip, will you, Samuel?"

"Absolutely not, Eclipso," the pleasant-appearing man in the burgundy cardigan sweater answered pleasantly as he rose to lead Stu Rosenberg out the door. "I'll have you home in a jiffy, Mr. Rosenberg."

"Have you ever taken a ride in a jiffy before, Daddy?"

"A jiffy isn't a form of transportation, Harriet dear!" Stu shouted from the French door entrance to the conference room. "That's just an expression meaning it will be fast!"

"I know, Daddy! Just kidding!" With that, Harriet gave her husband another high five.

Sally is not going to believe what I have to tell her. Just wait until she hears about Bonsai Gator, Stu told himself on the way to the faux tour bus. Somewhat ashamedly, he actually looked forward to sharing his bizarre experience with his wife as in: This might be fun.

"Okay," Stephen Feldman with his eyes closed meanwhile addressed Eclipso, "we've heard from everyone around this table about how friends and family are taking their participation in this ridiculous quest. When does it actually begin? Or are you going to break us up into smaller groups now to have a discussion about how we really feel about searching for living dinosaurs?"

Stephen reopened his eyes, only to find Bonsai Gator staring right at him, the gator's long snout slowly swinging from side to side as if to convey disgust. *Couldn't be that,* Stephen insisted to himself. *Oh, no. Just another unfortunate coincidence.*

"Impatience! I love it," said Eclipso. "By all means, let's not waste another minute before we see what I am putting at your disposal to facilitate our mission. And Mother, I believe Bonsai Gator is becoming restless for more reggae. Please to oblige."

Eclipso's selected team of dinosaur searchers found themselves filing out of the conference room to a reggae version of yet another old Beatles tune, this time, "I'm Looking Through You."

To their faint unease, Irene and a few others noticed that during Bonsai Gator's sway to the reggae beat, he seemed to systematically shift his attention from person to person, trying to look through each one of them. Or was that, as Stephen would have insisted, merely a trick of their suggestible imaginations?

Augie Matias recollected a summer training seminar his wife told him about. One of the seminar leaders had them write down on a slip of paper what they would have been doing had they not been mandated to participate. After volunteers read aloud what they wrote, everyone was ordered to crumple up their dreams of family vacations and the rest into little balls, disposed of in the nearest trash bin because none of that was going to happen.

Well, if Augie didn't know better, he would have sworn Eclipso, at his mother's encouragement, was about something far less cruel. His talk of returning to home base, his expressed interest in how each participant's friends and family dealt with their peculiar news...

Eclipso wanted his recruits to continue honoring and cherishing whatever meant the most to them. They didn't need to trash any of it in order to embark on a search for living non-avian dinosaurs.

To Augie's surprise, lost in his meditations, he had already been led outdoors. Eclipso took his chosen ones on a trail in amidst the yellow birches that ended in an open field back behind God's Toenail or whatever else one might care to label his mansion.

What Augie noticed next was an immense circular area of the field with its mix of wheat and other grasses completely matted down, flattened. A crop circle?

The blue sky above featured a motley assortment of fluffy cumulus clouds floating along picturesquely on warm, gentle breezes. Augie turned from this epic vista to Eclipso, and saw his pudgy hands holding what looked like a video game joystick control. He was manipulating it while focused heavenward.

That's when several of Eclipso's fellow travelers realized an especially majestic-looking cumulus cloud had inexplicably broken off from the general drift of the rest. To several gasps and pointing fingers, and Stephen drily observing, "This is an odd time of the day for a fog bank formation, but I am sure it is not without precedent," that cloud slowly but steadily descended.

It landed squarely middle of the circular area of matted-down grasses, whereupon everyone could hear a gentle whoosh. Whirlpools of condensing water vapor polka-dotted the enormous cloud, like several bathtub drains had just opened.

As the cloud dissolved away, the strangest-looking contraption Augie could ever hope to see, as large as two football fields, quickly came into view.

"Ladies and Gentlemen, I present you with your expeditionary vehicle, Cloud Nine. It's a steam-powered, room-equipped drone!" proudly announced Eclipso Sunray Smith, waving his hand unencumbered by the remote control towards the landed object.

"Yes," added Alistair Frump. "We stubbornly refused to throw in the towel after Cloud Eight still had significant issues. Didn't want any comparisons to the chaps who quit after Six Up!"

Chapter 12

"Wait," professional skeptic Stephen Feldman held up a protesting hand, and bowed his forehead into his other hand like he was experiencing a pounding headache. "I didn't hear you say 'steam-powered drone.'"

"Steam-powered, room-equipped drone, Mr. Feldman," corrected Alistair Frump. "Your ears weren't fooling you. Maybe just leaving out one detail," he added with a laugh.

"Room-equipped is even worse," Stephen lifted his forehead out of his hand to say haughtily, where Augie was concerned. "The amount of water you would need to store on board to power that thing's propellers would weigh too much. Lifting it even one inch off the ground would prove aerodynamically impossible."

"Not to put too fine a point on it, mate," said Alistair, "but you just watched your 'aerodynamically impossible' aircraft make a smooth landing after keeping up with the cumulus. Cloud Nine doesn't store any water aboard at all. Rather, it mooches all required moisture from the atmosphere, provided the humidity doesn't drop below a certain level. That's the genius of it. The solar-panel-powered heating of indrawn moisture spins its four-corner jet-engine propellers plus numerous additional stabilization propellers about its circumference. That results in dramatic vaporization from its exhaust valves, and Cloud Nine becoming literally engulfed by a cloud during operation."

"So it's not well-suited for flying over desert regions?" asked Bernie Coleman while others walked Cloud Nine's periphery for closer inspection.

The four jet engines Alistair alluded to did look like jet engines. Only, they were mounted vertically at each one of the square-shaped craft's four corners. A landing strut extended from each of those corners, and the many pieces of fuselage fit together at most peculiar angles, gleaming variously gold, silver, and gray.

Augie was reminded of the moon lander vehicle on display at the National Air and Space Museum in Washington D.C., which in turn had reminded him of a tiny spider. Only, if the moon lander was a tiny spider, Cloud Nine was one of those immense crabs netted off the coasts of Alaska and Japan.

"You need to avoid flight over desert regions," conceded Eclipso. "But fortunately, the places most likely to harbor surviving non-avian dinosaurs trend especially humid and swampy. Oh, and you will love how well the stabilizing propellers work. Most times aboard Cloud Nine, you won't even feel like you're flying, even on your way through turbulent weather short of a hurricane or tornado."

"Wait," said Stephen, looking like he was fighting a bad headache again, forehead back in hand and other hand raised in protest anew. "Obviously when the sky is full of fluffy cumulus clouds like it is today, your Cloud Nine is easily able to blend in. And presumably there's no problem hiding amidst thick overcast. But what about when we have to fly across clear sky? Won't it stand out? And in any event, aren't radars going to detect something more substantial than a cloud at its core? Or don't you put a premium on secrecy?"

"Oh, no!" Eclipso shook his head. "The less the general public is aware of our quest, the harder time hoaxers will have sabotaging us! Fortunately, Cloud Nine's steam-powered functioning confers most serendipitously incidental benefits where concealment is concerned.

You see, the cloud-concealing vaporization creates an atmospheric inversion that either fools radar into detecting no solid object whatsoever, or displaces Cloud Nine's location several miles away from where it's actually flying."

"That being said, your personal navigator, Samuel Longbottom, will make every effort to conceal Cloud Nine in amidst layers of stratocumulus, vapor trails, so on and so forth," said Alistair.

"But when it's out there all alone, flying across a clear blue sky?" asked reporter Laura.

"Meteorologists of Stephen's skeptical bent will argue it is simply a hitherto unnoticed, ultra-rare cloud formation akin to lenticular clouds that are sometimes mistaken for flying extraterrestrial spacecraft," answered Eclipso, his voice nasal as ever. "The fact that Cloud Nine either leaves no radar trace, or throws that trace miles away like it's a ventriloquist throwing his voice, certainly helps. Fancy a peek inside?"

Ample rest quarters, kitchen, fully equipped labs, and a navigation room specially designed to accommodate all the charts and maps Harriet and Harry had carefully compiled over the years, "This is undoubtedly a marvel of design engineering," Bernie Coleman shook his head in wonder. "But one thing still puzzles me: Engulfed by a cloud bank, how are we ever going to see where we're going, let alone spot a relic Apatosaurus or some-such?"

"Check this out," said Alistair, retrieving what looked like a foot-long hair follicle from inside his suit jacket. "Believe it or not, this," he stroked the bulbous end, "is a three-hundred-sixty-degree camera lens. Soon as Cloud Nine lifts more than ten feet off the ground, two of these extend below it, two above, and one on each side. They unobtrusively give you every view you could ask for, including night-time infrared as well as heat detection."

"We have also launched two satellites specifically dedicated to keeping contact with you, wherever on Earth your search should take you," added Eclipso. "We assume you'll want Harriet and Harry's compiled information aboard-ship, at your fingertips at all times. But should you have other resource materials, you might want to leave them with me rather than lugging them around. I'll make sure you can still access them on your navigation room control board screens."

"And we'll rent golf clubs along the way," inserted Alistair. When this curious declaration was met by abundantly perplexed looks, he added, "That is, should we want to test out the feel of a particular, hopefully dinosaur-infested area for golf resort development. But about those resource materials Eclipso mentioned, with your flash drives you...don't tell me you don't know what a- okay, forget it."

"Perhaps we should return inside God's Toenail, and get down to establishing your first destination, or destinations should you choose to break into smaller groups."

Chapter 13

On the brief trek back to Ankylosaurus Mansion/God's Toenail from marveling at the interior and exterior of Cloud Nine, Stephen Feldman hurried over beside journalist Laura Gómez. He hoped she'd appreciate his latest dry remark in his ongoing effort to come to terms with having sold himself out to join the search for living, non-avian dinosaurs. "For a moment there," he spoke in a confidential voice, though not really that concerned over who might overhear him, "I thought we would be sent home a second time, to ask ourselves how we really felt about Eclipso's quest."

"And what purpose would that serve, Mr. Feldman?" loudly asked Eclipso from several steps up ahead of Stephen. "Oh, I get it. You're trying to be funny. Ha ha."

Until then, Augie Matias hadn't really keyed in on Eclipso's nevertheless striking appearance. He remembered the enigmatic fellow's plaid shirt in the conference room, but that wasn't visible presently. In its place, or perhaps concealing it, was a high-collared velvet coat that could have been a queen's robe, especially stuffy-looking for the late-spring warmth of a sunny day in early June. And the way it trailed along the ground, concealing his legs and feet, he appeared to float more than walk across the mansion grounds and then the marble floors. Adding to this eerie effect, Augie couldn't discern Eclipso's footsteps. But presumably, the general hubbub drowned out what would have been muffled anyway by the robe-length coat.

Maybe his mother fitted him with it just before he left for outdoors.

Upon re-entry to the conference room featuring the swamp-embedded conference table, Stephen hesitated to resume sitting. Instead, he addressed Eclipso's mom, "Mother of Eclipso, I hate to see you standing there minutes on end while the rest of us relax in these comfy padded chairs. May I offer you my seat?"

From her usual demeanor, attentive yet with a distant, reflective look on her soft-featured face, Eclipso's mother suddenly perked up. Eyes shining brightly, she said, "Actually, I rather fancy remaining on my feet all day long after having to lie down all night long. Do not fear, Mr. Feldman. With Samuel Longbottom gone to bring home Harriet Letterman's father, I can always take his seat if need be."

The mother's voice had her son's nasal quality to an extent that reminded Augie of a squeaky mouse in certain cartoons.

Meanwhile, Bonsai Gator went from nodding his long snout seemingly at Eclipso's mom to shaking it side to side seemingly at Stephen.

"I don't think Bonsai Gator was very impressed with your gallantry," said Irene.

Roberta seated on Irene's left covered her mouth as she made a peculiar noise from stifling a laugh.

"Yes, and I could have sworn some dandelions grimaced at me on our way back indoors," Stephen reacted drily.

"So putting aside all inconsequential slights, whether real or imagined," said Eclipso, gesturing with another hummus-covered pretzel, "who wishes to step in first on the issue of where our search ought to formally begin?"

"'Step in' puts it quite accurately, I think," Stephen deadpanned. "You all might as well be stepping into a mountainous putrid pile of- okay, let's call it non-avian dinosaur poop – for how wastefully unproductive this quest of yours, Eclipso, is bound to prove. Although I suppose if we identify a couple new species of beetle or even a small frog along the way, well that will be something at least."

Eclipso stared at Stephen long and hard while he completely ground down his bit-off piece of pretzel, so it seemed, prior to swallowing. "What I shall delight in," he said at last, "is savoring the expression on your face, Mr. Feldman, the moment incontrovertible evidence confronts you that a non-avian dinosaur has indeed survived to the present day. The very prospect makes my close surveillance just that much more worthwhile. Doesn't it, Bonsai Gator?"

Willfully oblivious to Bonsai nodding, Stephen said, "I really do hope to see such evidence...the same way I hope that one day a leprechaun will lead me to his pot of gold."

"Far as claims of surviving dinosaurs go," said Bernie Coleman, eschewing the testy back-and-forth between Stephen and Eclipso in favor of answering Eclipso's original question, "I should think the mokele-mbembe of West Central Africa best fits the bill. Descriptions of a large beast with an elephant's torso, an alligator's tail, and a long, snake-like neck are identical to the morphology of a sauropod dinosaur such as the Apatosaurus or Diplodocus. Their purported habitat includes an unexplored region straddling Cameroon and the Central African Republic roughly the size of the Florida peninsula. Geologically speaking, that has been a rather stable region for the past hundred million years since its separation from the South American continent. Maybe has been a bit more variable in the weather department. But isn't the mokele-mbembe of special concern to your cryptozoological research, Mr. McDonald?"

"It better be," said Irene. "He just wrote an entire book on it."

Scott McDonald's attention shift from Bernie to Irene twisted him out of his chair. Only Bernie and Stephen's quick reactions prevented his falling into a misshapen heap on the floor, chair brought down over top. "Um, yes," he said after he finished flailing his arms, "the mokele-mbembe would certainly be a logical starting point. Like you indicated, Mr. Coleman, the possible range of the creature's movement is roughly the size of the Florida peninsula. My investigations suggest a northwest-southeast migration, dodging seasonal droughts in favor of wet weather patterns. In other words, the more easily we can penetrate a particular swamp, the less likely we will find it lounging around there. And the rainier and muddier the conditions, the better the chances we will sneak a peek. But there's a far more onerous problem I'm afraid has only been growing worse in recent years."

"You mean a problem even worse than the creature's lack of existence?" Stephen deadpanned anew.

"I know you and your magazine pride yourselves on blind skepticism of all things cryptozoological, Mr. Feldman, especially when the topic is non-avian dinosaur and sea reptile survival. But I strongly believe that if we exploit Eclipso Smith's vast resources to locate mokele-mbembe's migration route, definitive proof of its existence, including verification of its identity, would soon follow."

"Two problems," Stephen rebutted, raising two fingers for added emphasis. "One, Central West African geology might have remained relatively stable for the past hundred million years, but its climate certainly has not."

"As I indicated."

"As you indicated rather dismissively. The region fancifully populated with living sauropod dinosaurs has not remained tropical rainforest that entire time. Far from it. For long stretches it has consisted of savannah grasslands, a few especially arid epochs mixed in. Which leads to my second point: Your so-called mokele-mbembe, if it migrates at all, takes the same path as the gryphon, the unicorn, and other creatures that really don't exist. It migrates across people's fevered imaginations."

"Without taking sides, I do want to point something out, Mr. Feldman," said Dr. Roberta Quiñones. "Creatures that are used to tropical rainforest can adaptively evolve to a drier savannah habitat, and back again. That's not at all unheard of, provided the transitions between such climates aren't too abrupt. And even when our planet has undergone dramatically fast and extreme climate changes, as after an asteroid struck near the Yucatan Peninsula sixty-five million years ago, several creatures, including several reptiles, still did survive."

"A point well taken, Dr. Quiñones," conceded Stephen. "But that doesn't really address the fevered imagination point."

"Let's allow Mr. Letterman a word," said Eclipso, indicating with his lone remnant pretzel piece Harry Letterman's hand politely raised for a patiently long while.

"I wanted to say two things about mokele-mbembe migration," Harry proceeded in his groaning yet clear-enough voice. "Harriet and I will have to double-check. But I think you are correct, Mr. McDonald. Most of our recorded mokele-mbembe sightings are from wet season locations. The second thing, um…"

"The different names, dear," Harriet tried to remind Harry quietly, but spoke so loudly that everyone heard.

"Harriet sets off the alarm to wake up my brain whenever it falls asleep," Harry observed unabashedly before he went on, "Mokele-mbembe is also called mbokale-muembe, and from Zambia further east, the isiququmadevu and the mbilintu."

"They all are said to have a python's long neck, an elephant's big fat body, and an alligator tail," nodded Harriet.

"Yes," said Stephen, "when an elephant fords a deep river in the rainy season, I have read that it is likely to hold its trunk high. From any distance at all, someone can easily misperceive a long neck, with the elephant head the body to which it's attached. There is one old photo in particular, if you don't look too closely you might swear it captured an Apatosaurus wading across a lake."

"The swearing part," Irene quietly confided to Roberta and Laura seated beside her, "I feel that coming on, but for a different reason."

While Laura and Roberta strained not to giggle, Stephen went on insensible to that, "As for the various names for the same creature, Santa Claus also has various names, such as Old St. Nick."

"Uh, Mr. Stephen Feldman, sir, I have to call you out on that," exploded Irene, unable to contain herself any longer. "You're suggesting people who have lived their whole lives in tropical rainforests can't tell the difference between an elephant fording a deep river with her trunk lifted high, and a sauropod dinosaur taking a swim. I find that highly insulting to- Oh, what a coincidence – people who happen to be dark-skinned."

"No," Stephen shook his head emphatically, "I'm actually referring to fair-skinned Americans and Europeans who explore those rainforests with very little prior experience seeing elephants and other creatures in the wild. I wouldn't put it past some of them to mistake a feeding giraffe for a Brachiosaurus."

"And if you had carefully read Scott's book on the subject, you would have learned that the closest an outsider has gotten to seeing mokele-mbembe has been a heading sticking out of the water, or a distant large object blurred by high-humidity haze. The better views have been by the locals, exclusively."

"And none of them happened to have a camera at hand to document those better views," Stephen drily observed while Scott beamed contentedly over Irene having referred to him solely by his first name, and moreover indicating she'd given his book a close read.

"People are rarely equipped with cameras for these experiences," Bernie Coleman said softly, to dampen flaring tempers. "Strange creature sightings usually take place when least expected, the furthest thing from mind. And then people are often so awestruck, they either forget to film until it is too late, or they make some careless mistake. Didn't you write, Mr. McDonald, that a fellow thought he was filming one of these creatures in Lake Tele for a good five minutes before it sank below the surface? But then realized he forgot to remove the lens cap? An easy thing to do, I should think, when you believe you are in the presence of a living sauropod dinosaur."

"One of his colleagues confirmed he felt so embarrassed, he offered to resign his post at the Brazzaville Zoological Research Station," nodded Scott McDonald.

Fearing more implications of racism on his part, Stephen stifled himself from noting that the locals might be shamelessly hyping myths to promote tourism.

"But what I was going to add," Scott went on, "is that there's an even bigger obstacle presently to searching for mokele-mbembe, other than the usual poisonous snakes, bugs and plants, as well as – did I mention the number of vaccinations we will require? Anyway, civil war is simmering in both Cameroon and the Central African Republic. All the bribes we had to finance were bad enough before. But now in Cameroon, people who inherited French as their second language due to colonization are at serious odds with people who adopted English. They're at each other's throats. And in the Central African Republic, armed rebels are hiding out in the very areas that require traversing to reach those unexplored swamps. Yes, Eclipso, I know we can fly in directly on Cloud Nine. But if any rebels catch sight of us climbing down a rope ladder from an oddly low, stationary hovering cloud, well they do have missile launchers."

"In many an issue of *Turok Son of Stone*," reacted Eclipso, "Turok and Andar's quest for an escape route from Lost Valley is complicated by having to deal with the locals."

Oh boy, Stephen thought derisively, *here we go again with that ridiculous comic book. Soon enough he'll be referencing a particular issue like he's a Biblical scholar quoting ancient text.*

"Take 'Prey of the Flesh Eaters' from issue thirty of the original series, for example," continued Eclipso, his eyes roaming the elaborately paneled ceiling as he recalled one of Turok's many adventures. "Our Native American heroes save warring tribes from a volcanic eruption by persuading them to make peace. Only, those very same tribes then proceed to try sacrificing Turok and Andar to a herd of meat-eating dinosaurs."

"Okay, time out," said Irene forming a capital "T" with her hands. "I'm calling racism, maybe also including on your *Turok* comic book, for implicitly comparing Africans to prehistoric cavemen too stupid for their own good. By Scott's own admission, a lot of the conflict he describes goes back to the locals of West Central Africa having had to fight their way out of colonial enslavement."

"Nothing I am talking about could be any further from racism even if I tried, Ms. Irene McDowell," huffed and puffed Eclipso Sunray Smith. "For one thing, most of Turok's 'cavemen' are drawn with lily white complexions. For another, their prejudices and superstitions clearly are intended to mirror the shallow thinking of many contemporaries in these here United States. Indeed," snap! Eclipso apparently bit into another hummus-buttered pretzel, "you might say we are all stuck in a bit of a Lost Valley of our own. We seek exit from fear of the unknown, and willful ignorance, in which most people unhappily wallow, to joyfully enter a world where non-avian dinosaurs might still roam!" Crunch!

"Actually, there's a rumor concerning those African conflicts I've not yet been able to substantiate," said journalist Laura Gómez. "It has to do with a pending arms shipment to rebels in the Central African Republic. Supposedly, the freight containers have been bugged in the hopes of finally revealing whoever has been confiscating military equipment around the world without leaving even the tiniest clue behind."

"Now that could get very interesting," reacted Stephen as in the dinosaur quest, not so much, aside of course from the large amount of money he stood to gain from his participation.

"So maybe we wait for any West Central African expedition at least until that arms supply has been confiscated."

"And/Or tensions have subsided on the Cameroon end, between French and English-speaking forces," added Scott.

"Dr. Matias," Bernie Coleman spoke gently again, if also with a certain firm decisiveness, "your trip to New Britain Island off the coast of Papua, New Guinea: That is perhaps the most recent attempt any of us here has made to film or otherwise secure evidence of a living dinosaur, is it not?"

"Especially frustrating," nodded Augie, his heart suddenly racing with excited anticipation. "We had to pack up and leave right after a night-time encounter with something that caused trees and bushes to shake about wildly. Of course, we were dealing with strict deadlines filming a TV show."

"That hallucinogenic fruit the locals insisted you try before your search, I'm surprised you didn't see more than just wildly shaking vegetation," said Stephen.

"But the palms and casuarinas swaying about was caught on film," pointedly observed Bernie. "I doubt the locals forced their camera to eat any hallucinogens."

"So you did watch at least that episode of Mr. Matias's cryptozoology show, Mr. Feldman," noted Eclipso with a triumphant scoop of hummus onto the latest pretzel. "Very good!"

"At *Doubting Thomas*, we try to keep up with as many manifestations of superstitious behavior as possible."

"So tell us, Dr. Augustine Matias," said Eclipso, ignoring Stephen's mockery, "are there any obstacles we should know about? Which is to say, obstacles to a more thorough redo of your New Britain quest that approach the onerous level of what could stand in our way in west central Africa?"

"It's fairly stable politically, though lots of bribery is still required especially since they have no such thing as public land. Even the most remote swamps and shorelines are claimed by one group or another demanding both tributes and an audience. I'd say the single biggest threat to our safety would be a volcanic eruption. Volcanoes everywhere, there's always a small chance one of them could blow its lid off near us. And I do wish to avoid another forced indulgence of that hallucinogenic fruit you mentioned, Mr. Feldman. Think it left my stomach unsettled for several days afterwards."

"I might have a plan for that," Sherman Peabody lifted his chin off his neck just long enough to offer.

"I rather like making that region of the Earth our central focus," said Bernie. "It is certainly ground zero for some of the more unusual extant creatures such as the platypus of Australia. And incidentally, it's about as far away as you can get from where the large asteroid made apocalyptic impact sixty-five million years ago."

"You do understand that the particulate matter ejected into the upper atmosphere by that impact cooled the entire planet," lectured Stephen Feldman.

"Yes," conceded Bernie. "I also understand that several large reptiles did make it through, including the Komodo dragon native to Indonesia, as well as the tuatara native to New Zealand. And consider the large flightless birds of New Zealand and Australia, such as the moa that appears to have gone extinct in recent history. They most likely evolved from certain theropod dinosaurs. And let's not also forget that much of the flora in parts of New Guinea and north Australia are holdovers from the Cretaceous."

"Harriet and I have compiled reports of flying reptiles from islands near New Guinea," Harry Letterman finally worked up the courage to contribute to the conversation.

"And from northern Australia, we have a few accounts of a large, meat-eating reptile that stands on its two hind legs and is called the burrunjor," Harriet concluded with a that-should-settle-it slow nod.

"She completes me," said Harry with his kindly, bespectacled grin.

"I appreciate everyone's enthusiasm, but I think we need to really narrow our focus, isn't that right, Bonsai Gator?"

Bonsai nodded Eclipso's way, earning a new eye roll from Stephen.

"We could maybe return to the exact same spot where an exploration was initiated on *Cryptomonster Hunt*," proffered Augie. "It's near a mangrove swamp along the coast perhaps ideal for docking your Cloud Nine, Eclipso."

"And the frequency of possible dinosaur sightings in that general vicinity, Harriet and Harry, other than the report in their local news that spurred the *Cryptomonster* investigation?" asked Eclipso.

Harriet and Harry looked back and forth at one another in a seeming standoff until Harry finally said, "They are not many, but that's true of anywhere you look. And the reports we do have from there are very interesting."

"For example?"

"For example, Mr. Smith," said Harry, "there is a report of a large reptile standing on a boulder beside the sea. This was also along the coast of New Britain Island."

"It scooped fish out of the water with very long claws," added Harriet. "The description fits perfectly the Therizinosaurus."

"Which wasn't identified from the fossil record until five years after the sighting," concluded Harry, holding up his hand with five fingers spread apart for extra emphasis.

"He completes me," said Harriet with one of her bespectacled grins.

"Were there any other reports from New Guinea of such a creature?" Stephen asked challengingly.

"No," Harry shook his head. "That is the only report of such a creature from anywhere."

"Anywhere in our particular documentation," specified Harriet. "That doesn't mean other people haven't seen it."

"But such scant evidence is exactly what you would expect for a creature that doesn't actually exist," said Stephen on a conclusive note, "or when an ordinary creature has been mistaken for something else."

"I must say, New Britain Island off the coast of Papua, New Guinea sounds like a good place for embarking on our quest," said Eclipso, "and of course, Mr. Feldman, for putting some of your skeptical suppositions to the test. But this being said, Mr. McDonald, suppose you and at least one or two others here prefer to scout locales in the Central African Republic, despite the several onerous perils you would face. We could accommodate that. A second Cloud Nine is nearly ready for maiden voyage, and I can provide more than adequate connections and funding to deal with the worst corruption imaginable."

"Marvelous! Marvelous!" enthused Alistair Frump, slapping his hands and rubbing them together so zestfully, Augie half-expected to see smoke rise off them. "From that *Cryptomonster Hunt* episode, Augie, I could easily imagine a tropical links course snaking round the many swamps and coastal mangroves. The most adventurous golfers might expect to see an occasional saurian head poke out munching on coconuts like they're M&Ms. But I could also easily imagine," he abruptly turned Scott McDonald's direction, "the single most challenging eighteen-hole layout in the world, running along the edge of Lake Tele. It would feature water hazard carries where you can never be sure a surviving Apatosaurus won't raise its snakelike neck to snatch a golf ball out of the sky on its soaring journey to the fairway on the far side."

"I would- I would," Scott McDonald started over again, unnerved by the for-him most beautiful Irene McDowell focusing her full riveted attention on him, "happily see all our efforts centered on that creature with which Augie might have come so close to a full encounter, over in New Guinea. It is, um, maybe if and when we don't quickly answer definitively this question of non-avian dinosaur survival, maybe then we should consider operating parallel expeditions. In fact, to track the speculated migratory path of mokele-mbembe, um..."

"It can be near impossible to prove a negative," warned Stephen, "if you insist on exploring every last nook and cranny of the planet before you finally concede..."

"Then it's settled, good people," Eclipso cut off Stephen as though he didn't even realize he was saying something. "New Britain Island, Bonsai Gator?"

Bonsai Gator nodded his long snout emphatically. His frozen-in-place reptilian grin appeared to Augie even grinnier than usual.

"Excellent! So the quest begins!"

"Wait!" Stephen held up a hand in protest, while with his other hand he rubbed his forehead like he was back to dealing with a headache. "You do understand don't you, Eclipso, that when your misnomered Bonsai Gator moves its head about, that likely has nothing to do with its actually reacting in any meaningful way to something said?"

Rather than respond directly, Eclipso tipped his head Bonsai Gator's way, suggestive Stephen follow suit.

Bonsai Gator was slowly shaking its long snout from side to side at Stephen, in you-just-don't-get-it disgust.

Chapter 14

"There's your dinosaur!" Stephen Feldman shouted to be heard above the din of the cigarette boat splashily cruising calm turquoise seas, and propelled by a loudly humming, solar-charged, battery-powered outboard engine.

Augie Matias seated beside Stephen already noticed an enormous reptilian form, scaly ridges and all, break surface some hundred yards off the starboard bow. Glistening in the mid-morning sun, for precious seconds it had him wondering, *Goodness gracious, we're not ten minutes disembarked from Cloud Nine in search of definitive proof of non-avian dinosaur survival to the present day. Can we already be on the verge of success?*

But all too soon, even as he heard Scott say, "What's that over there?!" and Roberta ask Laura, "Do you see something?!" Augie realized that telltale eyes and nostrils had also emerged, of something not so dinosaurian.

"That's a saltwater crocodile!" said Stephen. "They can grow up to twenty-four feet long! A respectable size for a dinosaur! I'm guessing that's what all the fuss was about over there!" Stephen pointed towards the coral sand beach darkened to light brownish-gray by ash-fall from a volcano one decade ago.

Stephen and company were fast approaching the Gazelle Peninsula of New Britain Island off the northeast coast of Papua, New Guinea.

"The local women and one police officer described a pudgy-snouted snake's head on a long-ish neck!" rebutted Augie. "The rest of the body and tail they did liken to a crocodile, except that the hind legs looked a lot thicker than the forelegs!"

"Okay! So the crocodile's monstrous length came as such a surprise, they imagined they were seeing something different!" argued Stephen. "Maybe some dinosaur paintings got in their heads!"

Augie might have rebutted again, and Roberta Quiñones joined the fray. However, both found themselves too captivated by the saltwater crocodile's behavior...including a most curious aspect. Initially, the large reptile acted how both paleontologist Matias and zoologist Quiñones would have expected. The cigarette boat's outboard engine racket, probably totally foreign to the crocodile's ears, sent it on an adjusted course swimming away from them.

That course happened to head the large reptile directly towards swampy coastline replete with mangrove bushes towered over by areca and casuarina palms. A few yards later, though, it slowed to a halt and headed back out to the open sea, albeit on a diagonal ever more distant from the cigarette boat.

Augie and Roberta were struck by the same intuition. But wanting to avoid any accusation of wishful thinking, they kept quiet about it. Both sensed the saltwater crocodile thought better of coming any closer to the mangrove shoreline because of what lurked there. The dinosaur Eclipso's crew crossed half the globe to search for, perhaps?

Augie took his eyes off the crocodile, its glittering scaly back already hard to distinguish from the sparkling sea, so far had it swum away. He refocused on Cloud Nine's cloaking fogbank where it hovered mere feet above serene seas, miles in the cigarette boat's wake. *Imagine a relic Iguanodon or some such is hidden in that swamp,* he excitedly told himself. *Our approach from shore this evening, the other side of the swamp, might very well chase it out into the open for Cloud Nine to obtain definitive film footage!*

A half-year earlier, of course, the *Cryptomonster* film crew made the video Augie reviewed repeatedly to no avail, of palms and casuarinas knocked around in the night by some mysterious something. But there was nobody the other side of the swamp for the ambush Augie desired. Even worse, the TV show's tight budget and strict schedule necessitated flying home the next day. This time, though, suppose zilch happened the first night, or the night after that, or the night after that. Eclipso promised plentiful resources to keep waiting until they filmed whatever shook those trees so dramatically much. Either that, or until they were satisfied no more such dramatic event was liable to occur there; the dinosaur or whatever had moved on.

Jake Rumblehouse used to irritate Augie no end, how heedless he behaved of Augie's warnings where possibly scaring off their prehistoric quarry was concerned. Augie insisted it behooved the *Cryptomonster* team to behave as non-intrusively as possible. Make their presence in Lost World habitats as low-profile as they could, especially given the well-known shy, reclusive nature of most reptiles.

But Jake used to be all about grand, dramatic gestures. Augie still fumed over how the *Cryptomonster* team entered the very same swampy woodland the Eclipso-organized expedition was returning to presently. The first thing Jake Rumblehouse did was lead local guides and team members alike in noisily chopping down bamboo stalks to build a platform for hi-tech detection equipment, plus supports for a bright blue tarp to shelter said equipment from the elements. Moreover, motion sensors connected to infrared cameras were mounted on random casuarina and palm tree trunks.

Augie marveled that any large creature stuck around at all, to mysteriously send trees and bushes swaying overnight as it trampled through the underbrush.

This time would be very different. Zero commotion setting up base camp, no foreign objects sitting out in the open such as a tarp tent, or only partially concealed such as motion sensor cameras. No infrared beams to which a relic dinosaur might be sensitive to the point of scaring it off.

Instead, Eclipso's explorers would rely on evening heat lightning and near-full-phase moonlight. Hopefully those sources would provide sufficient illumination for head-band visual sensors feeding into video equipment aboard Cloud Nine.

True, they couldn't be sure their prehistoric quarry wasn't endowed with dog-quality sensory organs that could detect human scents a mile away. But they would be spritzing themselves with locally obtained agarwood resin perfume, just prior to trekking through the minimally explored underbrush. They hoped that would adequately mask such odor, maybe even attract the target beasties.

"I think," started Irene, intruding most purposefully on Augie's meditation. She'd sidled up beside him along the cigarette boat railing when Stephen moved across deck to get a closer look at the beach they were fast approaching. "I think our crocodile friend out there noticed my thermos bottle, and figured I'd bop his snout if he didn't steer clear of us."

"Actually," responded Augie, "I assume Bonsai Gator warned him not to mess with us, or he'd challenge him to a reggae dance marathon."

Irene noticed Scott out the corner of her eye emanating all-is-lost despair on having seen her sidle up beside Augie. So with the implicit excuse of still having to raise her voice to be heard above the din of the cigarette boat's whiny outboard motor, she shouted loud enough for Scott to hear, "Your wife is fine with you continuing on expeditions this far-flung from home?!?!"

"More than fine!" Augie shouted back. "As with some of my other creature searches, Vicky's making good use inside her classroom!"

"Really?!"

"If all goes well tonight, my headband camera will transmit to her classroom television simultaneous to providing video feed to Cloud Nine! Her fourth graders will join our dinosaur search vicariously!"

"Cool!" Irene emoted the same time she rolled her eyes, noticing a shit-eating grin overtake Scott's face. *So now he realizes Augie and I are not making a love connection after all. Someone needs to instruct him on not being so obvious. If he did discover a living Diplodocus in Central Africa, I wouldn't be surprised if he chased it back into hiding by excitedly exclaiming, "Oh boy oh boy oh boy!" Think I'll have Augie advise him to take it down a notch this evening.*

"Doesn't mean she doesn't fret about my safety," Augie went on, oblivious to Irene and Scott obsessing over each other. "Here," he held out his left arm, "these two cloth bracelets, they're good luck charms! My daughter Liz made the rainbow one, and she guided Vicky through weaving the green one!"

"Those are precious!" enthused Irene, leaning over for a closer look.

"Liz has quite the imagination!" Augie nodded proudly. "'Daddy,' she said, 'from a fifth-dimensional perspective, these bracelets provide a direct link back to us, like a leash. If either Mommy or myself senses you getting into big trouble, like being chased down by a hungry dinosaur, you'll feel a tug on them as we yank you to safety.'"

"Your daughter said that?! Wow! That is some imagination! Just how old is she, anyway?"

"Eleven!"

"More like eleven going on twenty-seven, I'd say! But speaking of leashes, um, yeah!"

"Say what?!"

"No," Irene shook her head more defensively than she intended, which was not at all. "I was just thinking that if they actually could pull you out of harm's way with those bracelets, might work better than trying to bop Mr. Dinosaur over the head with my thermos!"

What really went through Irene's head she thought better of sharing in range of Scott, even whispered. Had to do with a week earlier, the night before the faux tour bus brought her back to Ankylosaurus Mansion up in west central Pennsylvania to board Cloud Nine bound for Papua, New Guinea.

Skip took Irene to dinner at a Spanish tapas bar in Frederick, Maryland where he gifted what he termed a special survivor package. Included the thermos bottle as well as trail mix, mosquito spray, and tablets for water purification despite her having told him Cloud Nine was already well-equipped in that regard. Anyhow, fit snugly side-by-side beneath the other items were two little velvet boxes. At first, Irene pretended not to notice them, tried to get away with simply thanking Skip for the rest, but...

"No! Don't tell me you can't see what else is down in there!" Skip's voice cracked high register. "You're killing me!" he added, writhing about on his side of the semi-secluded restaurant booth.

"I was afraid those might be two large beetles that crawled in."

"Two large beetles with velvet shells? C'mon!"

"There are some really out-there animals out there," she quipped as she extracted the two little boxes from the repurposed Easter basket. But she also flashed Skip a look he could only read, to his sinking-feeling regret, as: I wish you didn't do this.

"At least open the larger one first, girl," Irene remembered Skip pleading.

"Okay," Irene remembered answering dubiously. And despite her profound irritation with Skip calling her 'girl' again, she snapped open the larger box, albeit slowly enough as though, Skip wanted to scream in despair, she hoped for intervention, divine or otherwise, to spare her going all the way. "Okay," she said dubiously again, lifting the revealed object on its silver chain. "So what is this exactly?" Irene had braced for some kind of jewelry. But she wasn't expecting a pendant that consisted of bones or bone replicas, tiny ones that looked to have come from some small creature's foot or paw. She might have joked about Skip resorting to witchcraft to cast a love spell on her, but in deference to his feelings...

"A sixty-million-year-old prehistoric rabbit's foot fossil replica," boasted Skip. "The Latin name is Gomphos Elkema."

"Huh."

"Modern day rabbit's feet are supposed to gain their good luck powers by consulting with underground spirits. So I figured a fossil rabbit's foot can bring you protection from modern-day dinosaurs by consulting with their underground fellow fossil spirits. Besides, I didn't think you would appreciate a modern day rabbit losing his foot, fur and all, for you to carry around. That is, even if the rest of him was eaten so his sacrifice wasn't entirely in vain." *Like the sacrifice of my dignity is starting to feel,* Skip told himself when he finally stifled his nervous prattle. *Great; those women at that nearby table nearly bumping their heads together for a secret chuckle, that's probably at my expense!*

Irene would have opened the smaller box to avoid comment on the good luck necklace. But she suspected its contents would provide something far more awkwardly onerous for her to avoid talking about. So she affected a nonchalance she wasn't really feeling to say, "Um, shall we see whether they still have that chocolate-drenched hazelnut ice cream on the dessert menu?"

His eyes watery, Skip silently nodded towards the smaller velvet box in lieu of making the least additional pleading noise.

Resigned to finally getting it over with, Irene relented on pushing for the dessert distraction, and slow-motion latched her fingers onto the smaller box. But soon as she did, Skip wriggled out from his booth seat, sinking to bended knee. This prompted her to set the box aside, which prompted Skip back up onto his seat, saying, "Go ahead and open it!" This triggered Irene with reluctant slowness anew to retrieve the box from where she set it aside, in turn triggering Skip back down on bended knee. Irene set aside the box again, which led Skip scrambling back to his seat again, saying, "I promise I won't move this time."

Irene gave Skip a long, pitying look, the corners of her mouth slightly downturned, before she said, her voice freighted with finality, "I'm really sorry, Skip, but I can't accept this." She slid the smaller box across the table to Skip.

"But you haven't even looked at it yet, girl!" he cried in near falsetto. "You might really, really like it! You don't know!"

"Unless it's a Bonsai Stegosaur for Bonsai Gator to play with, and for the rest of us to, well..." Irene almost would have said, for the rest of us to earn our millions without having to lift a finger. But she wasn't comfortable sharing that little tidbit even with her parents, let alone this guy actively wooing her.

Skip writhed about in his booth seat, flailing his head every which way. So much so, Irene pityingly imagined him as the sought-after dinosaur roped captive. Then he finally settled down enough to say, "But you'll wear the good luck charm, at least?"

"I thank you for the thermos and the rest. They'll come in really handy," Irene said in her gentlest voice as she slid the boxed rabbit fossil replica back across the table to Skip.

"It's just a fossil! Not even a real fossil! A ceramic-coated plaster cast! Okay, can I show you a convenient way to carry your thermos when you're traipsing through the jungle?"

"What would that be?"

Skip seized this opening to scramble out of his seat yet again, and fall on bended knee beside Irene, saying, "Hand me the bottle!"

That's when Irene, checking the bottle handle, realized Skip meant to slip it over her ring finger. "Off your knee, sir!" she said, pointedly swinging the thermos bottle on her forefinger. "I've got this, Skipper," she went on in a more tender voice as Skip lunged himself dejectedly back onto the padded booth seat with a whiney squeak. "I've got a lot to sort out, and on the verge of searching for a living dinosaur is no time for that, understand." Irene hoped that while she was gone, someone would come along more amenable – or was it vulnerable? – to Skip's attentions. Whatever fleeting feelings she ever experienced for him beyond simple friendship, she often wondered: Was this as far as it went for Mama when Papa was wooing her? But Mama finally just caved in to his pressure? Or back before her parents got married, did her mama feel something far stronger? So that what Irene felt for Skip, compared to true love, was like mistaking an elephant's trunk for the long neck of a sauropod dinosaur? The real romantic love, the real dinosaur, remained to be discovered in someone not yet explored? Or was that love for Skip yet to be found in an unexplored region of her heart?

Whatever, the next thing Irene knew, Skip tearfully complained, "You know, girl, I was perfectly okay with your traipsing off to New Guinea! I was perfectly willing to sit by and let you put your life in peril chasing after a dead animal, because I cared enough to understand that's what you wanted!"

"No, stop," Irene coolly raised a hand for Skip to cease and desist. But long before he got as far as he did, she had raised her chin proudly, defiantly. She could have been carved into the prow of a mighty sail ship braving stormy seas. "You were okay with me going to New Guinea?" she went on with continued cool, though Skip fearfully sensed a long fuse lil. He unwittingly lit it, and the resultant fiery little spark was speedily burning towards a certain powder keg. "You let me put my life in peril? Excuse me!! Who the fried fish made you my master?! You know, I was really starting to lose my appetite for dessert! I was really starting to think I'd have to be a psychopath to still crave that special hazelnut ice cream while your heart is breaking! BUT NOW I'M STARVING FOR IT!!

WAITER?!?! BRING ME TWO SCOOPS OF HAZELNUT ICE CREAM DROWNING IN EXTRA CHOCOLATE SAUCE!!!!"

Next thing Irene knew, "Skiiiiiiip!!!" emitted from the entrance to the tapas place.

Skip was admonishing himself.

Nobody aboard Cloud Nine might have heard a thing of Skip's derailed marriage proposal, hadn't journalist Laura Gómez gushed about a copper bracelet to Irene and Roberta in the women's quarters of Cloud Nine, halfway across the Pacific Ocean.

"Tom was so cute how he framed giving this to me!" Laura said, raising her hand to put the bracelet on full display for Irene and Roberta.

"I've got a feeling Tom is so cute how he does anything," snarked Irene. "Even picking his nose. Oh-oh; looks like too much of that copper leaching through your skin is turning your ears all red."

"That's...Stop it!" Laura laughingly protested. "He was talking about his first article for my 'woo-woo' column while I'm away from the *Puffington Post*. Has to do with a new study of health claims made about copper bracelets. He said, 'Let's make you a guinea pig.'"

"Or a New Guinea pig; oh yeah," nodded Irene. "And how romantic is that?" But this provided the opening for her to unload about Skip...after Roberta far more discreetly took the opportunity to call special attention to her necklace. Gifted her as a bon voyage present by her significant other, she explained its pendant consisted of two Welsh dragons. They faced each other with tongues entangled in a traditional Celtic design.

What made Roberta's own show-and-tell so discreet was all the psycho-drama she left out that transpired between her and Daniela. That led to Daniela making the necklace a peace offering just before Laura left their College Park residence bound for Pennsylvania and

Cloud Nine. "You have no idea what I went through to secure this," Daniela claimed about the dual-dragon pendant, in the throes of a new bipolar high. It was as though Roberta was supposed to believe that discovering such an artifact was at least as much of an adventure as discovering a living non-avian dinosaur.

Augie was curious as all heck to ask Roberta about her unique necklace. But he couldn't quite work up the gumption, unwilling at least yet to mention his great grandfather's autobiography. Vicky had pressed him on that, soon as he revealed Eclipso's quest to her. Nevertheless...

Anyway, the women might have been indulging gossipy show-and-tell aboard Cloud Nine, well en route to Papua, New Guinea. Meanwhile, though, Sherman Peabody was regaling the men with his close study of snake charmer videos.

"It's a cruel-beyond-cruel practice, mind you," Sherman advised his fellow males, including Jeremy Longbottom who looked over his shoulder at the computer screen. "The snakes are defanged, and kept in baskets where they can't move around much. Even worse, their mouths are often sewn shut save for just enough space to stick out their forked tongues. The result is that they usually die a slow, cruel death in aid of oblivious tourists' entertainment. In fact, the practice has been outlawed many places. That being said, I've noticed something from studying all these snake-charm videos. No doubt, their movement is mostly about a thwarted desire to bite their tormentors, something they are too weak for even were their mouths not sewn shut. However, their sway to the sway of the snake-charmer's flute suggests perhaps just a wee bit of entrancement despite poor hearing.

"Bottom line? I wonder whether we should, um...I am not a flautist myself. But perhaps we should practice swaying our bodies, see what effect that has on Bonsai Gator over Eclipso's video phone installed on Cloud Nine's flight deck. If it's put in a daze, then imagine this: We find a surviving non-avian dinosaur not too happy about being discovered, maybe even roaring displeasure and ready to attack. Might hypnotic dancing save us? Daze our prospective dinosaur, or at least puzzle it frozen still while we boogie ourselves away?"

"What kind of dancing would we do?" asked Harry, innocently intrigued while Stephen shook his head and rolled his eyes.

"Well, I was thinking something like this," said Sherman rising from his chair, then abruptly dropping his arms into a slow body sway.

"Oh, so you mean something like this," said Harry Letterman, pushing the bridge of his spectacles back up his nose before dropping his arms into his own slow sway.

"No, I think it's more like this," Stephen mischievously said before swaying, himself.

"No, no, no," Augie waved his hands and shook his head, entering onto the body sway floor. "Here's what Sherman is doing."

"C'mon, Scott," Stephen paused mid-sway to gesture towards the lone holdout, since Jeremy had already quietly joined in. "Show us how it's really done!"

"Jeeesus won't mind!" said Augie.

Scott laughed, stiffly swaying his arms one direction, then the other.

"That's it!" pointed Stephen. "The robotic hula!"

"No, oh, I get it," said Sherman, twisty as could be.

"Sisters, you've got to see this!" shouted Irene walking in on the sway fest totally unprepared. Then to Scott who on seeing her, abruptly broke off from the spectacle and stood over to one side, "Oh, no, Mr. McDonald, you don't get to pretend you were the lone wallflower!"

"Pardon my French, people," said Roberta, "but exactly what the f—k is this?!"

"We're charming a Tyrannosaurus out of eating us," explained Stephen still in full sway, mischievously not letting up.

"Yes, that's right," confirmed Sherman. "Didn't mean to leave you esteemed ladies out of the loop; please feel free to join in. But we'll have no idea whether this behavior should be taken seriously until we see how Bonsai Gator reacts to it."

"Well I for one don't think we should wait, girls," said Irene in a mock-earnest voice. She would have speculated that maybe this explained what Skip was up to, writhing about in the restaurant booth. That he was trying to hypnotize her into saying, "Yes." But with Scott in ear-shot..."Let's contact Eclipso on the video phone right now, find out if Bonsai Gator isn't too busy for Sherman's little experiment."

"I can operate the phone, Jeremy," laughed Laura as she headed over to a nearby communication port. "You just keep doing whatever that is you're doing. Ah! Connected already!"

Peering through the video phone, Bonsai Gator quickly latched onto the men's contorted gyrations lacking even the least coordination. Pursuant to which he turned his snout quizzically Eclipso's way.

"Please humor them, Bonsai Gator," Eclipso reacted, "even though their writhing about looks a far stretch from your reggae Beatles dance moves!"

If Irene didn't know better, she would have sworn Bonsai Gator shrugged his shoulder-less forelegs before he imitated the artless swaying revealed on Eclipso's video phone.

"You see that?" asked Sherman Peabody, nearly tipping over from stopping mid-sway to point at the Cloud Nine video phone screen. "It would seem our humble efforts have had at least a partially hypnotic effect on that minutely-sized alligator!"

Stephen also stopped swaying, to study Bonsai Gator's curious movements more closely...while trying to ignore an eerie sense that the look in Bonsai's eyes came more from bemused perplexity than from a hypnotic spell cast over him. It didn't help that the miniature gator suddenly froze mid-sway, threw up his forelegs in seeming scoffing dismissal, and then dropped back down on all fours to trundle off. Presumably, Bonsai returned to the swamp embedded into Eclipso's conference table.

"I don't blame him," remarked Harriet. "Sorry, Harry, but I didn't marry you for your dance moves."

"Hypnotic swaying is not the same as dancing," protested Harry, deliberately persisting with his own contortions when he had been about to give up. "We need all the practice we can get."

"His silliness complements my seriousness," Harriet announced to her fellow females with a big, bespectacled grin.

"I say, what is this?" asked golf-course designer and expedition co-financier Alistair Frump, storming into the Cloud Nine command center from a side room. "I couldn't help overhearing all this commotion. What, while I've been faithfully doing my yoga stretches, have you gentlemen discovered the best exercise of all for improving one's golf swing?"

"We're practicing how to hypnotize a Tyrannosaurus Rex so he won't eat us," explained Bernie Coleman in mid-sway, moving much more slowly than the others.

"Well count me in on not wanting to be eaten by a Tyrannosaurus Rex!" enthused Alistair. He leapt into his own contorted sway, Laura mused, like he was leaping into a swimming pool. "But why aren't our young ladies joining us?"

"If it comes down to a choice between a T-Rex eating me, and putting on a show like that," said Irene, "I'd rather die with my dignity intact."

"You say that now," said Stephen mischievously. "But...I suppose you're also going to demur from holding one of the special umbrellas I've brought along to shelter us from downpours of flying giraffe dung?"

"Oh, I won't demur from that at all," responded Irene, embracing the sarcastic moment. "That's a look I can carry off!"

"Okay, I think we can agree Operation Snake Charm would prove of limited efficacy at best," said Sherman, as usual making no eye contact with anyone, chin scrunched against neck. His note of finality led to a quick cessation of all contorted swaying. "But if other tactics fail to stave off a relic dinosaur pursuing us, I might offer up my personal spastic gyrations as a last-ditch distraction."

"You're assuming you don't scare off Mr. T-Rex with your air bags explosively inflating when he makes a grab for you," said Irene mock-seriously.

"You've got the sequence wrong," said Sherman, earnestly somber. "The prospective beast would set off my protective airbags after I lured it away from you with my gyrations, not before. As how am I to sway about, engulfed by inflated large balloons?

"Anyway, since I still have your attention, now is perhaps as good a time as any to explicate my far more practical plan for dealing with a separate issue. As many of you may already know, the Tolai people foisted hallucinogenic substances on Dr. Matias's Cryptomonster expedition as a rite of passage."

"It was either that, or no access to the suspected creature's reported stomping grounds," Augie confirmed.

"So give me a few moments, if you will."

Sherman Peabody retrieved a typical hiker's backpack from his corner work area of the Cloud Nine command center.

Meanwhile, the steam-powered drone rode the jet stream at a good clip high above the Pacific Ocean, looking like a jet contrail from sea level.

"I've learned all about what the natives forced on you, Dr. Matias," continued Sherman as he finished slinging his backpack over his shoulders. "It's a substance extracted from the buai fruit, named betelnut. Chew on it like on a wad of tobacco, and you stain your teeth red, and release a memorable flavor, to put it charitably. A stubbornly persistent aftertaste is accompanied by heightened alertness, and varying potential for distorted perceptions of reality. Incidentally, a high risk for mouth cancer when used regularly has made the betelnut a blight across southeast Asia."

"It probably has also led people to believe they're seeing dinosaurs," drily observed Stephen Feldman.

"So is there any downside?" Irene asked.

"Ms. McDowell," said Sherman, ever scrunching his chin against his neck, "I shall soon require protective layering from your acidic wit. I don't know how much longer I can endure the resultant hilarity without collapsing into a puddle of endless laughter."

"Oh, that really hurts."

"I suspected it might. But in any event, perhaps you would like to be the first to try my bait and switch for saving us from the betelnut rite of passage?"

"Will it involve swaying like an uncoordinated belly dancer?"

"In fact," Sherman pointed his forefinger heavenward, "uncoordinated belly dancing might prove perfect for feigning that we have succumbed to the betelnut influence."

"Only, the uncoordinated part of it won't be feigned, based on what I've witnessed here."

"True," agreed Sherman, chin too steadfastly pushed into his neck for him to nod as well. "But shall we get on with my demonstration?"

"I'm ready to get it on," said Stephen with just enough "hey-hey-hey" in his voice for Laura, Roberta and Irene to give him a wide berth as they crowded round Sherman to see just what he was up to.

Oblivious to the squirmy discomfort Stephen created, Sherman said, "For my demonstration, I thought it best to incorporate an actual slice of the dried betelnut pulp as I saw the Tolai hand to you and others on your *Cryptomonster* expedition last year, Dr. Augustine Matias. In fact, if I may…"

"Of course," nodded Augie.

"…let's pretend you are one of the Tolai. You dispense this dried fruit wafer to me, that I might deliver it to Ms. McDowell in my pretend role as humble servant. There you go. Just so…"

After Sherman handed Augie the betelnut slice, Augie handed it right back, pretending to have introduced it in the first place. He placed it in the palm of Sherman's hand the same way an actual Tolai placed one slice in the palm of his hand a year earlier.

Sherman apparently took the slice from the palm of his hand, and placed it in Irene's cupped hands. "Now without any hesitation," said Sherman to Irene, "you must deposit the wafer in your mouth, and start chewing."

"No, wait," protested Irene. "I thought you're going to spare us from having to experience this crap."

"I am. Trust me." Sherman looked up just long enough to make riveting eye contact with Irene before bowing his chin back down into his neck again.

Irene still couldn't help wondering how it was not a real slice of dried betelnut pulp Augie handed over to her. White with several brown streaks radiating from its center like bicycle wheel spokes, it sure looked like what she'd seen in a photo. But a certain something gave her the confidence to proceed with Sherman's directive. The object's texture varied significantly from what she expected, far more like something she knew quite well. "Mmm," she nodded with relief when she started munching away. "This is chocolate. Tastes like Belgian white streaked through with Belgian milk chocolate, plus cherry-flavored syrup at the center."

"Well discerned, Ms. McDowell; an educated palate, indeed! And I would add, it was hardened in a mold cast from an authentic betelnut slice."

"But what about that real one you showed us? Where'd it go?"

"Safely stored away in my little backpack, everyone." Sherman managed to pat his backpack while still keeping his chin bowed into his neck. "I trust everyone to keep their little backpacks strapped on so mine doesn't stand out."

"I gather you performed a magician's sleight of hand to switch out the real betelnut slice for the chocolate lookalike?"

"Another precisely correct discernment, Mr. Feldman," Sherman nodded into his chin. "A special tube, conveying from my backpack under my long-sleeve shirt, spit the chocolate lozenge into the palm of my left hand. At the same time, a special tube down my right arm vacuumed the betelnut slice out of the palm of my right hand."

"So in addition to keeping our backpacks on for the duration, we all must wear long-sleeve shirts under such hot and humid conditions?"

"Extra protection from mosquitos and the like, Mr. Feldman; not an unheard-of practice, you see."

"Just so long as we pretend we are totally spaced out after enjoying our sweet treat," said Augie.

"Maybe you could sway from side to side like we practiced for hypnotizing a dinosaur," Harry rose on his tippy-toes to suggest.

"I will probably be doing that anyway, lost in a Belgian chocolate rapture," mock-rhapsodized Stephen.

"Oh, one more thing," Sherman lifted his chin from his neck to say, on that one more thing absent-mindedly occurring to him. "Ms. McDowell, if you will bare your teeth like a monster baring his fangs... Does everyone see red food-coloring from the cherry filling? That mimics how chewing on real betelnut would stain your teeth, to far more rotting-out, carcinogenic effect. Most importantly, you should spit out some of it as though you were spitting out bits of betelnut not amenable to swallowing."

Presently aboard one of two cigarette boats fast approaching shore, Laura Gómez said something to Stephen that took Augie Matias out of his daydream recollection of Sherman Peabody's elaborate scheme for avoiding the hazards of betelnut ingestion. "If I didn't know better, Mr. Feldman," she said, remarking on Stephen's lofty, faraway look, "I would guess that despite all your entrenched skepticism, you are pondering the swampy coastline to ask yourself, 'Just what if a relic

Iguanodon is foraging about, somewhere out there, for tender betelnut pods to get high on?'"

"Well, Ms. Gómez, I hope you do know better. I'm just thinking about savoring that rich Belgian chocolate. Although I do fear this heat and humidity might melt it into a shapeless mess that gums up Sherman's backpack contraption."

"Didn't he say there's just enough carnuba wax mixed in to prevent that?" asked Augie.

"Oh, yes," acknowledged Stephen, his memory jarred.

A spectacle suddenly overwhelmed Augie's attention. Several young boys and girls were running down the mottled gray-and-white-sand beach from Pingapoovoo Village. And they were offering an ecstatic welcome to the strangers riding two especially sleek motorized boats. Sporting a random mix of t-shirts, shorts and sneakers donated by earlier strangers, they hopped about, cheering, though careful not to enter the gently shore-lapping surf even the least bit.

As he was struck the first time he arrived there with the Cryptomonster team, Augie was struck again, finding children at the edge of the unknown adorned by all manner of clothes from faraway places. Logo-emblazoned shirts featured everything from the Boston Celtics to the Baltimore Orioles, to random movie and music icons such as Godzilla and Jimi Hendrix. Moreover, these children's joy and enthused curiosity glowed brightly, even for a few who appeared to have had their growth stunted by disease and malnutrition. They might as well have been his wife's students welcoming him to talk cryptozoology.

For Augie Matias, the question once more reared its extraordinary head up out of a certain seldom-explored jungle: No doubt, these children in a small village along the coast of New Britain Island lived a harsher, more deprived existence than most children he knew in Montgomery County, Maryland back in the United States. But especially since they were clearly every bit as loved and cherished as his daughter Liz and her friends at home, in a certain sense were they really that much less happy?

At home, it went without saying that children wore t-shirts reflective of their interests, whether a favorite sports team or whatever else. But for the boys and girls of Pingapoovoo, might the joy feel immeasurably greater, to be wearing a fancy t-shirt at all? No matter what it depicted?

"I love it!" emoted Alistair Frump as he hauled to shore his bag full of brightly colored plastic golf clubs and golf balls from one cigarette boat, children already crowding around him. "These are obviously future caddies for the Pingapoovoo Golf Club: Jurassic Links! Who knows how many of them will go on tour some day?"

With that, Alistair upended his Santa's bag of goodies to spill them all over the beach. Pursuant to which, he teed up a spongy toy golf ball and send it sailing skyward with a toy driver that featured an oversized, kiddie-friendly club-head.

Scott McDonald rushed to help Irene unload medical supplies and food gathered in Port Moresby off the second landed cigarette boat. And he took that opportunity to try starting up a conversation with her, asking, "Um, isn't that wonderful, all the fun and joy Mr. Frump is bringing to those children? Not sure how practical he is, scoping out a place this remote for a golf resort," he added, trying to leave wiggle room to bail on enthusiasm for Alistair's doings if Irene expressed displeasure. "But..."

"Yeah," Irene huffed and puffed as she carried an awkward-sized box full of canned foods up the beach. "Nothing says respect for a people like littering their pristine beach with polystyrene."

"That is something to consider," Scott nodded. Before he could finish shifting gears to make common cause with Irene's concern, though, a short middle-aged man seized a box from Scott's hands. He lowered it gently to the sandy ground, then pointed at the gold-plated cross Scott wore on a silver necklace. "You are a man of God as am I, mate," he said with an Australian accent while extracting a small oval tin pendant from his jeans pocket.

The pendant had a crucifix stamped into it.

"Bless you, sir."

"Matthew," said the man with the tin pendant, in a correcting tone. "My family named me after one of the gospel authors."

"How wonderful," enthused Scott. "And isn't it also wonderful how the boundless love of the Holy Spirit makes everyone a person of God?"

"Everyone who believes," Matthew corrected. "I must bring you to our church, mate."

Scott sensed Matthew might as well have been saying he must bring him to a doctor for some sickness with which he was presenting symptoms.

"Um," Scott hesitated, looking from Irene to Matthew then back again to Matthew. "Um, we have other matters to take care of first."

"Other matters more important than going to church?"

"Not more important," plainly countered Scott. "But at this particular moment, my faith calls me out of church into the world."

While Matthew puzzled over Scott's response, Scott retrieved his load from him, to hurry over beside Irene already headed for a storage hut on short stilts.

"Well played, grasshopper," Irene whispered. "Glad I kept quiet, as I would not have come across so diplomatically. I would have told him he sounded like a dealer pushing opiates so you could join him being miserably drugged out."

Scott froze in his tracks. "I don't know how familiar you are with the history of New Britain Island," he said, unable to help bristling. "But not so many years ago, cannibalism used to be a real thing here. Not as widespread as certain racists back home would have you believe, but still...The advent of Catholic missionaries with their messages of love helped drive most of that away."

"Sounds like a motto in there for placing on a church sign: 'Christianity: At least it's better than cannibalism.'"

"Actually," weighed in Stephen Feldman with his authoritatively deep voice, so Scott felt to his growing irritation, "a deadly disease called kuru, contracted by eating human brains, was the major factor ending cannibalism across this region."

"Well, um, I'm sure Jesus's message that you should love your enemies, implicitly against eating them, certainly couldn't have hurt," Scott reacted, albeit feeling very lame.

"Well there's another motto for church goers," said Irene. "'Christianity: It certainly can't hurt.'"

"Unless you got in the way of the Crusaders or the Conquistadores," deadpanned Stephen. But the conclusion of his remark was lost to both Irene and Scott. A growing racket from tom-tom-like drums distracted them. And oddly attired dancers seemed to have suddenly materialized from nowhere.

No, Augie quickly realized. Before those dancers made a real show of themselves, they blended in with a stand of leafy, bamboo-like plants ornamented by white berries.

What Augie's thoughts referred to was the dancers' odd attire consisting of plump assemblies of large green leaves. They could have been dancing bushes if not for the narrow, conical wood masks atop them.

"How do they even see out of those things?!?" Roberta shouted to be heard by her fellow explorers, above the drums.

Just then, all three dancers leaned far forward and rotated from side to side like they were tumbleweeds being blown across the beach, Augie imagined.

"Maybe Sherman should glue those leaves to his airbag armor!" said Irene. "That way he can pretend he's just part of the foliage when our dinosaur is in hot pursuit!"

"But he won't have to if his swaying hypnotizes it!"

"Actually, who knows that a swaying bush won't prove even more hypnotic?" interjected Sherman before Augie could feel guilty over having piled on top of Irene's mockery. However, Augie couldn't tell whether Sherman was charitably joining in the fun at his own expense, or making a serious point.

Whichever, Laura said, "I learned about these guys during my prep for this expedition! They could belong to the Dukduk, a relic organized crime protection racket. Or they could be simply putting on a show for those tourists who expect to have their stereotypes fulfilled when they're in certain parts of the world like this!"

"Did you see them here before, on your first trip this neck of the woods, Augie?!" asked Irene, genuine concern in her voice as opposed to her usual snark.

"We were greeted by dancers! But they were of the more touristy variety you mentioned, Laura! Bare-chested with beads and feathers and the like! I must say this feels a bit more intimidating!" *Maybe one more dinosaur search party too many*, Augie couldn't help wondering.

Suddenly, as if to drive home Augie's concern, the three dancers moved aside, and a fourth dancer sporting the widest bush and steepest conical wood mask of all pranced forward. He danced around Augie, isolating him from Irene and the others.

That's when one of the shorter men loitering about approached Laura. He crouched towards her, and lifted over his head a thin cord strung end-to-end with beautifully polished cowry shells, shiny patterns of black, brown and white.

"A pretty hefty sum he's offering for my hand in marriage," Laura guessed, uncertain how to empathetically proceed with her rejection, especially since such a large audience had gathered.

"She's not interested," said Stephen in his deepest voice, literally stepping in between the suitor and Laura.

Augie wondered whether Stephen's reaction evidenced no small bit of jealousy.

"That is a no," Laura craned her head around Stephen to gently add.

Whereupon the suitor turned towards Roberta and made the same offering he made to Laura.

Okay, if at first you don't succeed... *This does diminish any pity I might have felt for him,* Augie reckoned as he looked past both the suitor and the dancer at a lanky young girl watching curiously. *That physique; she could be my daughter Liz. What future is in store for her here? The supplies we brought aren't going to make any major differences, although Alistair Frump's golf course might open up certain opportunities.*

Just then, one of the children who snuck up behind Alistair bopped him on the head with a green and pink plastic driver. He obliged by falling to the sandy ground, pretending to have been knocked out to the children's cheering, laughing delight.

"I have a proposal for you," Irene meanwhile said to the suitor wearing a faux tuxedo shirt, having stepped up beside him awaiting Roberta's response. "How about we slip off together behind one of those bushes, where I can shove those shells so far up your ass, I can pull them out your mouth like a plumber's snake?"

The suitor cowered from Irene, this time holding up before him his stringed cowry shells as protection rather than marriage proposal. "Sanguma!" he hoarsely shouted, confirming Irene's suspicion his reluctance to speak stemmed from not understanding English. Meaning she could probably vent without worrying about most locals taking any real offense.

"'Sanguma'?" Irene repeated to Laura. "Any idea what that means?"

"It means 'witch,'" answered the bare-chested man who had been dancing round Augie. He shed his conical-mask-crowned bush outfit without any of the American visitors noticing, their having been so caught up in the suitor's doings. "And by the way," he went on with a very British accent, "that was a rather impolite thing you said to Mr. Stanley Pickford over there."

Scott could make out the blush through Irene's dark complexion when she reacted, "Yikes! Sorry, I- There's no excuse for- Well a little excuse, maybe, which was how upset it made me watching a man, any man, try to buy a woman. I guess, at least he didn't ask which of these guys owned her who he would need to pay." Irene very quickly thought better of using as an excuse that she didn't think any of the Tolai people would understand. *Oh, yeah, there's Matthew with his church shtick!*

"Stanley!" the unclothed dancer shouted at Stanley, and went on in the Kuanua language of the Tolai, with a very reprimanding tone.

Laughter erupted, especially from the women, as Stanley slunk off looking very shame-faced. One of the women shouted something after him causing even more laughter, ever more lopsidedly from the women.

A lone man shouted in protest against the general hilarity over the twice-rejected suitor's ridicule, best as Augie could surmise.

"I explained to him that this young lady is not a witch," said the unclothed dancer while pulling on a t-shirt Augie hadn't previously noticed. The shirt featured in front a yellow silhouette of the bird of paradise against a red backdrop: one-half of the Papua, New Guinea national flag. The back featured the other half of the flag: stars set against a night sky symbolizing unity with surrounding nations such as Indonesia and Australia. "I might have said other things as well you don't need to know," he added while popping his head back into view through the top of the t-shirt. "She will want you to stay home caring for her children while she explores the unknown! You might have better luck with a wild boar! Distract her with your long string of shells while you mount her, and maybe you can take your pleasure while not paying the price!"

"When did you shed that costume anyway?" Irene indicated the bushy leaves topped by the conical mask, lying abandoned in a heap nearby. "One minute you're in Dr. Augustine Matias's face here, and the next minute you're stripped down to your waist."

"My name is Ambu," Ambu said with a broad grin, as though that explained everything. "Ambu comes from the ancient Sanskrit meaning water. That is how I am regarded, because whatever situation I find myself in, or costume too for that matter, I am able to slip through it like water slipping through one's fingers."

Augie decided not to note that Ambu didn't bother to explain that the first time he met him on the *Cryptomonster* expedition. Instead, he said, "I don't remember such elaborate costumes last year."

"You are back to resume your dinosaur hunt aren't you, Dr. Matias?"

This question made Augie recall the first time he met Vicky's parents, at their home for supper. "I'm guessing you didn't come here for my wife's cheesy-peppered asparagus," joked her father.

"Daddy!" Vicky said in a reprimanding voice, but Augie responded, "Actually, that does sound rather tempting." The loneliness in the father's voice did leave Augie feeling a bit guilty he wasn't there just to spend time with him and enjoy the asparagus, but rather had an ulterior motive, trying to gain approval of his beloved's family.

Ambu's question made Augie feel that much worse. Ambu's people lived in poverty, even if softened by the tropical splendor and easy availability of several nutritious fruits and veggies, not to mention strong interpersonal relationships. But Augie and company weren't there to address their deprivation, beyond the special supplies they brought and Alistair's harebrained golf resort scheme. That was all secondary to locating a living, breathing non-avian dinosaur. *Okay, guess I hope Alistair's scheme is not so harebrained; thriving Iguanodons nearby would attract major attention from the rest of the world, for sure.*

"Back for our dinosaur search, not hunt, yes of course," Alistair Frump agreed, smiling brightly. "But we are also here for you, all of you!" He turned around and spread his arms welcoming wide. "Even that young man over there who bopped my noggin with his club! Ambu," he came up close beside Ambu, "imagine this. Imagine your people working right here at one of the premier golf resort destinations in the world! Jurassic Golf, where one never knows when a Diplodocus might stick its long neck out from behind a palmetto bush! Then imagine that employment becoming a springboard for making their dreams come true. They could go on to work or study abroad, or stay right here and become golf pros themselves, headed for world tour competition!"

Laughter and cheers ensued to which Alistair took his bows.

Ambu would have none of it, shaking his head dismissively. "We dance about in our silly costumes that used to really mean something," he said once the general hubbub died down. "You chase little balls across field and stream until you can roll them into small holes in the ground. The only difference is, we dance to profit from your enjoying your prejudices being satisfied that us dark-skinned peoples are inferior beings who prefer our primitive ways to your modern convenience. Although it must be said," he kept glancing Irene's way, encouraged by her knowing nods, "that in the matter of medicinal remedies, your greed has kept you from the many benefits of herbal remedies. If such unwillingness to indulge something that works until you understand exactly why and how it works had been applied to your walking from place to place, you would never walk anywhere. Or fall in love either, for that matter."

This time general laughter and pointing erupted to mocking effect towards the foreigners from the United States.

"To continue," Ambu said loudly enough to silence his fellow locals, "while we only persist with our native dancing to please your prejudices, from what I've seen on television, you actually enjoy golf. Yes, some of you do play for money, but there have to be easier ways...the silly grins on your very best golfers' faces have not gone unnoticed."

"Exactly!" said Alistair as though Ambu just clinched his argument.

"Wait!" Ambu held up a hand to hold off Alistair. "What I was going to say about why the more elaborate costumes this time: You noticed during my entrance the noises from a deeper-toned drum?"

"And there was something tympani-sized over there. Yes, I noticed that too," said Augie.

"The smaller drums involve beating on stretched-taut iguana skin," said Ambu. "But the deeper-toned, larger drum, depending on who you believe, it's either saltwater crocodile hide, or from one of the purported dinosaurs."

"So might we temporarily remove the hide from the top of the larger drum to establish its identity?" Stephen queried.

"Ahh," ahhed Ambu. "For that, sir, we would need to substitute some other creature's hide, perhaps your own!"

"Then let's just assume it's crocodile hide," said Stephen with a wide grin.

"But if it is dinosaur skin," said Ambu, "my point was this: Some people here believe that the particular tone the iguana skin produces when pounded on is influenced by the departed spirit of the iguana who lost its life. So maybe if a dinosaur lost its life on the road to our larger drum, the sound it makes is a cry for help from the beyond. It will attract a living dinosaur your way, leading to your new expedition's success, Mr. Matias. But more talk about this after you eat!"

With that, Ambu led the Americans over to an expansive buffet-style spread featuring boiled taro root, various local fruits, and large, charcoal-grilled fish.

"Generous as always, Ambu," commented Augie. "But, um, you know the drill, Mr. Peabody."

"Indeed I do, Mr. Matias," Sherman responded. "So why don't you take your seats somewhere while I pile high your palm-frond plates. You see, Ambu," he turned Ambu's way to say, though still keeping his chin bowed into his neck, "I never should have snuck rabbit pellets into their rice and beans on a previous trip. Don't really know what got into me, but I have been paying the price ever since."

"Ahh," Ambu ahhed again.

The story felt ridiculous to everyone, once Sherman Peabody concocted it back aboard Cloud Nine. But nobody else had any better way of explaining why Sherman would be acting as serving intermediary, when betelnut time inevitably came up.

"Now one last thing before we confer about the particulars of tonight's dinosaur search," said Ambu, sure enough, on his last munching swallow of pomegranate seeds. "Mr. Matias, you surely remember our customary betelnut refreshment after every feast?"

"How could I forget? My former leader, Mr. Rumblehouse, ended up snorting like a pig, and trying to uproot a weed with his nose!"

"So your new team knows more or less what to expect? And that fellow," he pointed at Sherman, "will be doing the distribution honors, to continue atoning for his sin?"

One of Ambu's associates was already shaving down fresh, green buai pods to betelnut wafers.

"You better serve us before you serve yourself, Sherman," advised Augie. "As if there were any question of that in any event, given our special arrangement. But after you chew on your own betelnut, I very much doubt you will be in any condition to serve anything to anyone."

"Yes, I was thinking that as well," Sherman nodded into his chin as Augie and company returned to the long bench where they ate, from disposing their palm frond plates on a compost pile. They cupped their hands waiting for the cream-filled Belgian chocolate.

Ambu received the real thing first. Then the Americans followed his example with the sleight-of-hand switched-in chocolates Sherman served them. They chewed on the chocolates far more than necessary, and spit out bits of the cherry-flavored filling rather than swallowing it all. Pursuant to which they grinningly bared their teeth, revealing red food-coloring stains meant to mimic the red stains from fresh betelnut wafers.

Irene was first to brave rising from the bench to writhe about, faintly moaning as though she were reacting to a dizzying hallucinatory vertigo.

Pretty soon the others also rose to their feet, provoking much pointing and giggles from the Tolai. But when Sherman joined, things got interesting in a way nobody bargained for. Shortly after joining the faux vertigo fest, unbeknownst to Sherman an actual betelnut pellet fell from his small backpack to the hard-packed sandy ground, and then another, and another.

Ambu noticed immediately, and joined the collective moaning sway to bend down low and pick up one for a telling lick. Once he confirmed the pellet's identity, he feigned accidentally colliding with Sherman. That set off Sherman's protective airbags and in the process, sprayed both real betelnut wafers and their chocolate lookalikes everywhere.

While Sherman rolled around helplessly, onlookers scooped up as many wafers as they could.

Ambu quickly ascertained some wafers were not like the others.

"Guards!" he shouted with a snap of his fingers.

"I think there are enough chocolates for everyone," Sherman said defensively. His airbags had deflated enough for him to return not-so-swaying to his feet while two men emerged from amidst the villagers brandishing automatic rifles.

"Not one more word!" ordered Ambu as he had the guards lead the Americans at gunpoint into his shack on stilts.

Chapter 15

"Down! Sit down!" Ambu bellowed in no uncertain terms. He indicated the bamboo floor mats along the perimeter of his expansive hut's wood floor. "I have chased all the scorpions away! And you would have had nothing to fear from them in any event, if you treated them properly! Gently stroke their back sides, and they snuggle like field mice in the palm of your hand!"

As harshly as Ambu uttered these curious observations, Augie Matias found himself oddly comforted. He was reminded of his own father admonishing him decades ago when he brought home zero on a math test. Embedded in his father's complaint Augie had sensed certain love as in: He cared enough about his son to get angry at him for screwing up. Wasn't that same sort of love embedded in Ambu's complaint, even though he forced Augie and company into his hut at gunpoint?

Ambu stomped around the room until his foreign guests finished sitting down, and his guards exited to wait on alert just outside the front entrance. When he finally ground to a halt, he popped one of the chocolate betelnut lookalikes into his mouth. "Mmm, this is good," he nodded approvingly. "However," he resumed speaking harshly, "do you have any idea, any idea how much you have insulted us?!"

"You're right," said Stephen in a deep voice Laura had long since found irritatingly suggestive he fancied himself the ultimate authority. "We should have sampled your betelnut, taken our chances regarding its hallucinogenic properties rather than switching it out for chocolate by sleight of hand. I understand Augie Matias did that on his first visit to your tropical paradise, and he seems none the worse for it. And, as delectable as I found the chocolate replica, I must admit my curiosity leaves me partially disappointed I didn't sample the real thing."

"No," Ambu was shaking his head long before Stephen finished apologizing. "The real insult has nothing to do with your justifiable reasons for wanting to avoid chewing on the betelnut. It has everything to do with your bigoted assumption you couldn't explain why no betelnut for you because we would have flown into some irrational rage. That walks hand in hand with the other insult of your caring to be here more for the prospect of glimpsing a prehistoric monster than entertaining any least sincere concern over our personal well-being."

"I'm not sure that's at all fair, sir," protested Alistair with an exaggerated, hurt-looking frown. "I could see myself volunteering to give putting lessons to your bubbly sweet children!"

"Oh yes, that is a skill certain to add at least a full decade to their life expectancy, and correct their stunted growth into the bargain," said Ambu sarcastically.

"Long before we arrived here, Ambu, I argued for a major readjustment of the expedition," said Stephen. "In lieu of some vain search for the impossibly still-extant non-avian dinosaur, I argued the focus should be on learning more about amazing creatures of the real world. In your particular neck of the woods, for example, there's the seldom-witnessed mating dance of the bird of paradise that graces your national flag."

"What that still amounts to," Ambu bitterly reacted, "is your showering us with gifts in exchange for access to our natural wonders. In other words, you are still treating our rainforest as your whore."

As shocked as Augie found himself by Ambu's harsh comparison, it inspired a far gentler one. Whenever Augie first exited an air-conditioned jet into a tropical clime on Cryptomonster trips, and this time disembarking from Cloud Nine into a cigarette boat on Melanasian seas, there was a certain closeness to the warm, humid air that enthralled him with a special feeling of aliveness. Well now he finally understood why. The warmth, the closeness, was the same warmth and closeness he experienced from his sweetie pie Vicky's breath whenever they kissed. There was a certain intimacy, maybe with the spirit of a living planet.

"What complicates matters, it would seem," said Sherman Peabody in his usual clinical frame of mind, "is the question of when caring by members of one culture for members of another culture becomes more condescension than helpful. Can we be sure that we are not more miserable, most times, than the Tolai, in a dramatic offset of our longer life expectancy?"

"Mmm-hm," nodded Irene enthusiastically, embracing such emotionally detached analysis as a far safer place for the dialogue with Ambu to go. Better that, than further infuriating him. "Ambu, I've written extensively about the history of dinosaur hunts going hand in hand with colonial subjugation of dark-skinned peoples like myself and your self."

"Well good for you, young lady! And yet, here you are!"

For the very first time since their arrival to the village of Pingapoovoo, Augie saw Irene's eyes open super wide. A shadow of sheer terror crossed her face where previously, she had looked variously bemused, smug, marveling or eye-roll scoffing.

"The people who brought us here," said Stephen in his deep voice for conveying absolute gravitas, "they will be expecting our return to their aircraft at some point." *Don't think there won't be severe consequences if something happens to us.*

"My lookouts did notice your motorboats emerge from a most curious circular cloudbank after it descended to the sea out of a clear blue sky. Oh!" Ambu threw up his hands, palms facing forward, in mock epiphany. "You are sky gods, come to render judgment on us primitive savages! I must throw myself to my worshipful knees and beg for mercy!" With that, Ambu dropped to his knees and bowed low, his arms stretched forward. "But no," he suddenly broke from his mock obeisance to return standing to his full, albeit stunted height. He let the following silence simmer just enough to further unsettle his captive guests before he said, "The technique our ancestors passed down to us for preparing shrunken heads...Not you, Mr.—"

"Frump. Alistair Frump," Alistair assisted with what he tried to make his winning smile.

"Yes, Mr. Frump, you're too much fun for our children. For now, let them keep bopping you over the head, and you just keep pretending to have been smitten senseless to the ground. But what I started to say, a neat incision behind one ear, all the way around behind the other ear, allows for a clean extraction of the skull with eyes and scalp left intact. The tricky part, then, is to boil the skull just long enough to shrink it significantly, but not so long that the hair falls from the scalp."

"Our associates aboard ship have gone too much time without any communication from us. This detention has delayed a status report I was supposed to have sent an hour ago," said Stephen in his deepest, lowest, most serious voice yet, even as he was making up the whole thing about the status report. "Rest assured they will make quick contact with the authorities for an intervention far sooner than you might imagine."

"You're bluffing, I can tell," said Ambu, chin raised challengingly. "Oh, I don't doubt there will be a search party, eventually. But by the time they arrive, your corpses will already have long since been fed to the saltwater crocodiles. And for all that your 'authorities' know, your boiling heads could be boiling sweet potatoes. They could pass right by them without knowing the difference. As they have done in the past..."

"Now wait just a minute, there!" protested Alistair Frump, trying to subsume his own fear in anger. "My backers, who include two of the world's premier golf course designers, will not take kindly to my esteemed colleagues here ending up as shrunken heads! You'll have to kiss any golf resort goodbye!"

"So you think this is some kind of joke?" shouted Ambu with as much outrage as he could counterfeit. "Guards!?!"

"What about your Christian community?" asked Scott, like Alistair also trying to subsume his fear in anger. "They can't be other than condemning of these goings-on!"

By the time Scott completed his protesting speculation about the local Christians, Ambu's three guards had re-entered his shack, rotating their assault rifle aims from one foreigner to the other.

"Let's show them our crosses, guards!" said Ambu. With that, he pulled his own silver cross pendant on its silver necklace chain out from under his t-shirt. And his guards did likewise. "People here know better than to interfere with our activities, you see," Ambu went on. "And in exchange, we make this small accommodation to their beliefs." He held forward his cross to make perfectly clear that wearing it was the small accommodation to which he was referring. "But now, I think you would agree it is less painful, it's the Christian thing, for us to shoot you before we saw off your heads."

There could not have been a more pitiful sight than the lone tear sliding down off Sherman Peabody's chin onto his neck.

Noticing that tear was when Ambu and guards couldn't hold it in any longer. They couldn't maintain the deadly stern expression on their faces for even one second more.

They busted out laughing.

After Ambu nodded the guards out of his shack, he turned off his chuckling as though he'd flipped off a light switch, and seriously remarked, "Actually we should not be laughing so much."

"I agree," Stephen weighed in with the deepest voice he could muster. "It was extravagantly cruel of you to terrify us like that."

"But that is my whole point: You were so willing to believe you were dealing with your stereotypical savages. Even you, young lady of color," Ambu said directly to Irene. "No one else here looked more scared than you. Do you have any idea how absolutely insulting it feels to be suspected of capability for such cruelty?"

Irene's tears joined her companions' tears, this time in being sorrowful over their basic distrust of Ambu's humanity.

That is, save for Stephen. He protested, "In our defense, and I'm sure you know much more than we do: Head hunting was not an entirely unknown activity on this island as well as back on Papua, however much most people might have frowned upon it."

"Fair enough," conceded Ambu.

"Not fair enough, mate," Alistair shook his head, teary-eyed. "Where my parents come from in Bristol, there was only one way to end such a needlessly profound misunderstanding." With that, he picked up Ambu and enfolded him in a big bear hug.

Augie saw Ambu look over Alistair's shoulder with an expression mixing perplexity and discomfort as he patted the golf course developer most tentatively on the back. Then Augie joined everyone else, even Stephen, seeing no alternative but to pile on for a big group hug…

…from which Ambu crawled out from under, navigating through a thicket of legs.

Once Alistair realized he was left hugging Stephen, he looked around anxiously for Ambu. By the time he realized the fellow was standing to one side, watching, the group hug had dissolved.

"How did you do that, Ambu?" Alistair asked.

"Remember what Ambu means, which is water as in: able to easily slip through your fingers. But also allow me an apologetic admission, though not for my prank. Rather, for my own prejudice. You see, despite so many women in your party this time, Dr. Augustine Matias, I feared your return visit was for the purpose of raping our young women under darkness of night. Or abducting them for the southeast prostitution trade. But from what I've seen, you are all far too silly to engage in such evil."

"And let me guarantee you, Mr. Ambu, sir," said Irene. "Woe be it for any of these guys from whom I detected any least notion of that. He would have gotten a part of his anatomy other than his head lopped off by me, personally, then boiled until shrunken to peanut size!"

"Ouch," said Stephen, igniting much laughter.

With a head shake as in, *I don't want to deal with what Irene just said*, Laura said, "Perhaps we should explain, to put everything on the table. While the long-term risk to our health seemed pretty low, we still wanted to avoid any betelnut in our system. There was the added concern that its hallucinogenic properties could introduce an unwanted variable when searching for a living dinosaur.

But we should have just come out and explained in the first place, rather than engaging in subterfuge, sorry."

"I appreciate that, Miss...?"

"Gómez. Laura Gómez."

"Miss Laura Gómez. In fact, I personally avoid betelnut use as much as I find diplomatically possible. And every time one of our elders presents with a cancerous sore rotting a hole through his cheek, I make a big deal. I seize those opportunities to explain the cause and effect, and how daily betelnut use has created one of the biggest health crises in all southeast Asia. But do appreciate the difficulty getting that point through for people who depend on betelnut sales for their livelihood. Likewise for other people worked like slaves, or living in destitute poverty, for whom the betelnut's stimulating properties provide one of their few joys. But let us get on with the prospect that appears to bring you joy, of discovering a live dinosaur roaming swamps only a short trek from here. I have two asks before we proceed."

"Let's see what those asks are," said Irene after her fellow teamies turned to her for leadership.

"Thank you, Miss..."

"Ms. Irene McDowell."

"Yes, Ms. McDowell. So first, soon after our foray into the swamps, I should like to visit your flying fogbank."

"Don't even have to check in with our on-board crew to guarantee that," Irene shook her head. "Consider it done. Ask two?"

"My daughter Magdalena, you might have noticed her out there awkwardly taller and skinnier than the other children. She is reaching an age of high vulnerability here, foreign rapists intruding or not. I should like her to contribute her special expertise to your search, then join me for a visit aboard your flying fog bank for rather an extended period. Otherwise, some unscrupulous fellow far too old for her might sweep her off her feet, or kidnap her."

"You mean," said Roberta Quiñones, "so we can bring her back with us for a new life elsewhere?"

"You will find the extent of her self-education most amazing. I dare say that at twelve years old, she could already easily pass the admissions test to any college in Port Moresby. But she always has stars in her eyes when she reads about the Natural History Museum in London."

"Do you think your daughter might settle with the Smithsonian Natural History Museum in Washington D.C.? An internship there while she studies at the University of Maryland, or completes her high school education first, if necessary?" asked Augie. "My wife and I, we could take her in as a foreign exchange student."

"And my significant other and I live near the College Park campus of the university," chimed in Roberta.

Ambu's mouth hung open in delighted amazement while Laura operated her walkie-talkie.

"Samuel Longbottom here," crackled from Laura's device.

"Laura Gómez here, Mr. Longbottom; we have an unusual request to field before we put this show on the road."

As expected, no problem guesting Ambu aboard Cloud Nine. But as for Magdalena, Cloud Nine pilot Samuel Longbottom pled patience while he called "home base." "If you can hold on for just a few minutes more," Longbottom finally said after what felt to Augie like an interminable wait. "He's seeking Bonsai Gator's approval, hopefully a mere formality."

"Bonsai Gator?" repeated Ambu. "Someone's nickname, I presume?"

"This is ridiculous," muttered Stephen not softly enough to escape Augie's attention.

"It's an alligator's nickname, believe it or not," said Irene.

"But the 'Bonsai' part is a bit of a misnomer," jumped in Sherman, chin firmly tucked into his neck. "Rather than having been bred from parings of successively smaller alligators, he was discovered by our benefactor's late wife. She encountered him full-grown at the size of a pencil on a tiny island in the South Pacific near Fiji."

"And such an unusually small alligator really holds that much sway over the decisions of your expedition's principal financier?"

"One of this expedition's two most important financiers," corrected Alistair Frump. "I'm the other."

"Purportedly, Bonsai Gator is the entire reason we are out here," said Sherman, ignoring Alistair's correction. "He thought it was a good idea, so we're told. We just agreed to run with it."

Ambu furrowed his eyebrows in an expression of deep concern. "So much silliness," he said finally, "that is an extravagance none of us here could ever afford."

"Good news, gentle ladies and gentlemen," Samuel Longbottom's voice crackled from Laura's walkie-talkie anew. "Bonsai Gator has made his choice from among tens of songs, and it's a good one: 'She's Got A Ticket To Ride.' The answer is yes to Miss Magdalena's request. Even as we speak, I am assured that Bonsai has concocted entirely new, hitherto unseen dance moves to celebrate."

"Speaking of too much silliness, Ambu," said Irene, "Bonsai Gator also dances, a whole lot, especially to reggae versions of Beatles songs by a group named Yellow Dubmarine."

Ambu might have found himself amazed enough at Augie and Roberta's brainstorming over how they might accommodate his daughter Magdalena. But his mouth hung as wide-open as a cavern grotto, totally dumbstruck as he was by Irene's information. "If you really have such an amazing creature in your possession at home," he said, "that even bosses you around into the bargain, why on Earth do you also require the definitive discovery of a living dinosaur?! Shouldn't this 'Bonsai Gator' be more than enough?!"

"It's kind-of like going to heaven," said Irene in a tone Augie found dripping with sarcasm. "You can marvel at a dwarf gator dancing to reggae for only so long before you start to become bored and are after the next big thing, or not-so-big thing."

"But what does that have to do with going to heaven?" asked Scott, his perplexity overcoming his usual shyness about addressing Irene directly.

"Oh yeah, that. You see, Mr. Scott McDonald, no offense meant to what I know is your Christian disposition. But the vision some people have expressed about the hereafter, standing in a circle round the throne of God singing glory alleluia: that would grow very boring very quickly, forget about an eternity. I might prefer to raise a little hell, myself."

The pointed look Irene gave Scott was not lost on anyone, least of all Scott himself. He nevertheless worked up enough gumption to respond, "I'm actually counting on heaven to turn out far more interesting than you described. But don't tell my brother I said that."

"Maybe we're already there," proposed Stephen. "The entertainment value of these present circumstances is paradise enough for me."

"Very good," said Ambu. "But my Tolai brethren and I don't have the luxury to debate such imponderables. So let me bring Magdalena here for introductions."

Augie could have quipped that Ambu returned with Magdalena before he finished leaving to get her, bumping into himself along the way. That's how fast it went. Ambu's daughter must have been waiting just outside. And as Augie expected, she was indeed the awkwardly lanky girl who joined little girls and boys excitedly jumping about to welcome Eclipso's team ashore. Hair all frizzed out, she wore jeans and a blue t-shirt emblazoned with the orange Mercury sports-wear logo: a silhouette of a non-gender-specific someone sprinting out of the sun like one of its rays.

Augie and company had long since concluded that asking after Magdalena's mother would be too indelicate. But Augie suspected she had passed on, and that Ambu was still recovering from this loss.

"Magdalena, daughter of Ambu," said Alistair as the first foreigner to step forward towards her, "I want you to imagine something. I want you to imagine a stretch of your unexplored wilderness out there transformed into golf course fairway. And I want you to imagine that fairway winding through a swamp where someone's errant shot might come to rest beside a grazing Triceratops, or whatever strange unknown creature might still be wandering about from a bygone era."

Magdalena held her chin regally high, instantly endearing herself to Irene. And she darted her eyes from side to side as she tentatively said, "OOOOkaaaayyyy...." Then sensing a kindred spirit, she turned towards Irene and asked, in an unexpectedly strong Aussie accent to rival her father's, "Is he serious, mum?"

"He's something," answered Irene. Ignoring Alistair's taken-aback look, she went on, "Your father says you are especially interested in the creature we have come here to search for."

"Yes, mum, very much so."

"Have you yourself ever seen a dinosaur?" Scott bubbled. He couldn't contain his excitement over the prospect of a first-hand eyewitness account from a region outside of his more familiar haunts in equatorial Africa.

"What he means, Magdalena," interceded Stephen, "is: Have you ever seen a creature that could have been mistaken for a dinosaur?"

Magdalena shifted her gaze back and forth between Scott and Stephen as she worriedly answered, "I am sorry I cannot say 'yes.'"

"No need to apologize for that, sister," said Irene, turning her severe glare from Stephen to Scott as she spoke.

"But," Magdalena said encouragingly, looking every which way at her attentive audience, "I have spoken with two witnesses who confided in me shortly after your film crew left last year, Mr., um…"

"Matias, Augie Matias."

"Yes, Mr. Matias, I think they feared approaching you. Your expedition leader joked about paying for the younger one to be his bride with a long string of cockle shells he bought in Port Moresby."

"I didn't press them on the matter because it seemed enough other witnesses already came forward," added Ambu.

"But they noticed that, unlike many in our Tolai community, I didn't ridicule the other eyewitnesses after you left, Mr. Matias. I didn't treat it as a big joke just to attract tourism. Anyway, I promised not to expose them to any shameful teasing. So I am sharing their accounts with you in the strictest confidence, please, mum." Magdalena gave Irene an imploring look.

"Anyone here who violates your trust, Magdalena, will rather be dealing with a hunger-crazed Velociraptor than with me, uh-huh!"

To Irene's assertion, Magdalena noticed Augie and company nodding. So she said, "Very good, mum," and went on, "The older lady, I'm still going to keep their names confidential. She told me that nearly fifty years ago, early one morning as a little girl she wandered out alone to our beach, where she saw a creature as big as an elephant. Standing on his hind legs, he plucked a coconut off a palm tree by one of his big clawed forelegs, and plopped it in his mouth. Then he bit down so hard, he easily fractured it apart. That's when his gaze happened to turn on my aged confidante. What she kept emphasizing was how the coconut milk dripped and dribbled from his maw, and how his eyes widened, startled at seeing her. Quickly thereafter, he turned tail, a very long tail, and splashed into the surf, paddling away in no time."

"And this took place at the same beach where we came ashore," said Irene.

"The very same, mum."

"To a little girl, one of your wild pigs foraging for food could have seemed monstrously large," drily observed Stephen Feldman.

"So it was a long-tailed wild pig that reached into a palm tree to pluck a coconut with one of its cloven hooves, and then opened its mouth wide enough to crush the coconut apart. Don't know about you, Magdalena, but I think that might be an even more amazing sight than a dinosaur," said Irene, scowling Stephen's way as she spoke.

"For sure, mum."

"Maybe it was a pineapple the pig knocked off a pineapple plant, then crushed beneath its cloven hooves," offered Stephen defensively. "Or even a low-hanging betelnut fruit; that would be small enough for a pig to bite off. The mind can play lots of tricks on someone's memory over fifty years."

"I'll grant you the betelnut possibility, sir," said Ambu. "Areca palms sometimes bloom when they are still very short. But we have no pineapple plants growing anywhere near the beach. They were not even introduced here until the late eighteen hundreds."

"And it is unlikely my confidante saw a pig," said Magdalena. "Like many mammals, pigs are more likely to show curiosity than to be scared off at the sight of a little girl. Whatever she saw, its shy behavior is more characteristic of many reptiles and amphibians."

"You have done your homework," said Roberta Quiñones. "I'm impressed."

"Thank you, mum. Do you want to hear now about my younger confidante's more recent sighting?"

"Of course," said Augie, Irene, and Sherman in unison.

"Hers was only two years ago, and at this same time of the year, in September. She took me where it happened, so I will be able to take you there as well. Her description sounds similar to the other. She describes an elephantine beast reaching into a palm tree to snatch a coconut. But then it senses her presence, turns, and runs off through an adjacent swamp."

"Huh," grunted Augie.

"You said these sightings both took place in September," said Stephen.

"Come to think of it," interjected Augie before Stephen could complete his thought, "the Tolai who spoke with us also had their sightings around September, if I'm not mistaken."

"So what I was going to ask, Magdalena," went on Stephen, "is the betelnut harvest time."

"Betelnut harvest time?" Magdalena repeated quizzically. "Aren't they collected year round, Dad?"

"Their availability fluctuates, but that's pretty much the case," confirmed Ambu.

"Oh, I get it," Magdalena nodded knowingly Stephen's way, her chin regally lofted. "You're the professional skeptic. You're suggesting people magnify smaller animals into large dinosaurs when they are hallucinating on betelnut juice."

"It's a possibility you should consider before jumping to the conclusion you have a dinosaur living in your backyard," remarked Stephen most unapologetically.

"Well let me be completely honest with you, Mr., um..."

"Mr. Feldman."

"Yes, Mr. Feldman, here is the reality. My older confidante indeed chewed on so much betelnut over the years, cancer rotted through her left cheek. On removal of the tumor, doctors had to seal the hole with a latex skin substitute. She rarely goes out in public. My other confidante is also a regular betelnut user, despite my many protestations. But her beast sighting took place, again, when she was a little girl, long before she had her first chew. More importantly, there are two details from both my confidante's accounts that are intriguingly consistent. One, both report that the creature's head tapers into a long, duckbill-like snout. And two, what I find the most intriguing detail of all, both report that on each foreleg there is a claw situated like an opposable thumb."

"Hmm," Roberta and Irene nodded at each other, impressed with how easily Magdalena tossed around the anatomical term, "opposable thumb." But they were even more impressed by the remarkable consistency of such a detail in two unknown creature sightings, decades apart.

"Nobody would want to oppose my thumbs," quipped Ambu. "They're too likeable."

"Dad," Magdalena rolled her eyes. "What we're talking about would have presented something like this."

Making fists, Magdalena gave the "thumbs up" sign with both hands, and grinned broadly.

"Maybe our dinosaur was making an approving gesture regarding the flavor of the particular coconuts he mashed apart, for other dinosaurs to share," speculated Alistair.

"Neither of my confidantes reported any other creatures in the vicinity. And my real point is that those claws' morphology is consistent with the fore-claws of the herbivorous ornithopod dinosaur, Iguanodon. The duck-billed snout is more along the lines of a Trachodon or Hadrosaurus. However, for every dinosaur whose remains have been unearthed, there are likely at least fifty others still unknown to science."

"I will say this for you, Magdalena," said Irene. "Nobody can accuse you of not having done your homework."

"Thank you, mum."

"The bottom line is that my daughter is ready to lead us exactly where her confidantes think they saw a huge, unknown beast." Ambu's tone of voice made clear how impatient he'd become to finally move things along. "Dr. Matias, will your equipment for setting up camp be arriving on a third cigarette craft? You appeared to be travelling rather light, especially given your larger search party this time."

"We are travelling light this time," confirmed Augie. "Reflecting on my first trip here with the *Cryptomonster* crew, we went with the idea that base camp, motion detectors and the like left too big a footprint. They probably scared off the creature so that we were lucky to even see casuarinas sway on its retreat. As you indicated, Magdalena, if we are dealing with a reptilian beast, be it a dinosaur or some overgrown monitor lizard or Komodo dragon, it might instantly shy away from such unfamiliar intrusions. So we're not going to be hacking down bamboo to build a base camp where we can set up an array of detection equipment, nor any of the sundry other things we did before. Rather, we will depend on this peanut-sized surveillance camera mounted on our bandanas." Augie held one of the devices forward in the palm of his hand for Ambu to inspect. "Hopefully, multiple flashes of lightning from nearby electrical storms expected overnight will light the way."

"In addition," interjected Sherman Peabody, his chin ever embedded in his neck, "I have concocted a complex fragrance to be sprayed on each of us prior to entering your swampland. It should effectively mask our human spoor with the resin from your local aquilaria acuminate, what you know as ghara or eagle wood. Can't say I haven't noticed a touch of it carried on the occasional on-shore breeze."

"Pray it doesn't act as a sex attractant. I don't know how any of you would handle the purported strange beast trying to mate with you, forcing its attentions on you," cautioned Ambu. "If you're going to insist on going that route, a good thing none of us is in formal wear that might arouse such a creature even further."

"I think we'll take our chances," said Stephen.

"Very well, then," said Ambu. "Let's head outside and put your show on the road, shall we?"

Neither Augie nor any of the other foreigners expected such darkness, already, outside Ambu's electrically lit hut, increasing overcast notwithstanding. When they entered his hut, they were enjoying bright what they assumed was mid-day light.

"Good heavens, I don't remember exactly when we went indoors," said Alistair, checking the digital readout on his wristwatch. "But it's already seven eighteen. Where did the time go?"

Sudden breezes gusted through as though to put an exclamation point on how the time had blown by, Augie mused. And he couldn't swear he didn't hear a slight distant rumble.

More perplexing still was how some of the Tolai loitering about suddenly busted out laughing. What didn't help was the enigmatic smile Augie noticed play across Ambu's face.

"What's going on here, Magdalena?" Irene asked.

"I don't know, mum, but I'm guessing some sort of nasty mischief."

"What's going on," said Ambu plenty loud enough for all to hear, "is that perhaps I put you under a hypnotic spell inside my residence. And then perhaps under that spell I commanded you, one at a time, to not only kiss my ass, but lick it as well. That certainly would have gone on long enough to consume the remaining daylight hours. But the sun does set very quickly, close to the equator. And you were here for quite a long while before we went indoors."

Augie and company tentatively worked their tongues round their lips, checking for evidence.

"So, you still haven't gotten past your fear I might be some ooga-booga witch doctor or something! You are pathetic! Especially you!" Ambu pointed at Irene. "You thought you could slip your tongue in and out for your lip inspection fast enough for no one to notice, but not so! Davana! Let's go! Magdalena, lead the way!"

"Stop doing that, Dad!" Magdalena slapped Ambu on his arms as she strode past him.

Augie remembered the lyrics to one of the Beatles songs they'd seen Bonsai Gator dancing to, reggae style: "I'm Looking Through You."

Chapter 16

"We have a problem."

"Nice to see you again, too, Captain," responded Officer Kevin Smith-Park to Captain Helena Taylor of the starship, Smoke and Mirrors.

"Yeah, Captain," spat out Sergeant Fred Frankly. "How about at least a perfunctory congrats, even if you're not really feelin' it, before you launch into, What have you done for me lately??"

"Captain Taylor, I truly believe Sergeant Frankly deserves congrats for his proper use of 'perfunctory'," said Counselor Ali Magabu. But Helena Taylor absolutely spooked him with her dire greeting as he and the other two officers exited the shuttle pod.

Ali and company returned to docking bay aboard the Smoke and Mirrors thinking yet another successful mission to tamper with past-time events.

For nearly a year, assisted by extraordinary extraterrestrials named the Nuah-cherpels, the Smoke and Mirrors had been taking excursions into the previous century from the year 2064. They seized various weapons supplies, and left behind advanced technology of a more peacefully productive nature. By and large, those interventions were successfully redirecting Earth civilization on a more pacifist course. But occasional setbacks did require special adjustments. And that is exactly what the time travelers faced regarding an enormous storage facility in Yaoundé, Cameroon, along the West African coast.

From the late 1970s through the early 1980s, mercenary arms merchants had been intent on tapping into African oil money by equipping both sides of brewing conflicts ranging from Chad to Nigeria to the Ivory Coast. But Smoke and Mirrors intervention repeatedly, and easily, frustrated such efforts.

On the starship's past-time excursions, its crew found everything frozen still. According to first officer "Buddy" Leung, something he christened the quantum wave only put objects in motion in the ever-advancing present. In the ever-receding past, minutely thin slices of space-time continuum were left not only frozen still, but light as Styrofoam as well. Ali and company looked like superheroes, how easily they lifted tanks and battleships.

Entire battalions-worth of weaponry were chained together and hauled away by a mere shuttle pod with the greatest of ease; they could have been paper chains if not for their awkward enormity.

Solar panels and such were left in the wake of absconded armaments, though not a comparable amount given their "regular" weight.

True, the quantum wave inevitably backtracked to where these stealthy trade-outs were made, to set history in motion on a revised course. But by then the Smoke and Mirrors was well on its way through a wormhole rift in the space-time continuum back to the present. Either that, or it was approaching a wormhole. At worst, some outer-solar-system space probe detected the starship just before it vanished through a space-time rift, and it was labeled a UFO. The rare astronaut sighting was dismissed as a comet that melted apart before any satellite radar could home in on it.

Nevertheless, those aforementioned mercenary outfits were far from willing to throw in the towel, give up on tapping into the oil money just yet. In Cameroon, the Earthling mercenary arms merchants expected to thwart the mysterious disappearance of their destructive inventory, and spread it profitably through West Africa, after all.

To secure food supplies from the ravages of periodic flooding, the Cameroon government had constructed an enormous, circular storage facility on elevated ground just north of the hilly capitol city of Yaoundé. It was perfect for trucking containers full of arms labeled as grain, fruit and veggies. Bribes secured the deal, along with a pledge the Cameroon government could siphon off a portion of the destructive goodies to help suppress English-speaking dissidents against French-speaking domination.

Moreover, a mix of armed Cameroon and mercenary troops surrounded the facility, under orders to shoot to kill any unauthorized personnel who came too close, or who simply acted suspiciously curious in the general vicinity. Not only that, but the weapon-filled containers were chained to cement platforms, only a small handful of arms merchants trusted with the keys. War-enabling shipments would finally be made to any and all sides of West African conflicts, the more bloodily contentious, the better.

Of course, neither the mercenaries nor the corrupt government officials expected iron and steel chains to prove as easy to tear apart as one-eighth-inch-thick cardboard. Yet that was the reality in "completed" space-time after the quantum wave went through.

Moreover, inspired by the play-golf-not-war ethos of certain tree-creature extraterrestrials, not to mention the golf addiction of Captain Taylor's husband Chris, Ali Magabu had made a special arrangement. The away team replaced guards' automatic assault rifles and machine guns with putters and golf clubs. As well, they left boxes of golf balls and tees lying about, and cut four-inch-wide holes into the ground at random locations.

From one moment to the next, the guards experienced their guns beaten into golf clubs rather than plowshares.

As far as Ali Magabu and company knew when they re-boarded the Smoke and Mirrors, already well past Mars headed for the wormhole, their mission was accomplished once again without a hitch.

Only this time there was a hitch, a big hitch. A hitch implemented by the arms merchants...

"Of course, gentlemen," was going on Captain Taylor, "your efforts are always greatly appreciated. If more people were aware, ticker tape parades would happen way too often for you to attend all of them, celebrating your sabotage of numerous major wars round the globe."

"But we knew this f-n day was coming," nodded Sergeant Frankly grimly.

"We knew this day was coming," Captain Taylor repeated, surgically excising Frankly's curse word like it might as well have been another freight container full of machine guns and grenades. "Not ten minutes ago, Buddy Leung picked up short video transmissions back to Earth from what he determined were six separate surveillance devices mounted in six separate locations on the entrained storage containers. The transmissions he tapped into revealed full-length side-views of the Smoke and Mirrors."

"Damn," swore Frankly.

"Let me guess, Captain," said Officer Kevin Smith-Park, not waiting for her to call on him when he raised a forefinger to speak. "Once the backed-up quantum wave reanimated the past, satellite tracking triggered the surveillance devices. It told them the arms containers were suddenly out past Mars. And that set off those devices filming images of the Smoke and Mirrors, transmitted to the arms merchants."

"So we have to time travel to before those transmissions took place, Helena?" Ali Magabu comfortably addressed the captain in most familiar terms.

"Exactly, Ali."

"Captain Taylor?" Officer Leung's cheery voice crackled over the intercom, tinged by the same sense of urgency Ali noted in the captain's greeting.

"I've just broken the news to them, Buddy."

"And you've explained about the Challenger shuttle explosion rift?"

"Am about to."

"So having waited to cancel that particular historic tragedy is going to come in handy after all," said Kevin Smith-Park.

"A truly grotesque way of looking at it, Kevin," admonished Ali Magabu shaking his head. "But what's that you have to explain, Helena?"

"Traversing the wormhole located out past Jupiter allowed good-enough time-targeting precision for defanging the Cameroon military depot," responded Helena, no nonsense. "But now we must remove the surveillance cameras from some arms containers, just before you guys caravanned them off the Earth."

"And to zero in on such a narrow time frame will require traversing a smaller rift much closer to Earth," Kevin continued for Helena, her plan having dawned on him. "The Challenger space shuttle explosion rift should work."

"But our shuttle pod will have to go it alone," picked up Ali, not missing a beat. "Because that rift is too narrow for the Smoke and Mirrors."

Captain Taylor and her crew learned lots about time travel over their two years cheating light speed aboard the starship Smoke and Mirrors. Their most important discovery was that tragic events resulting in any loss of life always tore a hole in the space-time fabric. The greater the loss of life, the bigger the tear. Suppose you approach those tears at speeds greater than one-third that of light, at certain shallow angles comparable to those required for skipping stones across a pond. If you do, you neatly facilitate what used to be considered only an impossible science fiction dream.

"As we speak," went on Captain Taylor, "Buddy is loading the shuttle pod database with the exact locations of all six detected surveillance devices. He's also programming the autopilot program."

"At least this time travel run should be freakin' easy am I correct, Captain?" asked Sergeant Frankly, more than a little nervous. "We just peel off the surveillance devices, hammer them to smithereens, return through the Challenger rift to the Smoke and Mirrors, and good ol' 2064, here we come, all there is to it! Oh, shit!"

Well before Fred Frankly finished, Helena hunched her shoulders, a most sheepish expression playing across her face. She would have tucked her head inside her upper torso like a turtle retracting its head into its shell, were that possible.

"It's that f-n' conundrum again, isn't it?"

"It's that f-n' conundrum again," nodded Captain Taylor, this time not begrudging the sergeant his foul-mouthing. "If the devices aren't dismantled before they leave Earth, there is a bothersome chance the revisiting quantum wave will allow them to transmit significant info back to whoever installed them."

"So you're saying we will need to nip them in the bud back near Yaoundé, where we secured the freight containers in the first place."

"Captain," jumped in Kevin, "do we ever plan, or rather do Freamis-Framis and friends ever envision us revealing to our ancestors what we've been up to?"

"Especially were certain bad actors like those arms merchants to keep conspiring to undo our interventions, Kevin, I would guess that day is coming. For the foreseeable future, however..."

"But, okay, say we bury that surveillance crap at its more-or-less original location," said Sergeant Frankly. "No problem after that, zipping back through the Challenger rift to the S&M, can I hear an 'Amen' on that? NO?!" Frankly pounded his forehead into the palm of his hand, rather than against the nearest shuttle pod hangar wall.

"From what we've learned about timeline alteration conundrums," Helena started in a somewhat defensive tone, "it is likely you will find us gone, because we will not have had to return to deal with the surveillance devices in the first place. And for that matter, soon as you bury or destroy them in Yaoundé, you also will not have needed to time travel. Any luck at all, you should feel like you just came out of a daze back aboard the Smoke and Mirrors."

"But of course sometimes, for reasons even our Buddy doesn't truly understand," said Ali Magabu, "someone's caught inside the conundrum."

"Exactly," nodded Helena Taylor. "Which is why, once you leave for the Challenger rift, we'll head for that much larger wormhole rift out past Jupiter. After we traverse it, we'll return towards Earth for your retrieval, unless and until we wake up not remembering any of this, and all of you safely on board."

"One last question before we go, Helena."

"Just for you, Ali, I'll allow two last questions, even."

"A second question is probably unnecessary, unless one of you gentlemen..." Ali Magabu nodded towards Kevin and Fred.

"I can smell serious complications from a billion miles away, Captain Taylor, madam," muttered Sergeant

Frankly in a growly voice. "So my question is for you, Officer Counselor Magabu: What is the particular mess-up in my psychological character that leaves me chomping at the bit for more trouble? Especially when, hell, I could be safely sparing my better half from having to deal with our young punks' latest mischief-making?"

"You just answered your own question, Freddy boy," snarked Kevin. "You'd rather be risking life and limb than deal with your so-called young punks!"

"Ignore him, Sergeant," said Ali. "It's no mess-up at all. It's your sense of duty and honor, though I truly do believe you take certain pleasure living life on the edge. I suppose the challenge for you could become learning to enjoy yourself without teetering on disaster. You've mentioned your luck not suffering any post-traumatic stress or various injuries visited upon your fellow Marine Corps personnel who served in Somalia prior to our timeline alterations."

"Maybe you need to learn how to enjoy one of Chris's endlessly long symphonic rock epics," sarcastically offered Kevin.

"That's already my back-up plan for curing insomnia. But I'm guessing you better get on with your question, Ali, before Captain Taylor here decides time is already up," said Fred Frankly. "The meter's running on the quantum wave having caught us. And I suspect that certain of Professor Skepticus's earthbound partners in disbelief are already going into a conniption, trying to explain away the Smoke and Mirrors as just an irregularly shaped piece of flotsam and jetsam that strayed out of the Oort Cloud."

"Captain," Ali turned to Helena, "clearly we will have to snip off those surveillance devices from certain shipment containers in the direct presence of frozen-time slices of our own selves. Has Buddy offered any thoughts on how we should deal with that? If we don't avert our gaze, or even if we just accidentally catch a glimpse, are there any special, um, quantum peculiarities we should brace for?"

"I wouldn't wave hello at yourself," said Helena flippantly. "But seriously, Buddy doesn't expect such 'peculiarities' whatsoever. He even joked that you could have a picture taken alongside your frozen self like it was an image on cardboard of President Carey outside the White House, with absolutely no risk. The real danger could threaten, of course, were you to have your arm around yourself when the quantum wave caught up. Buddy admits that's a big unknown."

*

The tear-drop-shaped shuttle pod departed for a return to several hours ago through the Challenger shuttle disaster scar across the space-time complexion. And shortly thereafter, the starship Smoke and Mirrors accelerated to one-half light-speed, bound for a wormhole rift out past Jupiter.

The unique design of the Smoke and Mirrors, bathed in an electromagnetic field both ends, enabled formerly-thought-impossible speeds for most anything other than light.

Comprising the starship's rear was an array of micron-thin mirrors arranged in a maze pattern that mimicked a bloomed rose. Those "rose petal" mirrors bounced light around like pinballs, actually accelerating it thanks to the electromagnetic field. And that accelerated light impelled the spaceship forward like wind pushing against sails to send a seagoing vessel forward.

An asparagus-stalk-shaped hull conveyed from the starship's rose-bloom rear to its tulip-bloom prow. The "tulip petals" funneled light ahead of the spaceship through a hollow tube running its entire length, the photon exhaust shaft. Streaming all light ahead of the Smoke and Mirrors out its rear via the exhaust shaft effectively reduced photon friction to zero, enhancing acceleration.

A trail of sparkles always comprised the starship's light-speed wake, fairy dust that physicists guessed are photons forced to favor their physical over their wave existence.

"Chris, Officer Chris Olsen-Taylor, why am I suddenly noticing chocolate chip cookie crumbs all over the floor?" Helena Taylor swung around in her captain's chair to ask her husband, seated up behind her on the starship's navigation deck. They were both strapped in along with everyone else aboard, anticipating the unsettlingly odd tingly sensations always experienced whenever they traversed a space-time rift. "I thought we agreed that Effy and Effelia were only to be fed in certain limited areas, sealed off until every last chocolate chip cookie crumb had been burned to a crisp."

"We did agree, Helena Captain Honeybun!" replied Chris defensively shouting. He couldn't help himself, time travel tingles already giving him goose-bumps galore. "I honestly don't understand how...maybe through the air vents..."

"Captain, I did sense the presence here of an ephemeral dragon while you were in the shuttle pod hangar," said chief navigation Officer Yoon-hee Park-Smith, her eyes glued to the panoramic view-screen while her fingers played across her control console.

"Don't you mean, Officer Park-Smith," corrected resident physicist Professor Skepticus, "you felt the gaseous anomaly floating through, the same as one might feel a gust of wind?"

Yoon-hee rolled her eyes then simply went on, effectively ignoring Skepticus, "Effy or Effelia couldn't have tracked in those crumbs, could they?"

"That doesn't make any sense," reacted Chris. "I'm not aware of even one crumb ever having escaped being charred to dust by their blowtorch consumption. Unless...maybe this time, they tried tucking away cookies like acorns gathered by squirrels into their cheeks, but crumbs tumbled out. Although, why now when never before? Wow!" he suddenly exclaimed, snapping his fingers. "It all makes sense!"

"How wonderful!" other resident physicist Professor Aquinas clapped his hands in glee.

"Oh-oh," murmured Professor Skepticus under his breath. *Here comes another nut-job theory of everything.*

"Remember a few weeks ago when we puzzled over why Effelia was suddenly torching so many more cookies than Effy?" asked Chris.

"Didn't you speculate she might be pregnant?" Yoon-hee tossed in.

"Certainly seemed a reasonable possibility since Oodle-Noodle intuited she was a 'she,' wherefore naming her Effelia in the first place," nodded Chris.

"Better check all your feminine nouns in French and Spanish while you're at it," grumbled Skepticus beyond disgust. "Make sure none of them are pregnant!"

With a there-he-goes-again sigh, Chris went on, "So her appetite did just-as-suddenly return to normal. But what if she was pregnant after all? And she gave birth, and was unable to keep her babies from prowling all over the starship? So when she looked like she was torching that many more cookies, she literally inhaled bits of them for exhalation later, in places her brood might wander?"

"Yes! Of course! Why didn't I understand this before? It's all so clear to me now!" burst out Skepticus in mock epiphany. "All you said is true, Officer Olsen-Taylor! No need bother over repeatable experiments to establish any of it! We can simply believe it's true!"

"Okay, Professor," said Helena as in: You've made your point.

But Professor Skepticus was unrelenting. "Effy and Effelia were joined," he went on, "by Uffelia the ephemeral unicorn, and Hippophelia the ephemeral hippopotamus..."

"An ephemeral hippopotamus?"

"Yes, you're right, Officer Olsen-Taylor! An ephemeral hippopotamus? How absurd! It is actually Pigmalia the ephemeral pig! They're all working together to construct right here on the navigation bridge an invisible playground where those baby ephemeral dragons can swing on invisible swings, slide down invisible slides,-"

THUNK!!

For Helena at least, it seemed as though the starship had suddenly gone over an impossible outer space speed bump, talk about invisible things!

"Captain," said Yoon-hee as in heads-up, "we're not alone in this wormhole. Somehow our entire course trajectory has been entrained by an enormous object some hundred-billion miles ahead."

"'Entrained?!' What does that mean exactly, Yoon-hee?" Helena asked as she noticed some of the cookie crumbs seeming to spontaneously combust. In the flash of light from one orange flare-out, she discerned the filmy transparent specter of a dragon no bigger than a baby chic, complete with wings, a long tail and a reptilian head most elaborately ornamented by horns and scaly ridges. *Why do so many things always have to happen at the same time?*

"Captain, it's as though that object has created a whirlpool effect carrying us, sucking us down whatever drain it's going, so to speak. Here," she played her fingers across the navigation console at an even more rapid clip, "I'm going to magnify the view-screen so we can take a closer look."

A lone, distant flicker in an eerily starless wormhole rift suddenly ballooned much closer, taking up fully one-fourth the center of the view-screen.

Donut-shaped with fairy dust streaming out from around its circumference like the photon exhaust that streamed out the Smoke and Mirrors' rear, only in spiral swirls...

"What is that, Yoon-hee?" asked Captain Taylor in unconcealed puzzlement.

"It's certainly metallic, certainly intelligently designed, and certainly propelled by tiny mirror array units mounted all along its perimeter. And it's fifty miles in circumference. And, as its swirling photon exhaust would indicate, it's turning quickly enough on its donut-hole axis to provide sufficient gravitational pull along its rim."

"Fifty miles in circumference, oh wow!" Buddy Leung couldn't help giggling with childish excitement. "Captain, that could be a large outer space colony inside there!"

"And shouldn't we have emerged from the wormhole by now, Yoon-hee?" Captain Helena Taylor already knew the answer to this question, well before she asked it. Not to mention that Ali Magabu and company also ought already to have reappeared aboard the Smoke and Mirrors. Meaning they had indeed gotten stuck inside the conundrum, and required retrieval.

Captain, I don't wish to add yet another mind-bending situation to your already formidably challenging pile of them, telepathed Oodle-Noodle, one of two mobile tree creatures from the planet Oomb aboard the Smoke and Mirrors. *But perhaps this one adds an element of comic* relief that will enhance your calmer, more constructive reflection on the rest.

"I'm all sixth sense, Oodle-Noodle," said Helena resignedly. "Go ahead and hit me."

I've detected no fewer than five infantile minds having entered onto your navigation bridge coincidental to those out-of-place cookie crumbs having ignited. Given the winged reptilian shape I noticed during one of the flashes of light from the cookie crumb combustion, I surmise that Chris has guessed correctly the source. Effelia did indeed give birth to five additional ephemeral dragons.

Chapter 17

"Mr. Peabody, no one else here seems willing to address what you Americans might term the elephant in the room," said Ambu, breaking the silence of a steady procession led by his daughter Magdalena through waist-high underbrush. "So I find I must."

"The stench is certainly strong enough to rival that of an elephant in the room, if not worse even," commented Stephen Feldman, holding his nose by one hand while waving the other.

"Which approaches my point, Mr. Sherman sir," nodded Ambu. "I detect notes of certain fragrances, to put them far more charitably than they deserve, other than the ghara wood with which we trusted you to spray us."

"Yes, that." Sherman Peabody pushing his chin into his neck seemed to Augie Matias far more about avoiding eye contact than usual. "Well, so you see we needed to be about more than simply masking our human scents from potential non-avian dinosaur presences. We must also concern ourselves with dangerous creepy-crawlies we might inadvertently step on, especially wandering about at night."

Just then, a wind gust drew Augie's attention skyward, away from his darkened surroundings. Dusk had not yet faded enough that he could not still discern puffy gray clouds scudding quickly across a beautifully variegated backdrop of blues, purples, and even a few remnant streaks of pinkish red. And he couldn't swear he didn't notice a heat lightning flash, more of which the expedition would depend on for illuminating foraging dinosaurs as night fell to pitch black.

Again, teensy camcorders mounted on each expedition member's bandana produced video streams back to Cloud Nine, recorded for careful scrutiny later on. Better that, Augie kept reminding himself, than intrusive motion detectors mounted on random trees, together with a base camp setup he suspected of scaring off whatever-o-saurus on his first trip there with the Cryptomonster team.

"The important thing is, you're having fun," Augie remembered his late grandma feistily commenting years ago, when he told her about his journey to Brazil for dinosaur fossils younger than sixty-five-million years old.

"The two creatures that give me particular worry," went on Peabody, "are the taipan death adder and the giant centipede, both exceptionally venomous."

"And both exceptionally rare on New Britain," added Ambu.

"I've wandered around here barefoot for years without encountering anything more threatening than a saltwater crocodile asleep on the far horizon," Magdalena commented.

"You have to understand the enormous risk Mr. Peabody is already taking, unprotected from any small meteorite that might happen to fall his way," noted Stephen.

"It is true that the centipede is more likely to be found making house inspections for insects and small lizards. And that the death adder would have to swim over from mainland Papua," conceded Sherman Peabody. "But the risk remains far more plausible than from the meteorite you mentioned. And I remind you the meteorite risk does remain a stubbornly bit higher than absolute zero. And so, together with our ghara wood scent, I mixed traces of ammonia-laden fruit-bat urine, peppermint oil and clove oil. That should keep the death adder, the giant centipede and more scampering out of our way as we trudge forward. Although, I do recommend we continue at our present slow rate so we don't unwittingly corner one of them."

"Another advantage, Sherman," said Irene. "Any cannibalistic designs I might have entertained about any of you, well rest assured that's become the furthest thing from my mind."

Scott wanted to ask Irene about which part of his anatomy she might have had "cannibalistic designs," were Sherman's protective spray not so putrid. But he couldn't work up the nerve to match her snark.

"Just suppose, though, Ms. McDowell," said Ambu, bending aside a nuisance bamboo shoot with a pronounced crack! "Suppose the eau de urine-infused peppermint ghara wood had not so inhibited your appetite. You might still have found yourself perplexedly disappointed when you tried taking a bite out of Mr. McDonald or one of the others, as you found yourself chomping down on nothing more than thin air."

"And how would that have been the case, pray tell Mr. Ambu, sir?"

"Hypnotizing you into licking my bare ass, Ms. McDowell, would only have been the beginning. Of course, I would also have hypnotized you into feeling no pain when I neatly, surgically removed each of your lesser-used arms up to the elbow for roasting at our next big celebration. As well, I would have hypnotized you into permanently seeing that arm still attached. And feeling it there would be no issue, we well know from people's experiences of ghost limbs after amputations."

Not a one of Eclipso's team, not even Irene and Stephen, could help running and squeezing a hand along one arm, then the other. They hoped Ambu wouldn't notice in the rapidly descending dark of night, but no such luck.

"How pathetic!" Ambu complained. He knew full well what they were about without even looking, for the awkward silence that followed his mischievous remarks. "Your attitudes are clearly far more racist, far more bigoted than any of you would ever care to admit! Disgusting!!"

"Hey, people, shouldn't we be keeping it down a notch so we don't scare off Mr. Dinosaur by sound instead of smell?" asked Alistair.

"Should one of you deign to scream at the top of your lungs, well that's one thing," said Ambu. "Short of that, the profusion of buggy and froggy noises ought to adequately cloak and drown out our varied utterances."

"There's a real concern I'm having," said Stephen Feldman raising his voice because right on cue, the volume of wildlife chatter seemed suddenly ratcheted up a notch. "If one of us vomits due to nausea brought on by Mr. Peabody's cologne from hell, what effect might that have on any large creatures we come across out here? Although where non-avian dinosaurs are concerned, I've found that chanting a simple 'hunga-bunga-boonga' out my back door at home is always highly effective for keeping elephants away from my garden."

"So you keep a residence where wild elephants are actually a thing?" asked journalist Laura Gómez, suddenly very interested. "South Africa, perhaps?"

"No, just a small patio on the rear balcony of my condo in New Jersey," Stephen answered matter-of-factly. "No elephants of any kind there." To Laura's quizzical look he added, "That's the whole point."

"Ohhh," nodded Irene in mock realization. Then to the melody from when the Munchkins greet Dorothy in the film version of The Wizard of Oz, she sang, "Ho-ho-ho and a yuk-yuk-yuk and a froggy-boggy-boggy-boo; that's how we laugh the dinosaurs away when you're someone as skeptical as you!"

"Actually," spoke Sherman Peabody into his chest, even though in the near pitch-black gloom none would have been the wiser had he lifted his chin high, "I have read about one member of the hyena family that loves rolling around in vomit like pigs in a mud puddle. Nobody knows why."

Augie might have marveled at how Sherman seemed to effortlessly ignore what transpired between Stephen, Laura and Irene to return to Stephen's original expressed concern about possible vomit. However, his attention was drawn to a flickering light slowly crossing the sky. He felt reasonably sure it wasn't Cloud Nine even though it traveled just as silently, while a plane or helicopter would have produced a distinct racket. "Look up to your left, people," he said. "What is that thing?"

By the time Augie finished asking, whatever it was had already descended out of sight behind a distant stand of coconut and casuarina palms.

"On an island off the south coast of Papua," said Ambu, "the fishermen complain about a flying creature they say comes out at night to steal their fish. They call it the ropen, and claim it has large, leathery wings like a bat."

"A bat, in other words," drily said Stephen.

"No bat I know sports a long tail with a diamond-shaped tip, plus a long, pointed beak, guv'nah," emphasized Magdalena, irritated. "The ropen's morphology, especially that diamond tip, is far more consistent with the prehistoric flying reptile, Rhamphorhyncus."

"And it glows in the dark as well?" Stephen asked expressing his own irritability and rolling his eyes like crazy. "Are you sure it isn't Tinkerbell?"

"The best guess, guv'nah, is that bioluminescent sea plankton adheres to its belly when it dives for fish rather than poaching those already caught."

"Okay," said Stephen dubiously, "so you think we've stumbled into a real life Lost World? I hope you're right."

*

"A Rhamphor- What was that name again, Ms. Copplestone?" asked fifth grader Amber. She'd left her desk to grab a prehistoric animal guide out of Vicky Copplestone's small reference library in one corner of her classroom.

"Can you tell us where Mr. Copplestone and his friends are now, Ms. Copplestone?" asked José standing with his classroom buddy, Lucas, beside a world globe, both ready to search for the location.

"Okay, boys and girls," Vicky slapped her hands together, delighted at her students' curiosity and anticipation. "I've kept you in suspense long enough. As we speak, Lucas, Mr. Matias-Copplestone is with fellow investigators on New Britain Island off the north coast of Papua, New Guinea, well north of Australia. They are searching for a living dinosaur that is not a bird!"

While several students variously oohed, ahhed and giggled, resident skeptic Rachel looked to Vicky like she was suffering a headache. "Wait," Rachel said, holding up a protesting hand. "Dinosaurs went extinct sixty-five-million years ago!"

"I've found New Britain Island!" announced José proudly. "Is Mr. Copplestone near, um," he squinted to read the tiny lettering, "Port Moresby?"

"So the dinosaurs just dropped dead all at the same time?" Lucas challenged Rachel like José's question never happened. "That's ridiculous!"

"The dinosaurs didn't just drop dead all at the same time for nothing!" Rachel pushed back. "A giant asteroid struck the Earth, and then there were fires followed by an ice age that wiped out most life! Duh!"

"Most life except for alligators, turtles, frogs, birds, the first little mammals,-"

"And maybe some dinosaurs!" Lucas completed Jonathan's observation, to scattered laughter and applause.

"But Rachel does have a point," interjected Vicky Copplestone. "Some scientists estimate that at least two out of every three living things on our planet died off because of that giant asteroid. By the by, Rachel, can you share for us where it struck the Earth?"

"Are we going to be killed if there's another giant asteroid?" worriedly asked Simona.

"I don't know," answered Jack, "but I don't like our chances if there's another giant fart like I just smelled."

"Ew!"

"Ew!"

"That was you, Jack!" laughed Lucas as he pointed an accusing forefinger at Jack.

"If that was you, Jack," said Vicky, "what do you say?"

"You're welcome?"

During the resulting uproarious laughter for which Jack stood and took a bow, Vicky noticed Simona still looking very worried, and said, "Simona does raise a very good question. Could another giant asteroid strike the Earth, and do to us what the earlier one did to the dinosaurs?"

That question quieted Vicky Copplestone's increasingly riotous fifth grade class in a hurry.

"The good news," Copplestone proceeded, "is that the odds are slim, like one in a hundred thousand in our lifetime. But of course that's also the bad news, that the odds for such an event are not zero. More good news, though..."

"Please, Ms. Copplestone," protested Nelson. "Bad news, good news, bad news, and now more good news: You're making me dizzy!"

Laughter again as Vicky continued, "I promise you I am finishing on a good news note, Nelson. Which is this: Astronomers are searching distant heavens round the clock for possibly dangerous asteroids. Plus, applied physicists are working on plans to deal with such an asteroid if we ever find it. Open your science encyclopedia and look under asteroid search, and you'll find a big article on this subject."

Simona and four other students lost no time pulling out their science encyclopedias from inside their desks, then frantically turning pages to locate the article their teacher referenced.

"Around the Yucatan peninsula!" announced Rachel after her own hunt through the science encyclopedia, spurred by Copplestone's request. "That's where the asteroid hit!"

"Well that's on the opposite side of the planet from where Mr. Copplestone is looking for dinosaurs," observed Jonathan in his typically quiet, low-key voice that nevertheless always commanded attention, the few times he spoke. "That might have been far enough away when the asteroid hit. Some of the world's largest reptiles live there, such as the saltwater alligator and the Komodo dragon."

"But the ice age from the asteroid went worldwide! Duh!" said Rachel in prickly retort mode again. "And I think those large reptiles you mentioned evolved from much smaller reptiles that managed to survive."

"I've read that Komodo dragons can burrow in the ground and hibernate, like most reptiles and amphibians," Jonathan noted, again most soft-spoken. "Maybe some small dinosaurs also knew how to hibernate, and their descendants grew big again after they slept through the asteroid winter, just like the ancestors of the Komodo dragon."

Vicky found Jonathan's speculation mind-bending, for how well he synthesized various bits of info to get there. But before she could dwell on that, her remediation coach, Diane Mueller, who also happened to be the curriculum adviser, entered the room, evaluation clipboard at the ready. Most unsettlingly, how Diane leaned forward always reminded Vicky of a big blue heron stalking something in a pond.

Students conferred round the large, topographically molded world globe, intently pointing at it, and slowly turning it one direction then the opposite.

Other students were caught up reading and discussing science encyclopedia entries at their desks, while still others gathered up front round the television screen, seeing what they could discern during flashes of heat lightning over ten thousand miles away in a tropical swamp on New Britain Island.

Rachel and company were carrying on their debate, with Jonathan starting to say something about the platypus.

"Look who's here, students," said Vicky feeling an odd mix of pride over the lather she'd worked her students into, and nervousness over how the curriculum adviser would react. "Who would like to tell Ms. Mueller what's happening?"

Twenty hands shot in the air, to which Diane Mueller bristled, "You are all going to have to sit down and be quiet, first!"

*

"Is our transmission coming in clear enough for you, Eclipso?" asked Harry Letterman from the navigation room of the huge steam-powered drone, Cloud Nine.

Cloud Nine continued hovering nestled into a bed of its self-produced, softly hissing steam over South Pacific seas only a few miles east of New Britain Island's northeast peninsula.

"Can you see anything in the darkness when the lightning is not flashing?" Harry added.

"Even better than lightning, my fine Mr. Letterman!" burst Eclipso's ebullience through the navigation room intercom from over ten thousand miles away in his Ankylosaur mansion. "Surely you and the away team have noticed by now!"

"You mean the synchronous fireflies? They are pretty," nodded Harriet Letterman, awestruck at the sight on the large navigation room video monitor of thousands of fireflies blinking on and off simultaneously.

"Indeed they are, Mrs. Letterman!" Eclipso continued in a most ebullient mood, with Yellow Dubmarine's reggae version of the Beatles' "Here, There, and Everywhere" playing in the background. "And you should see how Bonsai Gator is boogeying up a storm to celebrate!"

Swaying languidly to the reggae beat, Bonsai Gator also started shaking his head "no" coincident to the Beatles' lyric about nobody being able to "deny that there's something there."

*

"All those fireflies in the same narrow location is an impressive sight," conceded Stephen Feldman, crouched down with the rest of the away team behind a convenient row of cycad bushes. "But of course it must be an illusion that they are lighting up in perfect sync."

"Actually it's not an illusion," corrected Magdalena. "Recent research has confirmed they flash on and off together. Entomologists guess it's an evolutionary adaptation."

"Of course it is," said Scott derisively. "Every oddball thing creatures do is always considered, by default, an 'evolutionary adaptation' that you can't prove otherwise because nobody was ever around to watch when it first happened."

"That doesn't necessarily mean, young man," said Ambu in lecture mode, "that there wasn't also some marvelously mysterious creative force at work, that delighted in the female fireflies being attracted to male fireflies by their glowing business ends!"

"Dad's right, kind of," said Magdalena. "But what I was going to explain is, well suppose the males flashed their rear ends at varying, uncoordinated times. Prospective mates would have really struggled to focus on who they are most attracted to."

"That's an impressive amount of information you've acquired about those fireflies, Magdalena," observed Dr. Roberta Quiñones. More and more, she felt that getting Ambu's daughter admitted to the University of Maryland at her tender young age might not be the most outrageous thing ever attempted.

"It is impressive," agreed Stephen. "I think I'm in love."

"Hey creep, get aroused by someone more your own age," severely lectured Irene.

"No, what I meant was, uh," frantically backpedalled Stephen in a fluster while Ambu gave him an arched-eyebrow regard. "The real purpose of our visit should have been to investigate further such natural wonders as these amazing insects, rather than chasing after non-existent monsters."

"Regarding those monsters, Magdalena," said Laura Gómez, not deigning to give Stephen's defensive explanation any more credit than as a useful segue, "is it possible the presence of those fireflies is going to keep them away?"

"Actually those fireflies could be good for our purposes, mum," said Magdalena, clearly invested in the dinosaur search rather than simply helping as a dispassionate enabler. "My older friend confided in me that her possible ornithopod dinosaur sighting decades ago happened on just such an evening as this. The fireflies were going at it, which in itself is rare to see unless you camp out here night after night. What also intrigued me from her report was that, as we are witnessing right now, the fireflies did their mating show amidst a mango tree, as they are doing now. And both my extra-shy eyewitness friends agree the creature went after the fruit and leaves of this particular mango tree, each time."

"Do you think maybe we should be a little quieter so we don't scare off the dinosaur, if it's approaching?" Scott asked gently. He intended his new tone to make up for how harshly he addressed Magdalena earlier regarding the subject of evolutionary adaptation. And he hoped Irene appreciated his effort in that regard.

"Yes, we could scare away all the little elves and leprechauns as well," said Stephen sarcastic as ever.

"Bugs and frogs are producing such a racket, the main reason I've been raising my voice, incidentally," said Magdalena. "I wouldn't worry about our dinosaur detecting our voices above the jungle din. Other reptiles possess varying degrees of hearing acuity, so I wouldn't be surprised if our quarry is somewhat deficient in that department."

"I only wish the bug and frog mating chatter could drown out the stink from that eau de crap you sprayed all over us, Sherman," complained Irene. "It will be my luck that when Mr. I'm-too-dumb-to-know-I-should-be-extinct-osaur finally rears its ugly head to take a bite out of a mango, I'll be too nauseous to enjoy the show!"

"Yeah," chimed in Laura. "How are Bernie and that nice data-compiling couple going to let us back on board in this condition?"

"If you want to take your chances with the snakes and centipedes," said Sherman Peabody in his now-you're-really-annoying-me voice, "you can always go wash yourselves off at the beach. Although, careful you not accidentally step on an aipysurus duboisi, a sea snake rated one of the three most venomous snakes in the world. Besides which, an attack by a moray eel-"

A sudden rumble just as suddenly quieted Sherman's litany of dangers from trying to prematurely undo his noxious handiwork.

"Was that thunder?" asked Augie, incredulous over the possibility such a distant-sounding rumble could have made the ground tremble so much.

"More likely it's Tavurvur feeling feisty," said Ambu.

"Tavurvur?" Stephen did a double-take.

"One of the island's more active volcanoes to the west of us," explained Magdalena. "West of Rabaul, actually. It's been in a rather persnickety mood lately. If I lived in Rabaul, I wouldn't feel especially safe."

"Well maybe Mr. Tavurvur can send enough sulfur fumes our way to drown out Sherman's anti-Christ cologne, cough!" suggested Irene. She made a point of sounding like the nausea was choking her, even though sporadic wind gusts from a drifting-about thunderstorm were carrying off the stench to more tolerable effect.

"Tavurvur is too far away for that, even if it goes full-on eruption," said Ambu. "But if I had eaten more eggs this morning…"

"Dad!"

*

"There's a volcano on New Britain Island?" Chelsea asked incredulously. She rose from her desk in Ms. Copplestone's fifth grade classroom to join three other students crowded round the world globe, already looking for Tarvurvur.

"According to this encyclopedia," said Amber paging through it at her desk, "Wow! There are at least eight of them!"

"Eight?!"

"Does each one have a McDonald's?" quipped Jack to general laughter.

"Ms. Copplestone?" said Simona raising her hand.

"Yes Simona," said Vicky, one eye on Diane Mueller furiously scribbling notes. Vicky suspected Diane commented on Simona not waiting to be called on. Part of her wanted to bend over, whisper in Diane's ear, *Please try to go easy on all the accolades; you're embarrassing me!*

"I'm interested in, how did they call them, syn-chro-nous fireflies?"

"Yes, that's right, Simona, synchronous fireflies." Vicky wrote "synchronous" on the whiteboard.

"What does 'synchronous' mean again exactly?"

"I've written it here so you can check in your dictionary."

"I'll explain for her, Ms. Copplestone," offered Jack. Then he turned towards Simona and said, "When I go trick-or-treating on Halloween, I pull down my pants so my firefly butt can light the way in the darkness. And synchronous is where both my butt-cheeks light up at the same time so I don't get confused."

"Jack Feuillet!" shouted Vicky reprovingly during much laughter to which Jack took several bows.

"Is that all you're going to say to him?" spit out Diane Mueller.

Vicky Copplestone bent down low to get in Diane's face when she responded, "Bite me!" This sent Diane into a raging paroxysm of more furious note-taking.

"So many volcanos would have wiped out all the dinosaurs there years ago, even if the asteroid hadn't already," said Paul, undeterred from making his point by Jack's foolishness. "I think that one guy is right; they should study those fireflies instead."

"If that is true," responded Jonathan in his usual soft-spoken manner, "then why does that same area have some of the largest known reptiles in the world such as the Komodo dragon and the saltwater crocodile?"

*

A faint rumble, then another gusty breeze, succeeded a fresh burst of heat lightning.

"Is this the plan, Magdalena?" asked Alistair Frump. "We stay crouched behind these cycads, waiting for the beast to make its move on a mango during a bright lightning flash?"

A new, stronger rumble, different from the earlier one of suspected volcanic origin, punctuated Alistair's question. Just before that, incidentally, an even brighter flash lit up the mango tree that all those male synchronous fireflies had turned into their own pickup bar, and made plain to see the many large mangoes ornamenting it.

"Patience is your friend, Mr. Golf Course Designer," counseled Ambu close beside him, "even if hours of lying in wait awards you with no beast at all, of any kind. That might also tell you something."

"Such results will only tell you what I've already been trying to tell you about the prospects for discovering a living non-avian dinosaur," said Stephen with no little amount of frustration. "But I am content to sit here for hours admiring the fireflies, marveling at the approaching thunderstorm, and counting how many different nocturnal critter noises I hear. Am even hoping to see a glow along the western horizon from that volcano you mentioned, blowing its stack."

"I'd be more content- Sniff! Sniff! Okay, whoever just farted under cloak of that bug and frog racket," Irene growled, "you'll have to do better than that if you're actually going to drown out the stink from Sherman's evil-smelling concoction!"

No sooner did Irene offer her mock-serious critique than a sudden new gust of wind, the strongest yet, nearly tipped her off balance where she remained crouched down behind a stumpy cycad bush.

"Maybe that was your dinosaur sending a fart our way," deadpanned Stephen as an even stronger rumble, definitely thunder, succeeded a new lightning flash.

"Wow!" exclaimed Alistair Frump breathlessly. "What that lightning just revealed for the umpteenth time is only now occurring to me: the makings for a palm-tree-lined fairway of a long par four!"

"You'll find several broken-off branches and stomped-on casuarina seedlings along both stands of trees, guv'nah," said Magdalena. She overheard Alistair despite the multiple continuing distractions of synchronized fireflies, loud nocturnal critter din, and the slowly encroaching thunderstorm with perhaps a muted earth tremor or two shuffled in. "My best guess is that the creature has been matting down your prospective fairway. Maybe there's a whole family of them."

"Well wouldn't that be something!" enthused Alistair rhapsodically. "Hey!" he snapped his fingers. "Here's a crazy idea!"

"You mean, even crazier than our crouching out here waiting to see a dinosaur in the first place?"

"Well that's a rather uncharitable way of putting it, mate!" Alistair protested with a hurt look on his face that would have gone for naught, had another lightning flash not accompanied it. "No, my crazy idea is, I take this glow-in-the-dark golf ball..." He shook the ball between thumb and forefinger to activate a soft green fluorescence at its core, then went on, "After placing it the middle of our proposed fairway, I give it a good thump with this seven iron! Launch it headed for glory towards our proposed green, just to the right of that synchronized firefly come-hither!" Alistair held his seven iron skyward, looking oddly victorious during the next lightning flash, so Augie thought.

"You're right, Alistair," Irene agreed, and chuckled in a voice huskier than usual for her. "There is a crazy idea! And you just happened to carry that seven iron all the way out here?"

"Can't say I noticed it earlier," said Laura.

"That's because I tucked it away, screw-together pieces in my backpack," explained Alistair. "I know," he added as he ventured out from behind the cycads for his golf shot. "Many experts consider fending off a dinosaur stampede to be more of a fairway wood shot, ha-ha!"

Augie and company too wondrous to offer protest, Alistair Frump lined up his shot. He took a few practice swings, giving his seven iron a good waggle during increasingly frequent lightning flashes.

Where Laura was concerned, discotheque strobe lights could have been capturing instants of a most bizarre dance rather than a golf swing.

Then Alistair said, "Now let's see whether my non-flashing, spherical firefly will encourage our dinosaur to show itself, AKA best golf resort tourist attraction, ever!" With one final swing, Alistair sent his lighted golf ball flying high down the trampled-down corridor between rows of palms, casuarinas and the occasional mango tree.

However, a new wind gust took the ball off course, sent it on a wild hook at the firefly-lit mango tree where with one mighty bounce, it disappeared in amidst the thick ground cover.

The rumble of thunder that ensued was notable for how little competition it met for attention from the varied nocturnal critter noises. The frogs and bugs had suddenly, unaccountably gone peculiarly quiet.

Even the fireflies had stopped flashing, as uniformly suddenly as though someone flipped off a switch.

"Wow!" gasped Alistair. "All those thngies that go chirp and croak in the night must have been awestruck by my shot, even though the wind hooked it! Still wish I tried a low-launch power-fade instead, though!"

"Sh!" shushed Magdalena in a sharp, harsh whisper. "Everything must have gone quiet for a special reason."

"Even more special than my seven iron shot?" Alistair whispered softly enough in Augie's ear for Magdalena not to hear over the steadily intensifying wind gusts from the imminent thunderstorm.

"I'm surprised these first, pelting raindrops haven't automatically triggered a spherical umbrella to encase Sherman Peabody," quipped Irene in Augie's other ear, also softly enough to not further raise Magdalena's ire.

Augie's subsequent loud noise from trying to suppress a chuckle might well have finally gained the young adolescent's reproving attention. That is, if not for a distinctive thwack! that issued from somewhere beyond the firefly-populated mango tree.

Alistair's lit golf ball came flying directly out from where it went bouncing in.

"Well isn't this always the case?" said Alistair, disgusted beyond appreciating the full import of what just happened. "Someone assumed their non-illuminated, dollar-a-dozen ball got miraculously transfigured into my expensive, glowing Champ Turbo 1! Or they just went ahead and hit it without checking to make sure it was theirs!"

"SH!" Magdalena repeated, even harsher than before.

"There must be a rational explanation," mumbled Stephen under his breath to no one in particular.

"You mean, aside from an Iguanodon using his tail like a wedge to chip Alistair's ball out of the rough?" asked Irene deadpan.

By then, the increasingly eerie quiet apart from the oncoming thunderstorm had everyone slowly, cautiously standing up from behind the cycads. They joined Alistair peering intently towards where his hit ball was mysteriously hit or tossed back out. Pelting raindrops eased the stifling muggy tropical heat.

Alistair made an additional step forward to retrieve his illuminated golf ball. But a sudden rustle of palm fronds and bushes from back behind the mango tree prompted Ambu to latch onto his arm and pull him back.

Subtle yet distinct tremors underfoot, unassociated with any rumble of thunder, caused everyone to rear back expectantly.

*

"Mr. Copplestone, your students are late for their lunch pickup!" burst from the intercom in Vicky's classroom.

"Awww!!"

"Shhh!"

"Nooo!!"

So went complaints from Vicky Copplestone's students.

"We're in the middle of something; can you give us a half hour?" pleaded Vicky.

"Second and third grade will be here by then! There won't be any place for them to sit!"

"They'll eat in my room! With me! No coverage necessary!" Vicky looked around her class as she responded, and was met by eager nods.

"We'll have the cafeteria line stretching down the hallway, but...okay," the cafeteria manager finally grudgingly agreed after Vicky didn't yield an inch during her pause after "but."

That's some epic you're producing, Vicky had to stifle herself from snarking at Diane Mueller, seeing her resume furious note-taking. Meanwhile, the students resumed their rapt attention via TV screen on a coastal jungle in New Britain Island over ten thousand miles away.

*

CRASH!

The loudest thunder, yet, and nobody in the search party even flinched, let alone gave a thought to heading for a safer locale. They were utterly enraptured by the prospect of meeting an enormous prehistoric survivor...and Stephen by the prospect of receiving ultimate vindication for his skepticism. They even crept closer ever so cautiously, close enough to the mango tree for Alistair to finally retrieve his ball, and then closer still, until they stood not twenty feet away.

The next lightning flash revealed the fireflies had long since fled, were no longer swarming nearby.

Accompanied by intensifying rustles, the mango tree was swaying. Augie sensed something large pulling at it, maybe trying to pluck off or bite into one of the mangos.

Casuarinas and coconut palms alike swayed just like this, one year prior, Augie remembered. That's when under far more benign weather conditions, the *Cryptomonster* crew had approached very close to where Eclipso's crew returned presently.

Augie was unable to discern whatever caused such commotion a year ago, either directly or by repeatedly reviewing the video. Would he have any better luck this time?"

CRASH!!

During by far the brightest, most prolonged flash of lightning Augie could hope for, there it was: Out from behind upper branches of the mango tree emerged the largest duckbill he had ever seen. Also larger than the largest entire duck he had ever seen, it swayed about, dripping wet and glistening orange-ish yellow. Stringy orange mango pulp hung from it like seaweed strands.

The next lightning flash, it was gone.

"Did you see that?!" Augie screamed, heedless of any danger or, on the other hand, his abrupt noise scaring off whatever it was.

"QUACK!!"

"That must be it!" Augie added. "Like a monster duck!"

CRASH!!

"You mean the sound trees made when wind gusts scraped them together?!" Stephen shouted to be heard above oncoming sheets of rain and additional crashes and rumbles of thunder, as well as noises that did sound like tree trunks and branches creakily rubbing against each other.

"Didn't see a thing!" Irene answered. "But I did hear the quack!"

"See what?!" anxiously asked Sherman, initiating his snake charmer sway.

"It looked like a gigantic duckbill!" answered Augie pointing towards the mango tree.

Thud! Thud!

Thud! Thud!

CRASH!!

"Was it my imagination?!" shouted Scott. "Or was one set of thuds coming from beyond the row of trees to this side?! While the other set of thuds came from the other side?!"

"Cloud Nine?! Do you hear me, Cloud Nine?! Over!!" screamed Irene into her walkie-talkie while joining her fellow explorers as they slowly, cautiously backed away from the mango tree.

Soon, everyone was trudging down the center of the muddy, underbrush-strewn corridor between the two rows of palms, casuarinas and mango trees.

"This is Cloud Nine, we hear you! Over!" answered Heidi Letterman.

"We have a developing situation here! Might be best if you extract us ASAP! Over!"

"We've got your coordinates and will be on our way fast! Over!" Heidi answered.

"Thanks! Over and-"

CRASH!!

Thud! Thud!

Thud! Thud!

"QUACK!"

"QUACK!"

"Okay!" shouted Laura. "Can someone assure me that whatever it is, there aren't two of them?! One each side, stalking us for an ambush?! Making the trees sway extra much, and making that amplified 'quack' as they lumber along?!"

"Calm down, people!!" shouted Stephen in frustration over both the foolishness of the others, and how unavoidably drenched he was from the thunderstorm's full fury. "Your imaginations are running away with you!!"

Thud! Thud! Thud! Thud!

Thud! Thud! Thud! Thud!

"Those things are pacing us!" disagreed Augie. He noticed that as he accelerated down the natural corridor, so did the frequency of the thuds, of a different character from the thunder and earlier on, the possible earth tremor. Said thuds also seemed disturbingly in sync with whichever trees were swaying the most.

"Our best hope might be those snake charmer motions I showed you for trying to hypnotize the- Whoops!" Sherman flipped over on his back from trying to coordinate his own motions with trying to keep up with the general retreat. Fortunately where he fell, the ground cover grew so thick, it cushioned him enough to keep his airbag from re-deploying. Augie had no problem bringing him back up onto his feet. He nevertheless lagged behind him, in case there were any more such incidents.

CRASH!!

"That must be Cloud Nine!" Alistair shouted enthusiastically. He lifted his seven iron pointing towards where a peculiar-looking cloud hovered unusually low rather than racing across the sky.

"I say, watch out!" Irene and Augie could hear Samuel Longbottom shouting into their earpieces from aboard ship. "I'm going to lower the conveyor belt rescue apparatus! Simply strap yourself in, one at a time, and hold on to the handle straps! We'll take care of all the rest if you please, over!"

Sure enough, the next lightning flash revealed a thick loop populated by straps and handholds at regular intervals. It hung out of the cloud generated by Cloud Nine, and rapidly grew longer and longer until finally, with wild wind-driven to-and-fro swings it scraped ground cover beside the soaking-wet expedition.

Oddly different from the rope ladder tossed from rescue helicopters on TV, Augie noted.

"Remember we have two extras along for the ride! Over!" Irene responded to Samuel before grabbing at a set of straps and saying for those around her, "Just follow my example!"

Soon as Irene strapped herself in securely, she tugged on the conveyor belt. It lifted her just enough off the ground for the next person, in this case Scott, to strap in.

Less than two minutes later, Irene and Scott were already safely unstrapping inside Cloud Nine. And Augie was strapping himself to the rescue conveyor, last after Sherman, who he worried might have his air bags accidentally go off yet again.

The conveyor loop steadily shortened, retracted back into Cloud Nine as it lifted the last people off the ground including, again, Augie bringing up the rear.

Some fifteen to twenty feet off the ground, however, swaying in the persisting thunderstorm wind gusts like he was a kid on a swing, Augie experienced a creepy feeling he was being watched intently from very close by. And then mixed in with the cooling storm wind gusts, he could have sworn he felt a large puff of very warm, fetid air. It was accompanied by a distinctive snort he associated with a bull he'd once seen roaming a fenced-in pasture back on a small farm in Gaithersburg, Maryland.

What happened next seemed almost beyond belief to Augie, in those final moments before the conveyor loop pulled him to safety. Something sharp pierced his pants, and briefly wedged in between his butt cheeks. For which he was thankful it didn't directly tear into one of them, instead.

All Augie could think of was the Iguanodon that Magdalena mentioned, giving a thumbs up. He stared down hard after he was lifted higher, into the cloud generated by the steam-powered drone vehicle. But stare as hard as he might, he couldn't make out a creature of any size, or some tall tree that somehow could have torn a hole in his pants, let alone a large dinosaur.

Chapter 18

"So you really think you were goosed by an invisible dinosaur on your way out of there?" Irene asked Augie, the expression on her face making clear she required every last ounce of self-control to keep from busting out laughing.

"Oh, come on!" scoffed Stephen. "Augie, you can't seriously believe an Iguanodon tore into your pants to give your business end a thumbs-up! Far more likely, the swirling thunderstorm winds sent some sharp projectile such as a loose branch flying at you!"

"So what branch has a sharp-enough point that a wind gust could make it do this?!"

Augie held up his ankle-length pants, meant to help protect against mosquitos, supplementing Sherman's putrid anti-critter spray. He pointed at where whatever-it-was tore a big hole.

The away team had long since shed their drenched clothes in favor of refreshingly dry outfits. And they congregated in the navigation room of Cloud Nine.

The steam-powered drone hovered five hundred feet above rough seas to the northeast of New Britain Island's northeast peninsula during the latter stages of the thunderstorm blowing itself out.

"I still don't understand how we stay level still with that storm raging outside," Scott commented to drone navigator Samuel Longbottom seated at the control panel. "And why it makes more sense to hover smack in the middle of it, rather than tucking ourselves away on terra firma."

258 | David Taylor

Scott's remarks were succeeded by a burst of thunder so loud, it could be heard inside Cloud Nine, albeit as a muffled rumble.

"Well it's really quite fascinating, Mr. McDonald," responded Longbottom with great zest. "You see, the vertically positioned jet engine at each of our drone's four corners, in addition to several mini-jets along its perimeter, allows for ever-adjusting modulations. But were we down anywhere near the rough seas below, such near-perfect stabilization would prove next to impossible."

"But again, what about terra firma, and what about a potential lightning strike?"

"Ah yes, terra firma. Well you see, that actually would leave us more vulnerable to your feared lightning strike, as the drenching rains could easily make for an uninterrupted line of conductivity. But well skyward, we benefit from the special plastic that constitutes the hull. It's reverse-engineered from an artifact left in the place of weapons by our mysterious other-worldly benefactors. It has no conductivity whatsoever, almost seeming anti-conductivity, if you will."

"But aren't the solar panels at least partially made from conductive metals?"

"We cover them over whenever we're in range of an electrical storm."

"Cycad leaves, I'm sure you must have noticed them, Augie," was going on Stephen Feldman. "Their needle-sharp points could easily have breached your pants, maybe even while we were crouched low. But you didn't notice until later. You're probably very lucky they didn't inject you with a neurotoxin, depending on what types grow here."

"But how could one of those have torn apart his pants to that extent?" pointed Laura.

"I should think it would have become stuck in there as well, rather than just falling out," Bernie Coleman overcame his timidity to contribute to the discussion.

"So an Iguanodon thumb is the only possible explanation," sighed Stephen. "Why not a unicorn's horn, then? Or the stinger from a monster bee?"

"You might recall, Stephen," said Augie, acid dripping from his voice like venom from snake fangs, Irene mused. "There were other things besides the tear in my pants."

"You said you felt something breathe heavily on you just before your pants were poked?" recalled Laura.

"If you've ever experienced exhaust heat from the outdoor unit for an air conditioner," said Augie, "it was something like that."

"I've been experiencing 'exhaust heat' to varying extents ever since we stepped out of Cloud Nine into the cigarette boat," said Stephen.

"Accompanied by a snort like from some mad bull, loud enough to be heard above the thunder and wind-driven rain torrents out there?" Augie couldn't help bristling. "But there's more than just that," he continued before Stephen could insert another of his ever-maddening dismissals. "As I announced on the verge of our retreat, I saw what looked like a giant-sized duckbill poke out from behind near the top of the firefly-infested mango tree. And I heard two incredibly loud quacks."

"I thought I heard one of the quacks, or something similar to a quack, myself," supportively added Irene.

"Ditto," chimed in Laura.

"Something similar to a quack, exactly!" pounced Stephen on Irene's wording. "Just because it looks like a duck and quacks like a duck doesn't necessarily mean it's a dinosaur that hits golf balls out of the rough, presumably with its tail."

"Maybe we should check in Port Moresby, see if a golf store reported fitting someone twenty feet tall with a set of irons," joked Alistair.

"Yes, and while you're at it, find out if the dinosaur has a credit history," spat out Stephen. "Or maybe those quacks you heard were unusual noises made by tree trunks and fronds when the wind gusts knocked them together! And as for your giant duckbill, Mr. Matias," he added, "maybe a rain-soaked palm frond or mango leaves glistening during a flash of lightning…"

"And the way all those trees swayed like something large was prowling behind them, on both sides of the beaten-down path, accompanied by steady thuds?!" Augie asked, far from ready to let Stephen just write off the entire experience as next to nothing.

"Isn't it possible," Stephen responded more tentatively, less insistently, as he sensed Augie's simmering testiness, "that your wild imagination made you misinterpret wind-blown trees non-causally accompanied by small tremors?"

"Admittedly, I was intensely focused on reassuring myself how slight the odds of experiencing a direct lightning strike," said Sherman, chin squished into his neck as always. "So intensely focused, in fact, I was mentally unavailable to notice either the giant duckbill or the loud quacks. However, I did intuit we were being stalked by something rather large. And that my swaying motions during our retreat may well have hypnotically slowed it down just enough for us to safely make it back aboard Cloud Nine. Incidentally, I'm far from convinced if only more of you, as opposed to none of you, had followed my lead, a beneficial result would not have accrued. Namely, maybe the something rather large would have been slowed long enough for your pants, Dr. Augie Matias, sir, to have been spared such mutilating penetration by whichever part of that something's anatomy."

"I love it when he talks dirty to us," whispered Irene to Laura and Roberta, eliciting snickers.

"We could review the videos we saved from your bandana surveillance cam, Augie," suggested Harry.

"And from Laura, Sherman and Irene's head gear as well," added Harriet, patting Harry's hand gently. "Any one of the surveillance cams could have recorded what the others missed."

"She completes me," announced Harry for the umpteenth time since the quest began, gently patting Harriet's hand gently patting his other hand.

Irene would have brought up that whenever Skip objected to something she was doing, she knocked him down as easily as playing whack-a-mole at an amusement park. Then she would have said, *If he were present here, he'd probably say, "She disses me."* However, as usual Scott McDonald was in hearing range. She didn't want to feel his jealousy...or was it that she didn't want him to know or misapprehend she was already in a committed relationship? And which was it, by the way? Know, or misapprehend?

"There!" Stephen pointed at the navigation room video screen. "Rerun the last ten seconds, and freeze it at the lightning flash!"

Once Harry complied, Stephen pointed again. "You see how that palm frond is lit up by the lightning reflecting off its film of rainwater? There's your monster duckbill!"

"But the duckbill was orange, not yellow," protested Augie. "And it was poking out from behind a mango tree, not a coconut palm. And it was wider than that. But other than those multiple differences, okay, I'll concede there's a startling similarity." Augie's sarcasm came effortlessly for how ridiculous he found Stephen's effort to explain away his sighting.

"Let me share with you the turning point experience of my life," reacted Stephen. "When I was a young man, standing on the balcony of my grandparents' retirement apartment..."

"I didn't even know they had balconies back then."

"Yes," nodded Stephen, taking Irene's quip in stride. "Might have been before the invention of the wheel. But anyway, out of a starry night sky I saw what looked like a saucer-shaped object descend closer and closer, silently closer, with multi-colored lights circling its rim. When it descended even closer, though, I could hear its propeller engine, and realized it was simply a landing biplane. The difference between what I imagined, and the reality, was stunning, and has stayed with me ever since. So all I'm suggesting is that maybe, just maybe what you thought you saw, Augie, colored by wishful thinking, was far removed from what you really saw."

"And so those quacks really were only tree trunks and the like rubbing against each other." Augie suddenly found himself struggling to automatically dismiss Stephen's conjecture, as unreal as his experience was starting to feel in the comfort of Cloud Nine.

"But there is something I noticed, if you could run Augie's bandana cam video a little further ahead," interjected Magdalena to everyone's surprise. "There!" she pointed shortly after Harriet obliged her request. "If you can stop the video and rerun those last twenty seconds, mum, I'll tell you where to freeze the picture, please."

Once Harriet obliged her new request, Magdalena stepped forward and tapped on the video monitor. "You see that mango tree branch pulled back into the darkness behind it during the lightning flash?"

"Yes I do," affirmed Augie as in, This is a significant revelation. "At that great height on the tree, something had to be responsible, some creature tall enough..."

Magdalena gave a clipped nod. "If I'm honest about it," she admitted, "I'd have to say your tall creature, guv'nah, was plucking a mango, or trying to."

"Or a microburst downdraft from the storm gave the appearance of something large pulling at that branch," insisted Stephen, continuing before anyone could object, "You've got an additional problem. At no point in this video is any such creature visible, even in small part."

"Lost in the night shadows maybe," proposed Roberta, shrugging her shoulders noncommittally.

"And what about those thuds we heard to both sides of us?" asked Scott. "Like you would expect such a large creature to make as it lumbered along? And seeming in tandem with the swaying palms?"

"Which were swaying anyway from thunderstorm wind gusts," Stephen retorted. "Gusts which would have passed from tree to tree if a microburst downdraft was ripping through, giving the illusion of stalking monsters..."

"But again, Mr. Feldman," Scott said undaunted, "what about those thuds?"

"What you suggested, Ambu," responded Stephen, looking to Ambu for a supportive nod, "ground tremors from one of Papua's many volcanos."

"You've got an answer for everything, sir," bristled Irene at Stephen. "The only problem is that all you are offering is pure speculation, no better than speculation we almost came to blows with a relic dinosaur."

"What admittedly has me perplexed," finally weighed in Sherman Peabody, "is how we could ever rule that what we experienced was a ghostly apparition from the

Cretaceous spirit world, haunting this region for seventy million years."

"Why would you be at all perplexed that such an absurd idea didn't fit the facts in the first place?" Stephen asked scoffingly. "I don't understand."

"But that is precisely my point, Mr. Feldman," spoke Sherman with his chin ever-scrunched into his chin, like Mr. Feldman was a button he was addressing on his shirt, Augie mused. "Based on what we know of ghosts' difficulty interacting very significantly with the physical world, it would be absurd to postulate a dinosaur ghost capable of plucking a mango from a tree. And even if a dinosaur ghost were capable of such a feat, what would he do with a mango? He certainly couldn't eat it in any efficacious sense of which I'm aware."

"Shake it shake it shake it baby now!" everyone aboard Cloud Nine heard Beatle John Lennon's recorded voice suddenly blast from the hovering drone's intercom. Simultaneously, Eclipso Sunray Smith's enigmatically plain visage appeared on a smaller screen beside the hundred-inch video monitor screen. "Well shake it shake it shake it baby now!" repeated Lennon even more emphatically as Eclipso turned his camcorder device on Bonsai Gator. Pencil-sized Bonsai was up on his two rear legs, facing away from the camcorder and seemingly shaking his booty in time with "Twist and Shout."

"I say, people," Eclipso spoke loudly enough to be heard easily above the Beatles' famous cover of a Phil Medley/Bert Burns song. "As you can see, Bonsai Gator grows quite impatient, waiting on your decision regarding what next for your New Britain Island quest."

"I- I was just about to suggest a sort of daytime pincer movement, Mr. Eclipso Smith, sir," hesitantly spoke Bernie Coleman, raising a tentative forefinger.

"Remember that the unlimited resources I offer mean you can take all the time you need," Eclipso reminded Bernie. "In addition, Cloud Nine provides you easy access to most anywhere on Earth, unless you think our quarry hides out in some arid region such as the Sahara Desert."

"Those of us who have formerly needed to sustain our cryptozoological obsession on a shoestring budget remain forever grateful, believe me," Bernie assured Eclipso seated before his swamp-embedded conference table some twelve thousand miles away. "But I am hopeful that my proposed pincer movement might reveal the object of our search economically quickly."

"That's great news, mate!" gushed Alistair. "Might my seven iron come in handy for this 'pincer movement'?"

Bernie looked long and hard at the golf club Alistair was brandishing before he finally said, "No."

Augie was uncertain whether the cryptozoology museum curator seriously considered how Alistair's seven iron could actually be of use. Or if it took him that long to recover from his shock over the absurdity of such a bizarre suggestion.

In any event, without skipping a beat Bernie went on, "What I propose would require us breaking into two groups. During daylight hours, one group would venture through the swamplands beyond our much-noted mango tree until we reach the shoreline, or collide with the other group venturing up the shoreline through the mangroves. Tell us Magdalena, are such treks doable?"

"Assuming we're sprayed with more of Mr. Peabody's uniquely formulated stink to scare off sea snakes and the like..."

"Although we would have to move extra slowly to allow any saltwater crocodiles adequate time to flee our presence. They'll lash out if they feel cornered," warned Ambu.

"Won't we possibly also thereby scare off whatever pulled at the mango?" asked Roberta.

"I'd worry about scaring off the leprechauns as well," deadpanned Stephen.

"You might think the observation of a huge duckbill is inconsistent with the Iguanodon morphology insinuated by my two friends' observation of a 'thumbs up' claw," said Magdalena, finally inserting a point she wanted to make earlier. "That our whole enterprise here is thrown into serious question, much as you seem to suggest already, guv'nah." She glanced Stephen Feldman's way. "However, paleontologists have only unearthed what, maybe five percent of the dinosaurs from during the hundred-forty-million years they flourished? The possibility of Iguanodons that eschewed the rather dog-faced heads suggested by known fossils, in favor of duck-billed visages more in line with the Trachodon or the Hadrosaur, is a prospect more to be yawned about than scoffed at."

"So are you endorsing my pincer operation?" hopefully asked Bernie.

"Provided we heed my father's warning, and mine as well regarding additional application of the stink spray, why yes, guv'nah, of course!"

"Don't know if any of you noticed when we arrived here on the cigarette boat," said Augie. "But a saltwater croc swimming towards the mangroves suddenly did a one-eighty, turned completely around headed back out to sea like it was avoiding something."

"Maybe it was scared of the leprechauns," said Stephen.

"Sounds like a most brilliant plan indeed!" exulted Eclipso, seeming to triumphantly bite into his latest hummus-lathered thin pretzel. "Bonsai?"

Bonsai Gator approached the monitor Eclipso's end, and nodded in sync with more "Twist and Shout" playing in the background.

"You see?!" exclaimed Eclipso. "Bonsai Gator couldn't be more excited!"

"Or he's sizing up a bug before he seizes it," said Stephen, once again in service of what he regarded as a far more conventionally palatable explanation for the small reptile's behavior. Where he was concerned, Bonsai couldn't possibly have understood enough, or even the least bit of what was being discussed, to have a celebratory reaction.

"You might have a point this time," said Irene. "I always nod my head, mm-hmm, before I dig into a mint chocolate chip ice cream sundae."

"Only Bonsai Gator is usually more a hummus-and-pretzel man than a dragonfly guy, like myself," said Eclipso.

"A hummus-and-pretzel man??" Stephen repeated incredulously with a pained look on his face.

Coincidental to Stephen's remark, Bonsai Gator went from nodding his head up and down to shaking it from side to side. But Augie Matias was a realist. He suspected that had far more to do with Bonsai losing himself in the rhythm of "Twist and Shout" than disapproval of Stephen.

Chapter 19

"Even though I can never get enough self-admiration of my own truly most rugged features," quipped counselor Ali Magabu, "we really are done here. It's time we return to the shuttle pod to wait on either hearing from the captain, or the quantum wave undoing the conundrum."

"Of course, Magabu," conceded Sergeant Fred Frankly. "But still can't help wanting to protectively take my cardboard double back aboard the pod, I mean our pod that hasn't gone feather-light cardboard."

"If I understand this quantum wave slash alternate universe stuff correctly," said Officer Kevin Smith-Park, "we need to leave our completed-time selves alone. Otherwise, they won't be here to spirit those storage containers full of armaments off the planet when the quantum wave reanimates this bit of history."

Kevin made a sweeping arm motion, from inside his envirosuit that protected him from fatally inhaling completed-time air with its taffy-like consistency. He was directing towards a long row of linked storage containers the away team had carried out of an enormous warehouse north of Yaoundé, Cameroon. "More importantly where our future viability is concerned," he went on, "Buddy Leung warned me of humongous trouble, were we to store away our past-time Styrofoam mannequin selves aboard our shuttle. They, I mean we, would not return to the Smoke and Mirrors in the past to have been able to come here in the future to edit the past. And that could mean a small chance we cease to exist altogether."

"Cripes, Smith-Park," growled Fred, "I think my brain almost ceased to exist, trying to understand all that!"

The Smoke and Mirrors away team successfully plucked every last surveillance camera off the storage containers. And they buried them together two feet underneath a patch of loamy soil within walking distance of the warehouse. When the quantum wave reanimated the past version of themselves delivering the weapons-filled storage containers to deep space, said surveillance cameras would not be on board for transmitting back to the arms manufacturers. In this rewrite of history engineered by future Earthlings' time travel intervention, the mystery would remain a mystery as to where the supplies disappeared for both sides of certain civil wars.

"I would prefer to wait on our departure for just a few minutes longer, gentlemen," said Ali Magabu to Kevin and Fred, back aboard the shuttle pod tucked away behind a grove of hardwood evergreens. "Realistically, though, we should expect those familiar quantum wave tingles any minute now. Kevin, I doubt the warehouse guards will think to hurl at our shuttle pod the golf clubs we left in their hands in place of their machine guns. Or that they will try launching golf balls at us. But we know the chances are good that when our younger selves are reanimated, our spirits will favor their bodies over ours, and we will soon fall into a trancelike state."

"I know where you're going with this, Counselor," said Kevin, already playing his fingers across the shuttle pod control console. "Best I program the autopilot now, rather than wait until we're air-born. Hey, just occurs to me that our twins out there are going to reanimate to a situation where the guards haven't been reanimated yet."

"You're right, Kevin," agreed Ali, thunderstruck. "We're dealing with a quantum wave inside a quantum wave, perhaps."

"You keep talking like that, and my brain might go into a 'trancelike state' before the quantum wave ever catches up to us!" complained Fred. "So quit your yappin' and get to work on that autopilot thingie, Smith-Park."

"Halfway there, Sergeant," Kevin assured Fred. "But I also wonder what it means that we haven't already woken up to a new reality aboard the Smoke and Mirrors, where what we're doing now precludes our having had to show up here in the first place."

"Only we did have to, Kevin," said Ali. "Those surveillance cams weren't going to remove themselves. No, I'm guessing conundrum physics still applies."

"Wait, Magabu," interrupted Kevin. "Before you blow Fred's mind any further, how's this sound? We program for seeking a large-enough sand dune in the Sahara Desert to burrow ourselves deep down while we await deliverance?"

"Better take off now, and finish that once we're air-born, Kevin," Ali answered worriedly. He felt tingles coming on, all too familiar from previous encounters with the quantum wave rolling back in like the tide.

"Oh, shit," were Kevin's last words before he slipped away. He did get the shuttle pod into liftoff mode, and alerted its artificial intelligence system to choose a safe place to hide away upon re-landing.

But Kevin didn't remain conscious long enough to program the Sahara part.

Location was left up for grabs.

Nevertheless, the teardrop-shaped shuttle pod, suitable for travel through both air and outer space, lifted skyward out from behind a thick grove of hardwood evergreens. As quietly as a leaf carried on an updraft, Ali might have imagined had he remained conscious.

The reanimated Cameroon warehouse guards reflexively aimed what had been their machine guns at the departing shuttle pod, glinting from late-day sun as though a behemoth pearl. Only then did they realize they were left holding various golf clubs. A split second before they reanimated, the earlier Ali, Fred, and Kevin had absconded in a flash with a civil-war's-worth of armaments.

*

Vicky Copplestone-Matias entered Diane Mueller's office expecting to be fired. She'd still walk away with the small fortune Eclipso allotted her and Augie, simply for Augie's participation in a dinosaur search. And she didn't face anything close to the possible dangers for her husband over in Papua, New Guinea. But no matter; she couldn't help the butterflies in her stomach.

The way Diane moved papers about her desk, not immediately acknowledging Vicky's presence, had a strangely calming effect. Vicky wondered whether the curriculum adviser was really that oblivious, or simply pretending total focus on her work as in: If Vicky had been focused enough on *her* work, she wouldn't have conducted such an outrageously out-of-control class as Diane witnessed, complete with a disrupted lunch schedule.

"You did want to see me at four?" Vicky finally asked.

Diane dropped the papers on her desk, and leaned her head into the palm of her hand to look up at Vicky with a what-are-we-going-to-do-with-you? look. Pursuant to which she directed her chagrinned expression towards the chair facing her desk as in: Take a seat.

Vicky couldn't help herself. "Say what you have to say," she cut loose before she finished sitting down. "I offer no apologies for what you observed. Kids who previously showed zero interest in geography could not have been studying the world globe more intently. I even overheard Sally discussing with Greg the difference between latitude and longitude. And before dismissal, we hammered out details for a debate on Friday over whether non-avian dinosaurs could have survived to the present day. Juvenile readers on cryptozoology, skeptical responses to cryptozoology, and travelogues about Papua, New Guinea...I might as well have been offering their choice of candy bars."

"Were those books on the approved list?"

"To my knowledge, none of them have been put through that process. But again, they were written for young people, and I skimmed them to make certain they didn't contain any inappropriate content."

"Oh, well, if you've checked that those readers are okay, what need do we have for some silly professional book review committee with their silly well-vetted standards?"

Sounds like something you've been rehearsing for just the right moment to spring on me, Vicky stifled herself from reacting. "If parents want to complain about something I am encouraging their children to read, fine," she said instead. "I'll happily suspend that part of my game plan for careful, open vetting of their concerns. Or the committee can speed up their reviews so teachers aren't left waiting until after the teachable moment has passed, and various time-sensitive lessons have to be abandoned. It's not like I'm painting the classroom using unregulated paint that might or might not contain hazardous lead."

"No, but you and your husband are encouraging children to seriously wonder whether dinosaurs are actually extinct. Some anti-evolution fruit-loop feeds on that, and the next thing you know, your students are also wondering whether the Earth is only six thousand years old. Isn't that hazardous to their mental health? Oh, but no worries; you'll just moderate a debate on the age of the Earth."

"One of those things is not like the other," Vicky insistently shook her head. "The Earth's four-and-half-billion-year-old age is well beyond debate, supported by literally a mountain of evidence. Evolution is a well-supported theory some of my students have been learning about as part of the fallout from following my husband's research, incidentally. In his quiet voice, Jonathan can explain how the discovery of living non-avian dinosaurs would do nothing to challenge evolutionary theory's more basic tenants. In case you didn't know, it's already baked in that more-ancient life forms such as fish can easily continue to survive while new life forms mutate and evolve into being. Believe me, if any of my kids became infatuated with creationist stuff, I'd have my husband nip that in the bud. He'd carefully walk them through how anti-science people exploit controversies about details within evolutionary theory to push seriously flawed arguments."

"You've been warned repeatedly about not burning off class time having your students follow your husband's 'research,'" reacted Diane Mueller.

Vicky strongly suspected Diane gave up trying to grasp what she was explaining, that she skipped over that to grind her ax instead.

"You mean, I've been warned repeatedly about making science and geography too interesting?"

"Can you tell me the reading level of each of your students? That information should be at your fingertips!"

"So what's more important: Inspiring children to read, or measuring their progress learning how to read? If you have to choose one, which is it?"

"You don't have to choose, Vicky. You can do both," Diane responded in her I'm-being-the-reasonable-one-here voice. "You can measure their progress while you're inspiring them."

"Really? Okay," Vicky extracted a reading curriculum ring-binder from her colorfully imprinted cloth bag bulging with lesson plans and student work that she lugged everywhere. She didn't normally lug the curriculum binders anywhere. But for this particular meeting, she anticipated Mueller's reading level question. "Let's look at one of these readings that should both excite our fifth graders and allow us to measure how well they're doing."

Diane couldn't help herself; a silly, twisted grin crossed her face as Vicky turned to a page middle of the ring-binder. *What does she think she's going to prove?*

"Ah, here we go: Hurricanes," announced Vicky. "Should be compelling, especially after that scare we had with Harvey last fall."

Diane nodded, grinning sillier than ever.

What Vicky read aloud detailed how hurricane winds intensify, the dangers from storm surge flooding, and how to stay safe when a hurricane threatens.

"Sounds interesting enough to me," commented Diane. "I for one was not clear before on why hurricanes weaken as they move north."

Seriously? Vicky stifled herself from reacting. "You might not have been clear on that," she went on instead. "But my resident weather hound Becky could have told you all about that, and more, before she ever read this. In fact, after I did the assessment months ago," back before the windfall from Eclipso virtually guaranteed Vicky didn't need the job, "she made a point of confiding in me afterwards. 'Ms. Copplestone, I like studying hurricanes, but that was the most boring thing about them I've ever read.'"

"Becky is special."

"They're all special," Vicky bristled. "But I found her comment particularly damning given her interest in meteorology. Anyway, I subsequently made a point of asking other students what they thought of the article. Jonathan's remark haunts me to this day. Word for word he said, shrugging his shoulders like this," Vicky demonstrated, "'It was something we had to read so we could answer questions about it. It was just a test.' 'Just a test,'" Vicky repeated. "Jonathan sensed that this reading was prepared more for the extrinsic value of asking multiple choice questions about it, and less for the intrinsic value of the content. For example," Vicky quoted anew, "'What is storm surge?' And here is the God's truth. Becky approached me a second time, much later on, to say, 'Ms. Copplestone, I know you can't discuss the test. But there was a question about storm surge where I am sure the test preparer wanted the right answer to be: 'Water that gets blown ashore.' But that is not exactly correct. Storm surge does involve wind, and it does move ashore. But it's actually a mound of water caused by a hurricane's unusually low pressure.' So I ask myself: If the people who prepared this assessment didn't care enough to make sure they were imparting precise information, what did they care about? Were they more interested in measuring student progress than in methods for promoting that progress?"

"And you took all of that away from one little part of one little assessment," Diane said dismissively. "So tell me, if we don't do any standardized assessments, how are we going to know what progress our boys and girls are making? I'm sure some of them cry when they're given vaccinations; are we going to stop giving them flu shots as well?"

"Again, one thing is not like the other. Vaccinations clearly, unquestionably protect us from disease. Without them, lots more people would become seriously ill. Understanding where my students are with their reading, however, is an altogether different matter. Far as I'm concerned, not knowing their assessed reading level, whether it's g, h, i, j, or k, would be like not knowing their horoscope, whether they're Pisces, Aries, Capricorn or whatever."

"Wait," Diane spasmed, "you're equating reading levels with astrological signs? You seriously put them in the same category?"

"I seriously put them in the exact same category," replied Vicky unflinchingly. "Are you familiar with the observer's dilemma in scientific research?"

"I'm too busy dealing with the dilemma you've created in this school."

"The observer's dilemma," said Vicky, undaunted by Diane's response, "is the difficulty collecting research data without yourself becoming a variable impacting the results. Astrological readings tell someone they have certain tendencies because of when they were born. That will often lead superstitious people to focus on those aspects of their personality, ignoring perhaps other more prominent aspects. Thereby are they falsely led to believe they've actually learned something. But at least the process can be quite entertaining.

"Reading level standardized assessments, however, I believe can prove quite damaging. The extent to which students find them a stressful chore- And don't try to deny that. You know as well as I do we've had children break down and cry in the middle of them, tremble visibly. I know of one girl who actually wet herself."

"Enough," declared Diane, leaning forward in her chair. "If that's how you feel about professional education, you never should have entered it in the first place. I'll have to discuss your unrepentant insubordination with Klondike, to do everything within our power to have you barred from ever entering a classroom, ever again!"

Vicky leaned forward in her chair also, set before Diane's desk, to say, "Bite me!"

"Grrr!" Diane couldn't help snarling in response, instantly regretting her lack of self-control.

"Grrr?" Vicky repeated quizzically, amused as she stood to leave. *Are you Dianosaurus Muehlex? Maybe Augie ought to have been conducting his dinosaur search here,* she stifled herself from remarking on her exit.

*

Thud! Scrrrratch! Thud! BAM! Splash!

It was the BAM! that finally roused Ali Magabu and company from their quantum wave slumber. Prior to that especially loud noise shaking the shuttle pod, it smoothly uneventfully landed and burrowed itself into a randomly selected location. Kevin didn't remain awake long enough to finish programming the autopilot to bring them down into a Sahara Desert sand dune.

"What the fried fish was that?!" asked Sergeant Fred Frankly, unbuckling himself to more easily, if apprehensively, scan the ceiling of the shuttle pod's cockpit window.

"I'm afraid the quantum wave caught up with us before I could finish programming the shuttle pod for seclusion deep inside a Sahara Desert sand dune," said Kevin, still shaking off the post-quantum-wave daze.

"Well that muddy water out there, for sure doesn't look like any friggin' sand dune I know! So where did that noise come from that shook me awake?"

"I'm checking." Kevin Smith-Park was already working the control console for their location.

A broad smile lit up Ali's face after he looked over Kevin's shoulder at the result.

"What?! What?!" Fred couldn't help his impatience, noticing Ali's delight. "Please tell me we landed at some water park in Disneyworld!"

"Not quite, Sergeant; we're embedded in a tributary of the Ngoko River in southeast Cameroon, close to the border with the Congo Republic," practically gushed Ali Magabu.

Kevin craned his head around to look up at Ali looking down over his shoulder. "What is this about, Ali?" he asked. "Why the shit-eating grin?"

"When I was a little boy in Nigeria, my grandparents told me about a strange creature reported to dwell in swamps of the Congo and the Cameroons, named mokele-mbembe. The story goes that it had an elephant's torso, but with a snake's long neck and a crocodile's long tail."

"A freakin' dinosaur, in other words," summed up Fred.

"I always wondered ever since, truly," nodded Ali. "And so here we are in Cameroon back country, woken up by some unknown force rocking our shuttle pod in a muddy tributary."

"Yeah, some damn elephant bumped into us on its way to wherever," grumped Fred.

"I know that's the more likely scenario," sighed Ali resignedly.

"So what about us?" asked Fred. "Why did we wake up stuck here rather than back aboard the Smoke and Mirrors?"

"We know strange things often happen whenever we've put ourselves the middle of a space-time conundrum," recalled Kevin. "I'm guessing the quantum wave has revisited where the surveillance cameras are no longer attached to the storage containers full of weapons. But it hasn't yet gotten around to revisiting when we time-travelled here to pluck the cameras off the containers."

"Perhaps Captain Taylor and company's memory has altered so they don't remember we came here to remove those cameras in the first place," added Ali, picking up the thread of Kevin's guessing.

"So they might be wondering why we've disappeared off the ship, and presently have no idea where we are," concluded Kevin.

"That I actually understood what you two were battin' back and forth like a freakin' ping pong ball might indicate my need for a tight-fitting straitjacket!"

EEEEEEK!!!! This odd noise suddenly permeated the shuttle pod cockpit.

"Whatever's straining the hull that much seems to come from overhead. Damn!" swore Kevin.

"An elephant pretending the shuttle pod is its inflatable pool raft?" suggested Fred.

"The biggest elephant in the world doesn't weigh nearly enough to create that much hull stress," said Kevin.

The dense peat suspended in the deep swamp water outside the cockpit window stopped swirling just long enough for Ali to catch a glimpse of...What would a tree trunk be doing out in the middle of a tributary? Or is it something's monstrous leg?

Whatever it was sent the shuttle pod rocking so abruptly, nearly threw Fred off his feet. "What the fried fish?!" he complained anew as the pod kept rocking from side to side, rhythmically.

"What, Ali, is your mokele-whatever treating us like an egg it's trying to hatch?!" said Kevin in a complaining voice like Ali could have done anything about it.

"Feels to me like we're not to the egg stage yet!" shouted Fred as he strained not to be thrown off balance by the increasingly violent rocking. "Feels more like that f-n' monster is tryin' to get it on with our shuttle pod!"

Chapter 20

"Excuse my saying, Stephen," said Irene, rushing ahead to get in his face. "But you look more distracted than usual, more like I'm used to seeing Sherman Peabody. Your khakis aren't about to inflate to the size of a Thanksgiving Day Parade float, are they?"

"Please. That might actually be an improvement. No, I was thinking about a bizarre nightmare I had this morning."

"Do tell."

"There was this small green gecko, more or less the size of Bonsai Gator. He stood erect on his hind legs, also like Bonsai."

"Huh."

"But he spoke with a strong British accent, trying to sell me car insurance."

"Car insurance? Well, Bonsai Gator must have inspired that. Or your brain tapped into an alternate universe where lots of weapons didn't mysteriously disappear all over."

"So without those weapons, we are not only spared various wars? We're also spared insurance ads featuring a gecko that spoke with an English accent?"

"Sh!" fiercely whispered Magdalena, Ambu's daughter leading the trudge across swampland. She was headed for where Augie Matias thought he saw a giant duckbill poke out from behind a mango tree the previous evening.

Stephen, Scott, Iris and Laura followed after "Maggie" while Alistair, Augie, Roberta and Sherman joined Ambu on the cigarette boat operated by Samuel Longbottom. The Longbottom contingent would be coming ashore amidst mangroves for the other part of Sherman's suggested pincer movement. Bernie remained aboard Cloud Nine with Harriet and Harry Letterman, however.

"The noises produced by our hike across this swampland should be impossible for our quarry to differentiate from the minor racket made by a saltwater crocodile or gang of wild pigs," went on Maggie less fiercely. "But your- There we go, mum, at ten o'clock if straight forward is noon!" she shouted abruptly, so much for the advice she was about to impart about speaking more quietly. She pointed left of the beaten-down trail through the swamp, at a coconut palm Scott guesstimated stood some two-hundred-fifty yards away.

Swirling morning mists of trans-evaporation variably blurred the tree...and what stood beside it. "I say, guv'nah," Maggie pointed excitedly, "is that our dinosaur?! Never seen anything before quite like it!"

"I'm taking out my binoculars," declared Laura, hurriedly fumbling through her backpack.

Scott McDonald stood transfixed, his heart beating a mile a minute. Whatever that figure was, it stood very tall indeed beside the coconut palm, and even jumped a couple times. Was it trying to snatch off a coconut? Scott wondered. Whatever it was doing, the sound of snapping jaws carried easily across the intervening distance. Scott also noted that the tip of its long tail was lost hidden amidst tall swamp grass. And the ridging along its back suggested something unmistakably reptilian. And, far more than anything else, a single detail suggested to Scott he might very well actually be enjoying his first, if admittedly hazy look at a living, breathing, non-avian dinosaur. During one preciously brief moment, the steamy, swirling mists cleared enough to make it out most distinctly, flush against the trunk of the coconut palm: the creature's left-most claw on its right forepaw in a thumbs-up position! Exactly like the comparably positioned claw on an Iguanodon skeleton! "You see that against the tree trunk, Irene?!" he turned around to exclaim.

Before Iris could confirm or deny she noticed what Scott noticed, Laura burst out, "Take a look, Maggie! Is that what I think it is?"

"I don't know what you think it is, mum," responded Maggie after she availed herself of Laura's binoculars. "Must admit having been a wee bit too carried away, meself. But now I see it is definitely a saltwater crocodile. What I want to know is why anyone would have gone to the dangerous trouble of stringing up that plucked chicken there!"

"Say what?!" exploded Scott snatching Laura's binoculars from Magdalena.

Scott's shoulders slumped dramatically after he focused on the magnified view of the crocodile. He couldn't quite make out the object that large reptile was going after, but could easily believe it was indeed a plucked chicken.

The chicken hung from string not at all visible past the swirling mists. However, the saltwater crocodile's snapping made it swing from side to side in a manner that could only mean...

"It's like that plane I imagined was a spectacular flying saucer, yes?" Stephen asked in his deep voice that this time conveyed profound empathy for Scott's crestfallen disillusionment. Before Scott could nevertheless defiantly respond, *Doesn't mean a dinosaur isn't out there!* Stephen turned Maggie's direction to ask, "Maybe this is what your eyewitnesses saw?"

On the loudest SNAP of all, the chicken disappeared, as witnessed by Scott still hogging Laura's binoculars, and the crocodile dropped down out of sight into the swamp grass. To Scott's further dejection, he realized that what he imagined was a thumbs-up from the hoped-for Iguanodon must actually have been one of the crocodile's fore-claws splayed against the palm-tree trunk.

"Don't think so, guv'nah," Maggie shook her head "no" to Stephen. "What my eyewitnesses saw was beside the mango tree, and they weren't standing all that much further away from it than we are."

"Did they see any raw meat hung from the tree? Or were they too freaked out to notice, letting their imaginations run wild like I'm afraid you were doing?"

Maggie's brows furrowed in clear bother over Stephen's suggestion. "Whatever they imagined, guv'nah," she said, "they definitely would have noticed meat going to waste, and made far more of that than of some prehistoric monster. What I want to know is who in their right mind would have made the dangerous trek over to that coconut palm to string up a chicken? Like there aren't enough snakes and fish out there already for any saltwater crocodile to enjoy a belly full?"

"Would someone in your village be doing that to create a sensation, attract more tourists perhaps?" wondered Laura.

"Nobody I know, mum," said Maggie. "Should we stick with the original pincer movement plan, and keep heading for the coast?"

"Maybe we can corner a snake," said Stephen drily.

"Yes, we should make as much racket as possible now, to keep the crocodiles away," said Maggie. "Where our safety is concerned, doesn't help that someone might be baiting crocodiles out here with plucked chickens."

"At least we have Sherman's fresh spray of eau de PU working hard to scare off anything and anyone with a sense of smell," said Irene. "If your nightmare gecko with the British accent were here, Stephen, he'd be holding his nose."

*

"There!" pointed Sherman, expressing uncharacteristic excitement in the cigarette boat carrying him, Alistair, Ambu, Augie, Roberta and navigator Samuel Longbottom towards a stretch of shoreline punctuated by mangroves. "What is that?!"

Something was definitely either floating or standing amidst the gentle aquamarine wavelets a good three hundred yards offshore.

"Whatever it is," said Ambu, "there are no reefs in that particular location!" He had to shout to be heard above the cigarette boat's electric outboard motor, excited or not.

"It's rounded, olive green, and I can't tell whether or not it's really moving!" After making these observations, Roberta Quiñones suddenly lowered her binoculars and turned to her companions. "Maybe it was only a trick of light. But could swear I glimpsed an orange stripe underwater."

Augie's mouth dropped open. What immediately came to mind were the splotchy orange stripes on Gila monsters, the thin green stripes on garter snakes...reptilian. And whatever was in the water, if it wasn't standing, wouldn't it have to be swimming?"

Okay, maybe it's a dog-paddling Iguanodon!

"I still can't tell whether it's moving or not!" noted Ambu. "Dare we approach closer before heading ashore?!"

"Wo!" Chin uncharacteristically lifted off his neck, Sherman Peabody suddenly leaned backward. "Was it just me, or did that thing rise and sink?!"

"Hard to know for sure with anything rougher than glassy smooth sea, I should rather think, sir!" responded Ambu.

"Well then maybe to stay safe," said Sherman with his chin curled back down into the comfort of his neck, "we ought to maintain our course headed for shore. There, I will deploy my petite helicopter camera drone to lend us a more intimate view!"

Oo, you're making me blush! Augie could imagine Irene snarking.

"Curiouser and curiouser," said Ambu on a narrow stretch of coral sand beach in between two mangrove clusters, while Sherman readied his camera-bearing drone.

"Too bad the thundershowers last night muddied their original shapes, but I find them very tantalizing all the same," remarked Roberta about two sets of tracks noticed immediately upon disembarkation from the cigarette boat. Both sets crossed the beach, and melted into the surf gently lapping at the shore. But one set came from in amidst long, thick grasses up along the shoreline, while the other set suddenly started mid-beach. Maybe the previous night's storm washed away the second set's lead-up tracks altogether, Augie speculated.

"And we're off!" announced Sherman.

Sherman's drone whirred high over the ocean into the bright morning sky, headed for whatever barely broke surface some couple hundred yards away.

Augie's distinct impression was that rather than self-generated, the olive-colored, orange striped thing's movement resulted from the surf's ebb and flow.

Sherman directed the drone with a hand-held device that reminded Augie of a video game joystick. Also, he glanced frequently at his laptop computer screen, to monitor whatever the drone camera revealed.

Sherman had mounted the laptop itself on a tray table unfolded from his backpack. An attached umbrella provided the shade necessary to prevent sun glare from obscuring the screen.

"Can't say for sure," said Roberta down on her knees to examine the tracks. "But both sets of tracks appear to present with something three-toed, far larger than an ostrich. And other than a dinosaur or some oversized lizard that dwarfs the Komodo dragon, I don't know what else it could be. But it's a big question why the tracks weren't washed away altogether."

"If the storm pushed the surf this far up the beach," offered Ambu, "a strong, narrow rip current could have completely erased some tracks, while sparing others."

"Okay!" shouted Sherman. "We're hovering directly over the mystery object! I'm going to slowly lower the drone to achieve a closer-in view!"

Ambu, Augie and Roberta crowded round Sherman's laptop computer screen, and Augie had an experience parallel to Scott's journey from thrill to disappointment.

The drone's overhead view, down into the crystal clear aquamarine waters, revealed two hefty legs supporting whatever superstructure bobbed on the surface. Augie also discerned the orange stripe Roberta glimpsed from the cigarette boat. The absence of a tail didn't yet register with him, so Augie found himself seriously contemplating the possibility a large dinosaur died there, maybe even the one that tore a hole in his pants the night before. Its corpse was left standing, rocked gently by the surf. Lightning wouldn't have had to strike directly to electrocute the creature while it took a swim. Water can conduct a charge from several yards away, easily.

The drone's closer-in surveillance rapidly, crushingly disabused Augie of any such fantastical notions. Not only did the lack of a tail become glaringly apparent, so too did the real nature of what Augie and company had been wondering over. Yes, the lower part clearly modeled powerfully thick legs that ended in the signature three-toed claws of either a bird or, at this size, a dinosaur. But the olive-shaded, orange-striped upper thighs left off in a gaggle of gears as of a grandfather clock's interior.

The entire unit comprised a robotic contraption.

"Goodness, someone has gone to an impressive amount of trouble to fabricate dinosaur tracks in the middle of a thunderstorm," marveled Ambu, shaking his head at what Sherman's laptop screen revealed from the surveillance drone. "All that, only to leave this mechanical monstrosity abandoned in the sea like a shipwreck!"

"And it wasn't just about the foot tracks," said Roberta. "They counted on us, or whoever else they were set on fooling, to glimpse that orange stripe. Although I'm guessing we were supposed to spot it through dense underbrush rather than out here, in open sea where it's clear there isn't a complete dinosaur."

"So what was that monster duckbill I saw poking out from the mango tree? Accompanied by a loud quack that Irene also heard?" asked Augie defiantly unwilling, yet, to relegate his unique experience to the annals of so-what hallucinations. "Was there a separate device for that?"

"You wouldn't think so," responded Sherman. "But it doesn't look like any upper torso superstructure broke off. Rather, all those gears appear meant to have been left unconcealed."

"See those dark things extending out from it, undulating in the water like seaweed?" Ambu asked.

"That mysterious light we saw early last night!" exclaimed Augie snapping his fingers. "Could that have been a small biplane or copter lowering the foot-track maker to the beach by a cord attached to those straps? But the storm caused the straps to unbuckle? Or they were disconnected from the cord because the storm swung the foot-track maker about too wildly? The biplane or copter would have crashed?"

Sudden underbrush commotion from where the beach ended in dense tropical rainforest drew everyone's attention away from Augie's question. Hearts raced on the possibility that despite discovery of a robotic foot-track maker, a large dinosaur might come storming out into the open, after all.

But only Ambu's daughter, Magdalena, emerged, proudly triumphant after one last branch-clearing, whooshing swing of her machete.

"Oh," ohhed Ambu with relief.

"Oh?" repeated Stephen quizzically as he followed Maggie out onto the beach. "So who were you expecting? Your thumbs-up Iguanodon? Because we just learned that some things are not what they seem. Far from it, in fact!"

Maggie and company shared their encounter with the saltwater crocodile, how it resolved into that identity after first being misapprehended as the prehistoric object of their pursuit. Then Ambu and his company related their similar adventure with the water-logged track-maker outfitted to give the appearance, when not inspected too closely, of some powerfully hind-legged bipedal dinosaur's lower torso, minus the tail.

"Well I think we can all agree," concluded Stephen Feldman, "that someone or some group has gone to great lengths to try tricking us into believing a dinosaur haunts this coastal area."

"But how would they have known we were going to be out here for tricking?" asked Irene. "It wasn't like Eclipso announced his intent to the whole world."

Everyone exchanged glancing, suspicion-laden looks while Stephen speculated, "Maybe whoever they were didn't need to know. Maybe they're members of your village, Ambu, who lie in wait to spring their hoax on any foreign visitors. They want to spread the word that there might be something fantastic awaiting discovery here, thereby increasing tourism. Such a tactic has worked for Loch Ness."

Augie might have squinted even without the glaring sunlight as he asked, "So what poked my pants last night while Cloud Nine was lifting me away? I had to have been close to twenty feet off the ground, but that robotic contraption out there in the surf can't be more than ten feet tall!"

"The sharp end of a broken-off branch sent flying at you by a gust of thunderstorm wind...Okay," Stephen read Augie's you've-got-to-be-kidding-me look, "that would have stuck in your pants, you think."

"I sensed an enormous presence behind me, and even felt a warm, powerful exhalation!"

"A different robot than that thing out there, then!" zestfully offered Stephen. "Tall enough to poke you plus blow warm air on you as well!"

"I can't say I have been aware of any fellow villagers tinkering with robotics out here, so far away from Port Moresby," Ambu pointedly remarked. "Or who would have even possessed the resources to indulge such a bizarre hobby, for that matter."

"And your monster robot built for breathing down someone's neck while it gooses him," scoffed Augie, "why couldn't I see any of it?"

"You mean in a torrential thundershower? And a dinosaur could have hidden more easily?" asked Stephen, sounding increasingly flustered and testy.

"A chameleon-type dinosaur could have camouflaged itself!"

"Well here's something unexplained we can all look at and measure," declared Laura, bent over with hands on knees. "The foot-tracks that emerge from the jungle swamp are twice as large as this set that starts and ends suddenly, mid-beach. Which set was produced by that contraption offshore? And what produced the other set? And anyway, that looks like a pretty expensive piece of machinery. Who would have left it to collect rust out there?"

"Maybe the same machine produced both sets of tracks," Stephen speculated, his testiness turning defiant. "With a closer look, we might find the foot-track size is adjustable. The hoaxers might have wanted it to seem a mother accompanied her baby. As for that thing being left out there," Stephen plowed forward before anyone else could get a word in, edgewise, "maybe it snapped off from the aircraft, and the storm became too violent to retrieve It."

"But the weather's fine at the moment," Augie observed. "Why don't we see anyone out here right now on a salvage mission?"

"And give themselves away to us? Oh, I get it," Stephen nodded knowingly. "You think they were scared off by a real prehistoric monster. They cut loose their contraption and ran, basically."

"Your words, not mine," Augie found the chutzpah to say while Laura noticed something that sent a chill down her spine despite the intensifying mid-morning tropical heat.

Back behind where the larger tracks appeared to have emerged from coastal jungle swamp, Laura saw a succession of palms looked pushed aside, with a few tops bent over and their coconuts all missing. Suppose the waterlogged foot tracker was set down inside the swamp, to come bursting out onto the beach leaving phony three-toed dinosaur tracks. Still wasn't tall enough to reach that far off the ground for such impacts.

"A hoaxed dinosaur and a real dinosaur are not mutually exclusive possibilities," asserted Sherman into his neck, leaving Laura to wonder whether he noticed what she noticed. "Why not both?"

"But the odds against such a coincidence must certainly be astronomically large," protested Stephen. "No, Occam's Razor suggests we must defer to the simplest, most elegant-"

"But there's nothing simple or elegant about those two sets of-"

"Quiet, people!" shouted Irene, hand to ear as she succeeded in shushing Scott McDonald. "I'm receiving a message from- Yes, Harriet, I'm listening...uh-huh...Oh...uh-huh...I'll tell them...Yes, I'm sure there will be a lot of discussion...Okay, thanks, see you soon." Irene dropped hand from earpiece to look around and say, "Eclipso reports the mystery weapons thieves have struck again, removing truck-loads of war-making equipment from Cameroon. A truce has already gone into effect across Central Africa. All sides have united with the common goal of finally locating whoever's been doing this for the past seventy years, rots of ruck. Either that, or building a bunch of golf courses."

"Oh?!" Alistair Frump suddenly sprang to life, after having so quietly tagged along with Ambu's seaside gang.

"Besides the usual assortment of solar panels and farming equipment, some Cameroon warehouse guards found themselves suddenly holding golf clubs in place of machine guns. Anyway, our pretzel-eating benefactor said that if political and social unrest was what kept us from initiating his dino-quest in Africa, he'd think no worse of us if we dropped everything here to head there like right now. I know African dinosaurs are your specialty, Mr. McDonald, so what's your first thought?"

Scott flinched at Iris's pointedly formal reference to him as Mr. McDonald. On second thought, though, he had to wonder whether the awkwardness spoke to her wrestling with feelings towards him other than wanting to strangle him at the first convenient opportunity for his involvement with a Bible museum. He could dream, couldn't he? Anyway, he responded, "I suppose we could hide out here, lie in secluded wait a couple more days to see who or what shows up: Mr. Thumbs-up Iguanodon, the hoaxers, or even both as you suggested, Sherman. But suppose there was a dinosaur lurking here that poked you, Augie, then headed off shore. No telling that it was not simply passing through, not to be seen in these parts again for months or years. Whereas over in the Cameroons, the info I gathered implied a more regularly present creature. So let's say we narrow down new mokele mbembe sightings to a particular swamp or section of river. In our numbers and with our resources I should think we would have a far easier time boxing it in to see exactly what we've got."

Chapter 21

"Oh, gee, Rachel, what happened?" asked Vicky, heart unable to help leaping out to her student.

Rachel hopped tearfully on one leg into the main office headed for the nurse, arm round other student Simona. She might have been in fifth grade, a big girl of twelve, but her fearful grief made her every bit as pitiable for Vicky as a five-year-old kindergartner.

"It's okay, Ms. Copplestone," Simona assured her. "Just a playground scrape, not from a velociraptor taking a bite out of her."

Rachel laughed through her tears at that remark while principal Marsha Klondike burst from the conference room saying, "Ms. Copplestone, you're five minutes late! Ms. Boland," to the secretary, "please keep it quiet out here, thank you!"

As Vicky entered the conference room, Sally Boland heard her explain to Klondike that she had to wait with her students on an art class running well overtime.

Klondike ushering her to sit one side of the conference table, Vicky wondered whether she shouldn't have lugged her entire backpack there rather than just one of her to-do folders. That way, she could have left straight for home after the inquisition, as she saw it.

Vicky imagined a long-term substitute teacher already reconnoitering her classroom.

In any event, the principal took her seat the opposite side from where she'd directed Vicky. Curriculum specialist Diane Mueller and counselor Steve Stickleback sat on her left. And flanking her right were fifth grade team leader Lisa Smith, plus a red-faced fellow Vicky didn't recognize. But from his gray pin-striped suit and paperwork set before him, she figured he was legal counsel. She also figured his paperwork had to do with ending her professional teaching career.

Marsha Klondike gave Vicky a teary-eyed look that conveyed how little stomach she had for what she felt compelled to do. Vicky also sensed her feeling betrayed as she said, "We'll start with introductions for our guest." She nodded towards the red-faced guy Vicky didn't recognize. "I'm Dr. Marsha Klondike, principal."

"I'm Bruce Weller, attorney for the superintendent's office," said Red-faced Guy in what Vicky found an unexpectedly squeaky, cracking voice. It oddly reminded her of the loud quack Augie reported hearing in a rainforest swamp twelve thousand miles away. She strained not to smile at the thought of the attorney sticking his head out from amidst a mango tree.

As introductions continued, counselor Steve Stickleback dutifully took notes. In Vicky's estimation, Steve was a good guy who made valiant efforts to try bridging the gap between her and her colleagues. But ultimately he needed to watch out for his own career. He lacked a mysterious benefactor to fall back on, a la Eclipso. So if Vicky was facing the executioner, figuratively speaking, he needed to watch quietly from the sidelines, merely documenting that event. Nevertheless, Vicky was certain that adults treating another adult this way went against every fiber of the man's being. Especially so over it being made to seem criminal, providing too much educationally stimulating experience for children without trying to exactingly quantify any resultant academic progress. Maybe, Vicky mused as introductions concluded, Steve pretended he was an anthropologist watching evangelical fanatics handle poisonous snakes. He knew that trying to stop it only ran the risk of getting bitten himself. Ditto, were he on her husband's dinosaur expedition, and seen an Iguanodon trying to fight off a saltwater crocodile. He would have conceded there was little they could do to protect the dinosaur without putting themselves in peril.

"Before we proceed any further," said Dr. Klondike, extra loudly to stop Vicky from psychologically distancing herself, "I want to make sure you understood something, Vicky. You were allowed to have a union rep or other form of legal counsel present."

"Well understood, Marsha, and am waiving that right."

As Klondike turned to attorney Bruce Weller, he shoved one of his papers and a pen across the conference table towards Vicky. And he squeaked, "Okay, so, this is not a document waiving your rights to legal representation at some future date. It is simply for you to affirm having refused legal counsel at this particular proceeding, if you will sign and date at the bottom."

"Of course."

"Okay, sooo," principal Klondike slapped her hands on the conference table as Vicky Copplestone pushed the signed document sliding back across to legal counsel, "can you summarize why you've been called here, Vicky?"

"We're having a significant disagreement over what is in children's best interest where their education is concerned."

Klondike inhaled deeply and exhaled slowly, trying to center herself before reacting, "If you want to join me for drinks after hours, we can dialogue on best practices all you want. But when you are at work, under county contract, there is one item from which you were specifically prohibited, months ago, ever again exposing your students. And not too many weeks ago, if I recall correctly, Diane here, acting as your mentor, advised you likewise regarding your daughter, what her teacher Stephanie reported she brought up in class."

"Yes," Vicky nodded, "my husband's research in cryptozoology. You seem to fear that allowing children to explore the possibility non-avian dinosaurs are not all extinct is equivalent to encouraging them to believe the Earth is flat, and only six thousand years old."

"You were warned never to bring that up in your class, ever again!" burst out Diane Mueller impatiently, her voice hitting shrill upper registers. "And yet, not only did you bring it up again..."

"Diane's correct," interrupted Klondike, "but there's something far worse that Lisa uncovered. Lisa?"

Fifth grade team leader Lisa Smith lifted then dropped back down on the conference table a collection of folders set before her. "Vicky," she said, "I was going through your files to recover test data for your ESOL student, Chung-yun. I noticed that for the past three weeks, you had absolutely no updated reading data, no formative assessments...It's not like what you collected previously wasn't spotty at best. But for the past three weeks, nothing. So I randomly checked five other student files, and found the same thing. Your neglect appears to have started when Mueller was assigned as your mentor."

"Yes, that's right," Vicky casually admitted while reaching down for papers and grade-book from her backpack. "I decided the time had come to drop all my admittedly lame efforts to accommodate hurtful strategies, and just go with what my experience and research made clear were more nurturing ways to work with children. In our discussions, Diane, I told you what I thought you wanted to hear, and then went my own way. For example," Vicky spread an array of papers across the conference table. She might as well have been revealing her poker hand, counselor Steve thought, while Diane gaspingly turned from Vicky to Klondike and back to Vicky. Isn't the principal going to say anything to short-circuit this outrage? "These are just some of the tests I designed personally, to see how my students are coming along. I can cite numerous studies that conclude teacher-made tests provide far more useful data on children's progress than standardized tests. You will be hard-pressed to find any studies that suggest otherwise, if you have ever checked for yourself. Standardized assessments do show, very generally, that privileged children perform better than disadvantaged children, duh, but that's about it. Anyway, the results are recorded in this old-fashioned grade-book." Vicky unceremoniously slapped her grade-book down on the conference table. "The test papers themselves are quickly returned to the students."

"Nobody is saying you shouldn't be doing all that and more, Vicky," insisted Klondike, "including placing photocopies of the results in the student cumulative folders, in addition to the more formalized assessments."

"And during what hours of the day was that going to happen?"

"Welcome to the teaching profession!" exclaimed Klondike. "There's nobody here who isn't overworked!"

"So it's that grim for you, is it?" Vicky asked, feeling an almost out-of-body detachment. "Ever hear that saying, 'If you really enjoy what you're doing, you'll never work a day in your life'?"

"Well maybe you need to search for that magical occupation that doesn't have any downside whatsoever," suggested Diane. Her mouth puckered how Vicky imagined it would have, had she just sucked on an especially tart lemon.

Counselor Steve Stickleback winced, and held up a cautioning hand Diane's direction before saying, "Vicky, I wish you would have come to me at some point with your concerns. In any large workplace, there are inevitably going to be disagreements, passionately argued by those who care enough to feel so strongly."

"Mm-hm," Vicky nodded noncommittally while thinking, *That sounded pretty well-rehearsed.*

"It's just a shame you didn't come to me about this early on, so we could have worked something out," went on Steve, "have a chance to at least defend yourself before things reached the point of no return."

"I'm not the one who should need to defend herself. You see, what really worries me is, I'm a big girl and can let this wash off me like water off a duck's back. But when you're getting on a child's case, Diane, like when you tried to get on my daughter's case about the possibility of dinosaur survival..."

"Wait!" principal Klondike held up a hand for Vicky to stop. "For your information, Vicky, none of us are the ones on the hot seat here. I'm turning it over to you, Bruce."

"Okay," squeaked attorney Bruce Weller as he lifted a paper off the table apart from the one Vicky just signed. "It's Ms. Vicky Copplestone, is it?"

"Yes."

"Okay, Ms. Copplestone, I have another paper here that does three things, really. One, it advises you that the superintendent, upon thorough review of recent events, is seeking your immediate dismissal from the county school system, plus revocation of your teacher certification. I understand, Dr. Klondike, you have already arranged for a long-term sub to pick up Ms. Copplestone's students from their arts rotation?"

"We've got Mr. Nicely ready to do his grandpa routine."

"Excellent. Okay, then, Ms. Copplestone, number two, this form also advises you of a hearing on a motion for your dismissal and decertification. A jury of your peers plus other professionals from the board of education will convene at a date and time you cannot in any way amend except under certain extreme circumstances.

"Number three, I strongly urge you to obtain the listing of your legal rights, including the right to counsel at that hearing.

"Now please initial on the line beside each item, and then sign and date at the bottom."

In her oddly detached, nearly out-of-body experience of her persecution, Vicky was oblivious to the growing commotion just outside the conference room. But by the conclusion of the attorney's third point, it had become too much for Dr. Klondike to keep ignoring. "Excuse me," she said impatiently as she rose from her armchair to approach the conference room door.

Too late; a short, plump woman in plain black dress and with her long, auburn hair in complete disarray burst in, followed by Ms. Boland the secretary muttering, "I moved too slowly to stop her."

The woman's husband brought up the rear, wearing long olive khakis and a t-shirt, and his face unshaven for days. He imploringly tearfully beseeched his wife, "Por favor, Myriam! Calmate! Calmate!"

"No!" Myriam screamed at her husband before continuing on her mission. She pointed what Vicky took to be an accusatory forefinger at her, and shouted "You!" with her 'y' sounding like a 'j.'

Oh crap, Vicky thought. Is this woman about to land me in so much trouble, even Eclipso's fortune won't save me from serious peril?

"I so sorry!" Myriam placed her non-pointing hand over her chest to apologize most tearfully. "Looks like you are busy with an important reunion. But you are my Jonathan's teacher, yes?" She nodded anxiously at Vicky.

"Jonathan Santiago, yes, of course," confirmed Vicky. Her fearful, pit-of-the-stomach dread of what horrific event could possibly have put Myriam Santiago in such miserable shape overrode any concern she had for her own circumstances...and led her to that-much-more-appalled wonder at what she caught out the corner of her eye. Diane Mueller and fifth grade team leader Lisa Smith were exchanging smirks as in: Vicky must really be in for it now! It's about time!

"My precious boy went to join his grandmother last night, from what his doctor call a brain hemorrhage!" Myriam wailed.

"Oh, no!" Marsha Klondike threw a comforting arm round Myriam's shoulders, accompanied by a gentle nudge meant to guide her out of there into Marsha's office, presumably for settling down.

But Myriam would have none of it as counselor Steve rose to his feet, figuring his services would be needed. "I want you to know," she went on, firmly standing her immovable ground, "this journal," she held forward a standard-issue composition book, "Jonathan shared with us every night what he wrote in it about your husband searching for a dinosaur!"

"We can talk about this-"

"Never I hear him read so much before!" Myriam grievingly cut off Dr. Klondike to continue. "And he write so much, too! He explained to us what he learned about the difference between latitude and longitude! He said he hoped your husband would succeed, that he want to see a living dinosaur, but is not so sure how realistic is that!" Myriam laughed through her grieving. "Anyway, I have to thank you, thank you, thank you, teacher Mrs. Copplestone, for providing my son so much joy and wonder in his final hours before Dios takes him from us!" Myriam rushed out of Marsha's grasp down over beside Vicky. Her big embrace left them sobbing into each other's shoulders. Vicky was wondering why Jonathan was absent that day, but didn't think much about it. *How horrific!*

"There must be something we can do," sputtered Diane helplessly.

"Ms. Copplestone did everything anyone could possibly do!" Myriam looked up over Vicky's shoulder to declare defiantly. "The rest is in God's hands!"

"Dr. Klondike, I know when it rains, it pours," said secretary Boland rushing back into the conference room while Myriam's husband mumbled, "I so sorry about my wife." "But it's the superintendent on the phone. Apparently Mrs. Santiago stopped by his office earlier this morning before she headed over here. He wants to make sure that the employee action form he signed off on is shredded immediately; he is revoking his approval. Also, if you have already initiated the legal process against Vicky, he wants you to issue her a formal, written apology on behalf of the entire county school system. And that's just for starters. He'll be waiting on the phone to discuss the rest once you've done that much. I'm only the messenger!" Boland added since Klondike glared at her in stunned disbelief.

Vicky made eye contact with Diane over the still urgently grieving Myriam Santiago's embracing shoulder, to silently mouth two words Diane read her lips most easily to understand. *Bite me!*

Chapter 22

"So they are going to let Maggie test for placement in upper school?" Augie asked Ambu. Dockside on the Thames close to London Bridge, he read Ambu's beaming grin to mean only good news.

"Better than that, even," Ambu sure enough responded. "Five minutes into skimming my daughter's hobby treatise, a Mr. Albert Taylor resolved to call Cambridge University. And the bottom line is, she has an interview tomorrow for admission to study organic chemistry."

"Did you say 'hobby treatise'?"

"For the past two years, Maggie has been running makeshift analyses of our local herbalists' favorite concoctions. She compared the active ingredients with those found in a very technical medical treatise I secured for her from a bookshop in Port Moresby. You see, Mr. Matias, she wants to learn enough to find a means for wooing our people off their very lethal betelnut addiction."

"Wo!" Augie didn't expect to hear anything from Ambu that would make him marvel any more than he was already marveling. How dramatically the man had shed his old gear, going from loincloth and off-brand sports t-shirts to navy-blue long pants and a gray polo shirt! But the news about his daughter...! "You'll have to tell us a lot more on our flight down to Cameroon," Augie finally reacted at greater length. "I'm sure Eclipso will be thrilled to learn he's a part of that."

"Eclipso is thrilled. And he's putting us both up at the Mercure Hotel here in London until his agent can secure a more permanent residence in Cambridge."

Augie's mouth dropped open when the import of what Ambu said sank in. "So you won't be joining our expedition to Cameroon?"

"I am slipping away from you like water cupped in your hands slipping through your fingers, faithful as always to my name," grinned Ambu. "What I have done shamelessly, not a thought given to any apology, is humor you all to get my daughter this far. Truth be told, my sympathies lie far more with your skeptic-in-residence, Mr. Feldman."

"So you don't believe any dinosaurs or other large undiscovered animals might inhabit the swamps near your village," said Augie as an observation rather than a question.

"Nothing the occasional saltwater crocodile doesn't explain. One of them scratching at an itch by rubbing against the lower part of a tree trunk can make the entire tree appear knocked about by some much larger creature. Or maybe it was the people responsible for dangling that plucked chicken to lure a crocodile up on its hind legs. Maybe they gathered round the base of that mango tree the night before, during the thunderstorm. And they used string to pull on one branch, make it look like your dinosaur was trying to pluck off a fruit."

"And somehow they also stuck out a large, paper-mache duckbill from in amidst other branches whilst producing a loud quack?"

"Mr. Matias," said Ambu in a reproving tone of voice to accompany his stern look at Augie, "where the duckbill and the quack are concerned,-"

"Irene and Laura heard it too."

"They thought they heard it too. Can any of you be absolutely certain the strobe effect from frequent lightning strikes, combined with intense scraping of truck against trunk caused by high winds, didn't fall you both prey to your highly suggestive imaginations? And we do know the hoaxers went so far as to use that robotic foot-track-making contraption, in addition to baiting the crocodile into posing like an Iguanodon. Isn't it fair to assume they would think nothing of adding a monster duckbill plus loud quacks to their bag of tricks?"

Augie didn't see any sense bringing up again the distinct sensation of something enormous breathing down his neck just before something sharp tore a hole into the seat of his pants. Ambu would just explain those realities away as casually as he did the rest of it, making Stephen proud. So instead, he didn't interrupt Maggie's father continuing, "The real mystery for me is why anyone would go to all that trouble. They even taunted you by leaving behind their foot-track-making contraption. Although, at least where they left it will provide a good foundation for a new coral reef."

"Plus they went to the trouble of two different-sized foot tracks. And they snapped upper branches and palm fronds in the swamp from where the larger tracks were made to appear to have emerged."

"My Maggie noticed that detail as well. She's not as convinced as some of you, but she is certainly more agnostic than I am. Anyway, I have read of certain elements within British society going to ridiculous lengths to provide a different sort of mystery they call 'crop circles.' I suppose it's something to do." Ambu shook his head.

"So you think we're wasting our time?" After Augie asked this question, he glanced sideways down towards Samuel Longbottom keeping the cigarette boat close to dock, and gave him a what-can-I-do? shrug.

"Absolutely not!" answered Ambu in no uncertain terms. "Had you never ventured on your quest in the first place,

Magdalena wouldn't this moment be preparing for her interview at Cambridge! Who knows what other good you might also inadvertently accomplish? To paraphrase Shakespeare if I might, what other directions out might you uncover by the misdirection of searching for a living prehistoric monster? I really can't afford the luxury of such foolishness, but you are enjoying yourselves, yes? That's the important thing. And I earnestly do hope you prove me wrong, leave me with mud all over my face, as it were, by coming across a grazing Triceratops somewhere."

"Did you happen to tell Eclipso how you regard his quest?"

"I did in fact."

"How did he take it?"

"Funny thing about that, Mr. Matias. I prefaced my assessment, saying, 'I hope you won't take this the wrong way.' And he responded, his very words were, 'It doesn't really matter how I take it. Say whatever you have to say to Bonsai Gator, because he's the one who thought this would be a good idea.' And then this alligator, the smallest alligator I've ever seen, walked up on his hind legs beside where Eclipso remained seated while munching on what I believe was a pretzel dipped in hummus. The creature stood perfectly upright like I've never seen an alligator stand before...Oh, you know all about him?"

"Of course. So how did Bonsai Gator react after you admitted your skepticism? Wait." Augie held up both hands. "I might be holding out hope of a surviving non-avian dinosaur out there somewhere. Nevertheless, I remain very doubtful Bonsai Gator can understand even a half of what Eclipso thinks he can. What I really meant to ask was, how did Bonsai Gator react to Eclipso's demeanor after you admitted your profound skepticism?"

"Monsieur Petite Gator shook his head in what could have been construed as a most disapproving manner. But a delightful reggae version of a Beatles tune with which I am familiar, entitled 'We Can Work It Out,' was playing in the background. And who knows what small bug might have been attracting his attention in the foreground, out of camera range? So I really have no idea whether he was about to pounce on six-legged prey, or actually expressing disapproval, or drifting off on the reggae beat."

www.ingramcontent.com/pod-product-compliance
Lightning Source LLC
Chambersburg PA
CBHW030344020726
47493CB00003B/672